That's when something barrels into me
from behind. I go down hard on my face.
There's something on top of me. Something
heavy. As I start to lift my face up,
it growls. A low, wet hum.
Then it clamps down on my leg.
I scream.

First published in the UK in 2025 by Usborne Publishing Limited, Usborne House, 83-85 Saffron Hill, London EC1N 8RT, England, usborne.com.

Usborne Verlag, Usborne Publishing Limited, Prüfeninger Str. 20, 93049 Regensburg, Deutschland VK Nr. 17560

A CIP catalogue record for this book is available from the British Library.

ISBN 9781835401026 JFMAMJJ SOND/25 9771/1

Printed and bound using 100% renewable energy at CPI Group (UK) Ltd, Croydon, CR0 4YY.

FSC www.fsc.org MIX Paper | Supporting responsible forestry FSC® C013604

LOGAN-ASHLEY KISNER

THE TRANSITION

USBORNE

This book is for you.

I wish I'd been a better friend. I wish you had been, too.

A NOTE FROM LOGAN-ASHLEY

In 2024, over 660 anti-trans bills were put forward across state and federal legislatures in the United States. When I write this, halfway through 2025, the new number has already climbed to 940. The overwhelming majority of those bills target trans children's access to medical and social transition. And in the United Kingdom, similar rulings and bans continue that same pattern of rabid cruelty.

For an untold number of youths across the world, the horror of forced detransition is very real. Beyond this page, please be aware that you will be reading about transphobia, sexual harassment and assault, body horror, and the death of several animals, both on- and off-page. For more detailed information on the contents of this particular story, you can go to loganashleykisner.com.

To those who read on – to the trans kids in particular – I want to say that these real-world horrors are not new. That does not make them any less terrifying to face. You have every reason to be angry, upset, or afraid.

To steal a quote from Larry Mitchell: there are two important things to remember about the coming revolutions. The first is that we will get our asses kicked. The second is that we will win.

I hope this story gives you courage. I'm here to tell you it's going to be okay. It's not going to be quick, and it's not going to be easy, but it's going to be okay.

Logan Ashley

Logan-Ashley Kisner, June 2025

1

A couple weeks before my top surgery, I curled up with Michael Dillon's memoir in the corner of the school library. He was the first transgender man to undergo top surgery, all the way back in 1942, but he wrote very little about the procedure and what to expect of it. What he did write was this: the anaesthesia made him vomit for nearly a full day afterward, and he was so *happy* to finally be "rid of what I hated most".

I don't know all the ways that top surgery has progressed since 1942, although I have to think that the anaesthesia has gotten better.

For me, the worst part has been the drains. Drains are these round, softball-sized bulbs hung by pins from the compression binder and connected to these tubes that disappear into my chest beneath the incision marks on my pecs. They have to be emptied twice a day. I've been doing it myself for the last two and a half weeks, measuring as the blood has gone from a vibrant, syrupy red to a thick, sluggish black. It's done a lot to solidify my belief that the human body is truly disgusting. Today, at last, I'm getting them taken out.

"Now, this will feel weird, but it shouldn't hurt." The nurse – whose name I've already forgotten – pulls a glove over each hand. "Are you ready, Hunter?"

I come back to the moment and nod. This doctor's office is like every other, small and sparse and blindingly white. I sit at the edge of the exam table, bare-chested and avoiding eye contact with my dad, who's sitting a few feet away in a plastic chair.

Being shirtless in front of him is strange because my chest doesn't look male. Not when you compare it to, like, a cis guy's chest. The nipple grafts are scabbed over and most of the skin is still numb to the touch. It looks weird and feels even weirder.

The nurse puts one hand on the side of my chest while the other wraps around the first tube. I wince at the strange sensation and watch as she slowly pulls it out. She's right; it doesn't hurt but it feels *weird*. Like a magician yanking scarves out of his sleeve.

Except I don't think scarves are supposed to squeal. I can tell the nurse hears it too, because she makes a face as she finishes pulling it out: *woOP!* Like a slide whistle.

Fresh blood dribbles from the new, dime-sized opening in my chest. The nurse calmly tapes a cotton ball down on it.

Then she drags her finger along my ribcage, and I realize there's something else there.

"That's coagulated blood," she explains, holding her gloved finger up into the air. "Totally normal, looks like you just had some left in the tube."

My blood fits perfectly on the pad of her finger. A small black worm. Even my dad's nose wrinkles when the nurse holds it up in his direction.

After the second drain is removed, silently, the nurse explains a few things that I already know: don't pick at the scabs, don't lift my arms above my head for a while, and any questions should be phoned to the office, not typed into Google. I almost roll my eyes, but I notice Dad nodding along, so I let the nurse prattle on.

On paper, my dad and I look something alike: blue-grey eyes, reddish-brown hair, and a slightly upturned nose. But my dad seems like he should be military: buzz cut, flat mouth. I'm still waiting to outgrow the puffy face I got from starting testosterone.

Traffic isn't bad for a Friday afternoon in Chicago, and it gets better as Dad drives us away from the surgeon's office and towards Naperville. He's a first officer for Southwest airlines, and travels in total silence. It's just us and the Duran Duran song playing on the radio, which all feels very normal considering we watched two tubes be pulled out of my body a few minutes ago.

Eventually, though, Dad clears his throat and turns the volume down a few clicks. "You're back to school on Monday, right?"

"Yep."

"You feel…all right?"

That's as close as he's gotten to asking about my chest since the surgery. "I'm fine."

He nods curtly. "Good. Well, sorry I won't be here to see you off."

"It's just coming back from winter break."

"Your *last* winter break," he corrects me. "High school only happens once."

Thank God, I think.

He continues, "Anyway, my schedule is going to be rough for a while. Trying to make up for being grounded the last two weeks."

He leaves *because you had to go and get an expensive fucking surgery* unsaid, but I can still hear it hanging in the air between us. Irritation prickles across my skin.

I came out as trans when I was thirteen. Testosterone wasn't an option at that point, but there were puberty blockers. Mom was willing to sign off on it. Dad had "safety concerns". So our relationship *really* sucked for the three years that my body bled and my breasts grew, and sometimes one of us will go back to scratch at that scab.

I could do that now, but I'm not in the mood to spend the

rest of the drive home rehashing this. The prickle fades into a buzz. I sigh and stare out the window.

There's nothing like Chicago in the thick of winter. The dead trees look like scratch marks at the bottom of the cloudless, blindingly blue sky. I love this time of year, although a large reason for that is the excuse it provides me to layer up and hide my body. We're all androgynous blobs when it drops below freezing. It dawns on me suddenly that since I have the chest of a man, I might not hate summer any more.

It's a strange thought. I can't visualize myself in a tank top.

"Oh, make sure you keep an eye on Norman." Dad's voice drowns out the radio again. "Annie's been talking my ear off about predator…migration. Something."

"You're listening to Annie, now?" I joke, pulling out my phone.

Most of my messages are from last month, people wishing me a speedy recovery right before I went into the hospital. My mom and younger stepsister, Maddy, are among them. Nobody's really checked in since then, which is fine. It's not like I *want* to tell Maddy all about my scabbing nipples. I just text Gabe, my best friend and one of only two people I've kept in the loop for every horrible step of this.

drains OUT

see you Monday :)

"He's *your* dog," Dad answers.

"Yeah, I know."

"Hunter." I look up and he's staring at me. "Seriously, I know we joke, but she's not crazy."

Yeah she is, I think, *that's why she's Animal Annie*.

Annie Searchwell lives in the house opposite ours. Every time our local news station, Channel 17, needs someone to talk about local wildlife or adoption drives or whatever else, they call Animal Annie. I'd be surprised if they didn't send her an honorary pay cheque every now and again.

"We're not in the inner city," he continues. "That preserve is right there and—"

"It's the *Evil Dead* forest, I know." I relent. "Yeah, I'll keep an eye on him. I always do."

My dad nods. "Thank you."

My phone buzzes in my hands. It's Gabe.

LET'S GO! 🎉

Animated confetti explodes across the screen. I stifle a laugh.

Marcy Calico is sitting on the hood of her maroon Sonata when my dad finally pulls onto our street. She's impossible to miss.

Mars is the name she actually goes by, which I think prepares you for the rest of her. She's a half-Filipino girl who's six months older than me. Her arms are covered in tiny stick-and-poke tattoos and her hair is turquoise from a failed attempt to dye it Christmas green. My dad parks in the driveway, and as I step out, Mars clambers down from her car and runs towards me, boots crunching on the snow slush.

I brace myself for impact. Instead, Mars stops a few inches in front of me, arms held threateningly open. "Hi. Hug?"

I consider her for a second. "Gentle, please."

She doesn't give me the usual bear hug, but she still comes pretty close to crushing me. I deal with it. It's been two weeks since I last saw her, and hearing her giggle in my ear breathes a whole new life into me.

"Hiya, Frank." She lifts one hand and waves at my dad. "Mind if I steal him?"

I can't tell if my dad likes Mars or not. I think he's mostly thankful that she gets me out of the house sometimes. "All yours." He nods. "Just bring the dog with you. He needs a walk."

Norman hates walks and only willingly goes outside to pee. I still nod and let my dad open the door. My fat nine-year-old Chihuahua runs out and does one circle around my legs before he tries running for the house again.

Mars scoops him up before he can. "Thanks, Frank!"

We walk down to her car, where I slide into the passenger

seat and Mars puts Norman in the back to sleep for as long as we're out.

When Mars gets behind the wheel, there's suddenly a Tupperware container in her hands. She grins and holds it out to me. "Congrats."

I try to give her a disapproving look, even though I'm smiling as I take the tub. "You didn't need to get me anything."

"Uh, *yeah*, I did." Mars makes a face. "Your hang-ups about gifts are *not* shared. I missed you. You get a gift. Suck it up."

Then she sits there, expectantly, so I pop the lid off. Two cupcakes stare back at me. The frosting is a strange shade of yellowish brown. A single raspberry sits atop each one.

It takes a second to process the joke: they're boobs.

"You like 'em? Figured you should get a last bit of enjoyment out of, y'know, *having tits*." Mars giggles as she grabs one and takes a giant bite out of the frosting. "The raspberry is the nipple!"

I laugh, though it's more out of shock than anything else. I take a small bite for myself. The frosting is some kind of maple.

When I don't say anything, Mars's eyebrows knit together. "Are they good? Or do I need to kick my own ass?"

I smile. "No, they're good. Really good, actually."

As quickly as it went, her grin returns. "Awesome. Hazel helped me make 'em. The maple was her idea."

Hazel and Mars have been...well, *dating* isn't the right

word for it. Seeing each other? Screwing around? I don't know. Hazel is two years older than us and works at this flower shop two blocks down from the movie theatre where Mars and I work. Mars owns one of their shirts, a cartoon Venus flytrap with "Grounded Gardening" in big bold letters across the chest. A part of me wants to shrivel up and die thinking about her and about my chest, but I take another bite of cupcake and swallow the thought.

Before we peel out of the neighbourhood, Mars connects her phone to the radio and grins at me. A second later, "deathwish" kicks in.

If the cupcake surprise had me tense, then "deathwish" puts me back at ease. It came out around the same time that Mars and I met, and it's become the first song we listen to when we go anywhere together. It's the most serious religious rite I've ever been a part of.

We don't have to go far. You could stand on my porch and spit and hit the Springbrook Prairie Forest Preserve. Mars drives long enough for "deathwish" to finish before she finds one of the alcoves they keep clear for tourists. We park, keep the car running for Norman's sake, and then we climb onto the roof and lie there, side by side, like frozen sardines.

Mars balances the rest of her cupcake on her chest before taking her vape out and offering it to me. She's got a Dunkaccino sticker on it that's faded into nearly nothing.

"Can't," I tell her. "Smoking's bad for the healing process."

Mars looks aghast. "Lame."

"Well, I don't want to lose a nipple."

"*Well*, I thought we had an agreement about dying in an iron lung together."

"Oh, that's still on," I promise.

She grins at me, takes a puff, and exhales. Then she scoots a little closer. There are two jackets between us, but I swear I can feel the heat from her arm where it's pressed against mine.

I used to have the worst crush on her when we met. Hard not to, I think. Mars is the kind of person everybody has a crush on at some point in their life. She's pretty, funny and effortlessly cool in a way that nobody ever is.

"So, Flat Stanley, drains are out," Mars says. "How do you feel?"

I shrug. "Good. I think. I don't know. There's a lot."

Mars looks at me. "Anything you wanna talk about?"

I shake my head. "I wouldn't even know how to describe it."

Or, rather, I don't know how to describe it to *her*. Mars is great, but she's not trans. Even though she nods along, I'm not sure she understands how deep dysphoria cuts.

It's like finding out that for your whole life, you've been driving with flat tyres. You just assumed life was supposed to be like that, but then, one day, you drive a car with inflated tyres, and it's like – *holy shit*. Or it's like *knowing* that you're driving on flat tyres, knowing that you're gonna drive into a pole and kill yourself if you don't get them fixed, but you have to fight the mechanic to even look at your car. And while you're doing that, random people will try and convince you that driving on flat tyres is, like, *part of being a woman* or something.

"It's weird," I finally say. "I mean, trans guys really only get two major surgeries, and now I'm done with one."

"Anticlimactic?"

I look down at myself. It's hard to notice a difference while I'm wearing a jacket, but I take a deep breath and I can *feel* it. "Just weird, I think."

"Why weird?"

I almost start laughing. "Because like, what if something tears, or a nipple falls off, or—"

Mars's shoulders drop. "Dude. Come on, be happy for yourself for five minutes."

"I don't want to end up looking *wrong*. I've only got one chest."

"So? If you need to borrow a nipple, I can spare mine." I glare at Mars for this, but she doesn't start giggling. "I am telling you, as a rational third party, that you are gonna be fine."

She's not a rational third party. What she means is that she hasn't spent two weeks totally paranoid that she was going to stretch and rip her chest apart, and this *is* a valued perspective.

I sigh. "Thanks, Mars."

She smiles and nods and continues picking apart her cupcake.

"So, uh, how's work been?" I ask, drumming my fingers against the roof. Trying to get the conversation off of me.

Mars laughs. "Oh, sweet Jesus. Still bleeding holiday hires. Three different kids threw up on my shift last weekend. A coyote ate Tammy's dog."

I stare at her. "A *what?*"

"Well, that's what she says, anyway. There wasn't actually a body, so I don't know how she knows that. It could've been a wolf or a bigger dog."

"That's horrible."

Mars opens her mouth to say something, but before she can, a coyote howls in the distance. There're plenty of those out on the preserve. The sound still stops us both for a moment.

Then Mars starts laughing. "Oh my God, that's some sick cosmic timing." She turns her face to the sky. "Give Tammy back her corgi, you mangy fuckin' mutt!"

I elbow and shush her, like the coyote is gonna hear her and come over to tell us off. We're both giggling, and I can smell her breath. Raspberry and maple-scented.

"I'm back next week," I promise, bumping my shoulder against hers. "Tuesday."

"Mm-hm. Are you planning on any more cool body mods?"

"Only if you're paying for 'em."

"Baby, I'm gonna have you looking like transgender RoboCop by next year, you wait."

2

Mars and I met about two years ago. We're pretty close, as far as work friendships go, but we go to different schools so our time together is limited. She's a senior at Bolingbrook, while I go to Asena High School with Gabe, my best friend since we were twelve years old.

"How long until you can actually, like, *do stuff* again?" Gabe asks as we walk into the locker room on Monday.

"A couple months," I answer on the conservative side.

He makes a face. "Jeez. I'd be bored out of my skull."

"Yeah, well, I'm either bored, or I split open and bleed out. Hard to choose."

Gabe grins. He's a tall, athletic Korean dude, whose hair has grown long since I last saw him. It hangs along the curve of his jaw, uneven and messy but decidedly a good look for him. He turned eighteen last week and is wearing the Chicago Blackhawks hoodie I had shipped to his house (one of the few designs without that stupid, racist mascot on it).

We met on a seventh-grade field trip to a skating park:

I tried to join his game, he told me that "girls can't play hockey", and I picked up a stick and chased him around the rink until our instructor noticed and benched us together until it was time to go home. We've been best friends ever since. Guys are weird like that.

Gabe also was the first boy I ever truly had a crush on. I didn't just want to *be* him, I *liked* him, though the crush has mostly fossilized into an embarrassing artefact of being twelve and ridiculously closeted.

The letter I handed in to the nurse's office today excuses me from "intensive physical activity" for the next eight weeks. I've only followed Gabe into the locker room to put my bag away. The room is filled with chatter as everybody catches up with their friends. I set my backpack on the bench and take my lock in hand – 15-45-30.

Gabe opens his locker beside me and changes quickly into the standard grey athletic shirt. Down at the far end of the room, a group breaks out into laughter. Just as quickly (and loudly) they shush each other, which is what makes me glance in their direction. I don't immediately recognize anybody in the sea of faces.

Then I pull open my locker and something goes *POP!*

I scream. Even Gabe jumps. An uneasy hush dampens the room as the sound echoes against the tile.

Confetti comes raining down on my head a second later. My heart is beating so hard that my chest feels hollow, even as the surprise curdles into anger. Some kids around us start giggling, but most remain silent as they try to figure out what's happening. My head spins straight for the end of the lockers, and the same cluster of guys, now watching me, burst into laughter and run for the exit doors.

The first face I recognize is Damien Hulme. He's small and loud and his freckled nostrils flare when he laughs. It's the second face I recognize that makes my stomach twist. Brown eyes that are a little too small for his head, a grin that snakes up to his ears.

Ethan Adams. Riley's boyfriend.

I turn back to my locker. Before I register the images on the poster, I read the text:

WELCOME BACK, FRANKENTITS

God only knows whose boobs they put on this poster. I'm also not sure what they used for fake blood. Jam? Either way, it's red and thick, fresh enough that it's dripping onto the floor. They've even replaced the nipples with little Frankenstein's-monster heads.

Gabe slams his locker shut. "Wait here."

He takes two steps before I grab him by the sleeve. "*Don't.* Just – grab me a trash can."

"Are you serious?"

Near the front of the locker room, Nick Riedling, the assistant teacher whose entire job is watching the locker room, chirps his whistle. Two-minute warning. Most of the boys hurry outside. Those who remain are staring at us, or poorly pretending not to.

"Just help me get rid of it," I mutter.

After a beat, Gabe walks off. I rip the poster down and crush it in my hands. The jam smells like raspberry. Then I hear something being dragged across the tiles, and a few guys hurry to get out of Gabe's way.

He puts the bin down between us and I throw the wad of paper into it before hoisting my bag into my locker and slamming it shut. There are bits of confetti still stuck in the door.

The nice thing about Asena is that it's a big school. The main building itself is divided up into five wings, neatly alphabetized A–E. It's the kind of big where you have to really, really try to stand out. Most people barely know that I exist, let alone care that I'm trans.

Key word: *most*.

The anger has already decayed into a faint sense of nausea at the back of my throat. Gabe drags the trash can back, and I silently trail behind him, pressing my knuckles into the underside of my jaw. The pressure calms me in some deep, primal way I don't fully understand.

"Seriously," Gabe says, letting the trash can go. "You say the word and I'll lay him out."

I shake my head. "Don't be stupid."

"What?"

"*What?*" I echo him. "You get into another fight, and the first thing they'll do is expel you. That's your whole life out the window."

Gabe has the audacity to shrug.

"And all it would do is make *me* look like a pussy," I add.

He stares at me. "How would *me* punching him in the face make *you* look like a pussy?"

"Because everybody would know that you were doing it for me."

The argument ends there because Gabe knows I'm right, even if he won't admit it. Gabe knows I'm right because he *has* punched Ethan. It was years ago, and he still claims it was an ordinary ice hockey fight that got out of hand, but the only thing it earned Gabe was a two-game suspension and a threat that the school would be involved if anything like it ever happened again.

We're among the last to shuffle outside, where the teacher in charge – Ms Bailey, a short, stout Black woman – tells me to walk laps around the length of the track field. I peel away from the group, keep my head down, and walk.

As the second lap bleeds into the third, I start to calm down.

Everything considered, I'm lucky. Sure, I might not have ever *needed* top surgery if my dad had let me go on puberty blockers, but I am still lucky. I've been on hormones for almost two years now and I've had top surgery. With the right amount of skill and luck, I might not even look trans in a year or two.

On lap four, I pull out my phone and scroll through Twitter (or whatever they're calling it now) and get a glimpse of my alternate realities. Horrible ones. Some friends are tweeting about a Florida lawsuit related to transition care, except there have been *so many* that I'm not sure which one they're talking about. One girl I follow is raising money for facial feminization surgery in the UK. I open the link, donate twenty dollars, and retweet.

One article making the rounds is about the bleak reality of being trans in Texas. I've read it already. Mom sent it to me earlier this morning. She's lived in Fort Worth ever since the divorce, with her no-longer-new husband, Gary, and Maddy, and I think she's still holding out hope that I'll someday join her. Her Facebook page is full of local news stories about Texas-brand transphobia and rallying cries to speak at city hall every time someone tries to introduce a ban. She's... *really* into it.

The thing is, though, while my mom is very vocally proud of her trans son (a descriptor that makes my skin crawl), Illinois isn't trying to forcibly detransition me. The thought of my yearly summer visit to Texas has started to give me more anxiety than I can stomach. I haven't even posted anything about my top surgery online. Things seem too bleak for me to want to celebrate. Like, in the heat of all these terrible bans, at least *I* got *my* surgery.

My heart flutters with something like guilt and…not regret, exactly, but the fear of it.

What I told Mars is the truth: I'm scared of ruining my new chest. But I think I'm more scared of looking trans for the rest of my life. Always looking *wrong*. Feminine. Disfigured. Mutilated.

I shake my head and, briefly, manage to dispel the swarming barrage of words and associated images. I won't look trans for ever. I won't look mutilated or feminine, because my chest is going to heal and it's going to heal *right*.

At lunch, Gabe and I sit with some of the guys in the school's ice hockey club: Tanner, Eugene, Josh and Taylor. They talk exclusively about hockey, or things very closely related. I listen to most of it, although I never join in. After everything that happened in gym, I'm good to let Gabe do the talking for both of us.

We sit near the cafeteria's floor-to-ceiling windows, which provide an unobstructed view of the school's front lawn. The district spent a whole bunch of money last summer ripping out the old sidewalks and planting new trees, so now there's only this giant concrete circle in between the front doors and the bus drop-off spot. It all looks the same under the snow, though: flat and white and depressing in a way that only high school can be.

Eventually, I'm able to spot Ethan walking down the paved path towards the student parking lot. There's a girl walking next to him. My hand instinctively goes to my breastbone, where my fingers find the silver chain around my neck. I follow it down to its end, where a wire wrap holds a misshapen chunk of grey-and-white howlite stone.

Riley and I used to be friends. We aren't any more. That's the shortest and simplest explanation of why catching a glimpse of her makes me clench my jaw until my teeth ache.

I suppose that's another thing about Asena: it's big enough that, most days, I never have to see her and remember the friendship that my transness *did* completely ruin.

After school, the sight of an empty driveway is something of a relief. My dad is usually gone for five or six days at a time, and the two weeks he just spent with me is maybe the longest he's been home for in years. I'm looking forward to having reign of the house with Gabe again.

Gabe obviously doesn't live with us, but ever since we started high school he spends just as much time at my house as he does at his own. It's a rhythm that feels as normal as breathing. We settle back into it as if we haven't had three weeks apart. We spend maybe an hour on homework, then call it a night and order pizza.

While we wait, Gabe helps me do my t-shot.

When I turn eighteen in April, I'll have been doing these shots for two years. It's hard to believe; I still look nothing like other trans guys I see online. The ones who have thick, even amounts of facial hair and hard jawlines. The ones who get periareolar and have these perfect scarless chests. It makes me want to draw the whole vial up and jam the syringe into my forehead.

"Stop tensing," Gabe mutters, taking the safety cap off with his teeth.

I shut my eyes. Ethan's stupid poster continues to float around inside my head anyway, Boris Karloff's face haunting me like the world's lamest ghost. Ethan's grin growing out of my pectoral scars. Then comes pressure as Gabe pushes the needle into my arm, and Ethan and Karloff are both washed away with a flood of testosterone cypionate.

"Thanks," I breathe.

It's an oddly intimate process. Gabe holds my arm to keep it steady, and his hand is practically the size of my entire bicep. If I was still a twelve-year-old girl with a crush, I would be losing my mind. But I'm incredibly normal about Gabe now, so I wait to feel his finger smooth out the Band-Aid on my arm before I open my eyes.

Then the doorbell rings, and Norman starts yapping with excitement.

An hour later, the smell of pizza grease continues to cling to us. I missed this, too: being crammed onto the couch with

Gabe, screaming at each other over the same *Cuphead* level we've been stuck on since November while Norman loses his mind and runs circles around us.

I think it's only after our fifth unceremonious death that Norman finally shuts up. I look at him, now sitting in front of the TV, staring back at me with his big, dopey eyes.

I sigh. "Want something?"

Norman barks.

That's what I thought. I drop out as Gabe restarts the level. Maybe Norman would stop being so lazy if he ever had to walk anywhere on his own. I football-carry him to the mudroom anyway and let him outside.

The mudroom is minuscule, barely able to fit a bench and an umbrella stand. I linger in the house, where it's warm, and stare out at the yard. It's a single white oak tree and a bunch of grass currently buried under the snow, all surrounded by a chain-link fence that my dad put up when he bought the house. A cheap wooden hockey stick is mixed among the umbrellas in the stand. It (and the fence) is Dad's idea of animal control.

Norman's paws have barely hit the snow when I hear Gabe call me: "Bambi, phone!"

I roll my eyes. *Bambi* is an especially stupid nickname that should've been a one-week joke. But you suck at skating in front of a bunch of hockey players *one time* and you've got a nickname four years running. I find one of my snow boots to prop the screen door open before hurrying back. My phone is buzzing in circles on the end table.

In her contact photo, Mars's hair is dark red, and she's standing in front of a poster for *Titane* with her hand covering it, so it looks like it says *Tit*. Her mouth is open in fake outrage.

"What's up?" I answer, right as Gabe falls off a ledge and shouts, "Shit!"

"Uh, hi?" Mars half asks. "Seth put his shift up for next Wednesday. You still looking to grab some extra closes?"

"Oh, thanks." I put her on speaker as I open our scheduling app. "From five to close?"

"Yep, that one." Mars sighs. Then I hear her gurgle and spit.

I frown. "Are you brushing your teeth?"

"Yeah. Why?"

"Rinse your mouth *away* from the phone, that's why."

Norman starts barking, and I glance in the direction of the mudroom. Then Gabe smacks my arm. He's at the final boss again. I put my phone back against my ear and focus on the TV.

"Ha. Did you beat the dragon yet?" Mars asks.

"Nope. Gabe's going at it right now."

"What phase is he in?"

"At the end of the first."

"Which would be easier if I had my player two," Gabe chimes in.

"I think I hear your friend telling you that he sucks." Mars sounds like she's smiling.

Mars and Gabe are aware of each other, in that friend-of-a-friend-that-you-follow-on-Instagram way, but they've never properly met. No reason why not, really. School is one corner of my life and work is another. Though I also think that Mars and Gabe in particular would kill each other within an hour.

Outside, Norman finally goes quiet.

I grin. "I still think you cheated to beat this."

Mars sighs. "Skill issue, Hunter. Skill issue."

One of the little fire orbs jumps into Gabe's sprite. He sucks his lip between his teeth.

Then my brain taps me on the shoulder. Norman's gone quiet.

My stomach pitches. The kind of anxiety that hits when you've gotten all the way to school and realize you left your final essay on the kitchen counter. That feeling of *too late*. I think Mars says something, but I don't hear a word of it.

I run to the mudroom. My boot is still holding the screen door open. I step into the doorway and look out into the yard. I can't see Norman.

"Hey, thanks, Mars," I say. My voice is warped with panic. "I gotta go."

I hang up, grab Dad's coat from the rack, and slip into my tennis shoes.

"*Gabe?*" I call out.

He doesn't answer and I'm not waiting. My toes already feel frozen by the time I hit the snow. The porch light is humming above me, but I turn on my phone flashlight anyway.

The chain-link fence has been peeled back the way I imagine you'd skin a giant orange. Like someone walked up to it and tore it open. My face tingles. I realize it's begun to snow.

"*Norman?*" I call out into the dark.

I carefully step through the hole. The snow is disturbed, like *something's* been through it, but there aren't any distinct footprints. No paw prints. Not even any blood. The fact that I'm already looking for blood makes something in my mouth taste rotten.

Please, God, I think, *I know this dog is hopeless, but please don't let him be dead.*

A long field stretches out between my backyard and the neighbourhood behind us, overgrown with tall grass and weeds. We're a corner house, and our only next-door neighbour is out of town for a month-long Mediterranean cruise. The house on the other side of the no man's land has been empty for the last three months. There's nothing but darkness and silence out here.

I wrap my dad's coat tighter around my body and push forward. If that dog isn't already dead, he'll freeze if I don't find him. "*Norman!*"

Flakes cling to my eyelashes. The snow is up to my ankles out here. I look back at my house. The porch light hangs in the dark like a ghostly lantern. Like an idiot, I left the back door open. My fingers are numb. Why the hell didn't I grab gloves?

Then, suddenly, I remember my chest. I'm out here in sweatpants, a T-shirt and my dad's coat. In a word, *severely* underdressed. Could I freeze a nipple off? I grind my teeth, trying to keep from screaming. "You stupid goddamn dog."

Something to my left snaps and I swivel towards the sound.

My phone's flashlight is garbage. The most I can make out are some bushes and a towering pine tree. I want it to be Norman so badly. I want Norman to come out, frozen solid and mad as hell, and I want to haul him back inside and lock him in my bedroom.

Another twig cracks. I glance in the direction of my porch light again, glistening like a faraway star. I wonder, if my life depended on it, how fast I could get back to it.

Then I see something running towards me.

3

In theory, I know how to handle a wild animal. You make as much noise as possible, try to appear tall and imposing, and, if all else fails, that's why you keep a hockey stick near the door. But when the coyote comes charging out of the darkness, I just scream and fall backwards.

The coyote stops and stares at me, like *I* surprised *it*. I stay on the ground, unable to do anything but stare back. It's a tiny little thing, but before I can get a better look, it takes off again, running right past me and deeper into the no man's land.

I stay motionless until I can't hear its paws hitting the snow any more. It's only then that I realize I should've checked its mouth for blood. *Shit.*

All I know for sure is that there was a coyote. Still no Norman, and now I'm wet. I sigh, pick up my phone, and brush the snow off it before I roll onto my knees.

That's when something barrels into me from behind.

I go down hard on my face. It's mostly ice underneath me, and my cheeks burn from the sudden cold. There's something on top of me. Something heavy. As I start to lift my face up, it growls. A low, wet hum.

Then it clamps down on my leg.

I scream. It's more out of panic than pain, because although I can *feel* the heat of a mouth locked around my calf, my brain blocks out the hurt. Adrenaline hits a moment later, and I start kicking. *Survive*, my brain spits, *get up*. I try to claw my way forward even though my fingers are too frozen to grip anything. I can only slap uselessly at the snow.

Then I'm suddenly twisted onto my back. Snow clings to my eyelashes, but it'd be impossible to miss the teeth coming straight at me. I instinctively throw my arms over my face. Those canines clamp down around my arm. I hear them puncture my skin with a wet *crunch*.

I scream again. *"Get off!"*

The animal shakes its head back and forth like it's telling me *no, I won't*.

In flashes, I catch glimpses of what it looks like: white and brown tufts of fur. Round, bulbous amber eyes. A bloody snout with massive, jagged canines that are tearing into my forearm. It seems way too big to be somebody's dog, but I'm going to die if I stop to try and classify exactly what's ripping me apart.

I try to punch it with my free hand. Its jaws lock tighter around my arm, tongue whipping against my wrist like wet fire. It feels like it takes for ever before I finally jab my thumb into its eye. The animal lets go of me with a yelp.

Survive. Get up.

All I have to do is make it forty, maybe fifty yards. My eyes lock on the porch light and the door under it. All I have to do is make it back to the house.

I barely manage two steps before my leg buckles and I fall into the snow. The animal's teeth clamp down on my leg again. As it drags me back, I watch the snow around me darken. When it drops me, I cover the back of my neck with my hands and curl into myself. Slobber – or maybe blood – leaks through my fingers and down the sides of my face as it starts sniffing around. My entire body is shaking, and I've got no idea if it's shock, cold or blood loss.

All I can think is: *I'm gonna die*.

Then the animal suddenly yelps into my ear and jumps off. Like an idiot, I drop my hands and spin around to see what happened.

Gabe doesn't even have a jacket on. He advances on the animal, the wooden hockey stick raised to strike. "Get—the—fuck—*off!*"

Each word punctuates another swing, and on the final word, I hear the stick break with a heavy *crack* against the animal's skull. It yelps.

Then, it growls.

Gabe grabs me by the collar and drags me to my feet. "*Go!*"

He keeps ahold of me, which is probably the only reason I don't immediately fall. My leg still buckles on every step, and

I'm slowing us down, and I can hear that animal behind us snap its jaws before I hear it pushing through the snow after us. I'm gonna get us both killed. The field stretches in front of me like a nightmare.

It's only because of the porch light that I know we're not running in place. The light hurts as it gets brighter and brighter, until it's suddenly right over my head. Gabe flings the screen door open and pushes me in ahead of him. I collapse on the floor and take a gasping breath before I think to drag myself forward. Just a couple of feet, but enough.

My left hand is *wet* with blood, my body throbbing as it tries to adjust to the change in temperature. Gabe drops the splintered stick and throws the door shut behind him. Half a second later, the animal slams into the door and the whole *wall* shudders. Then, it goes quiet.

I slowly prop myself up against the bench. The throbbing starts to feel like *burning*. Each breath comes out as a wheeze.

Gabe slowly back-pedals away from the door. "What the hell was *that?*"

The only thing I can come up with is: "I think it killed Norman."

Gabe turns to me, and he must finally see the whole extent of whatever I look like. I don't know how else to describe the expression of horror that takes over his face. "Dude—"

The animal slams into the house again. A giant split cracks down the middle of the door and plaster dust flies into the air.

We both jump and stare in shock. Gabe starts to pick up the broken stick, before he suddenly stops, turns and runs. I watch him disappear down the hall.

It slams into the door again and the split worsens. A dirty brown paw presses against the wood. A large, bloody maw is not far behind.

As quickly as he left, Gabe runs back into the room. He flings the door open, and I hear the animal *shriek*. I see the whites of its eyes before Gabe presses forward. Spraying something, I realize. Gabe keeps going until he's outside, and that horrible noise goes shrill.

Then, quiet again. Gabe lingers in the doorway for what feels like hours before he finally steps back inside and shuts the door. A few more chips of wood clatter to the floor. He lets a small can of pepper spray fall from his hand.

I look down at myself. Both of my shoes are missing. There's an actual pool of blood forming underneath me, and unless my eyes are playing tricks, there's either a chunk of snow clinging to my leg or that's *bone*.

"Is it gone?" I ask.

Gabe kneels in front of me. "I think so."

I want to tell him: *go make sure*. But a childlike panic is wrapped around my throat. Gabe can't die. He could've died just now. For *me*.

"Okay." Gabe starts nodding. "Bathroom. Let's go to the bathroom, okay?"

As soon as Gabe places his hand on my biceps, a horrible pain shoots up my arm. I reflexively punch him with my good hand. "*Don't*, that—"

"I'm sorry!"

A whining noise pushes up against the back of my throat. I realize a moment later that I've started to cry. Despite everything that's just happened, that somehow manages to feel like the worst part of this whole night.

I track bloody footprints from the mudroom to the bathroom. While the tub fills with water, Gabe helps me undress. It's like peeling the wrapper off a chocolate bar that was left in a hot car; going slow hurts but going fast is worse. By the time I'm down to my briefs and get into the tub, I don't have the strength to wash the blood off. I just sit there.

Beyond the initial sting of sinking beneath the water, I'm in less pain than I expected to be. That freaks me out more than anything else. What does shock feel like?

I carefully lift my leg out of the water, which has already gone a strange, salmon shade of pink. The mark on my leg doesn't look much like a bite. There is the smallest, slightest sliver of bone visible. A stupid voice in my head tells me I should touch it. I quickly put it beneath the water again.

"Which is the closest hospital from here?" Gabe asks. He's sitting on the floor beside the tub, gripping the broken stick like he's expecting that animal to come through the tile.

I think there's an ER on the other side of the preserve. I'm not sure; the last hospital I was in was all the way in downtown Chicago. My arm has stopped bleeding, and the skin looks like it's already starting to bruise. I flex and it doesn't hurt. Not severely, anyway.

The voice in my head tells me again: *touch it*. I don't know why I listen to it this time, but I lift my finger and prod gently at a bit of loose skin. The feeling is *weird*. I flinch. But I realize that it doesn't *hurt*. I frown and run my thumb along what I think is a sliver of muscle. It tickles.

Gabe finally notices what I'm doing and grabs my good arm by the wrist.

"No, hey—" I put both of my hands up. "It doesn't hurt."

Gabe's frown only deepens. He lets me go and stands. "Okay, that's *shock*."

"No, it doesn't hurt," I insist. "Look."

I take my leg out of the water again and focus on the visible bit of bone. Before Gabe can stop me and before I can think twice, I slam my hand down onto the wound. I *want* it to hurt.

It doesn't. I mean, it hurts like it would if I'd smacked my leg on any other day. Not like I touched my exposed *bone*. Somewhere in the back of my mind, I realize I'm not bleeding from here, either. I'm not bleeding *anywhere* any more.

I look at Gabe, who's staring at me like I've grown a second head before suddenly averting his eyes. The *Cuphead* theme is playing in the living room on a mind-numbing loop. "I think I'm okay," I whisper, like the universe might hear and realize its mistake. I *shouldn't* be okay.

Gabe shakes his head. "This isn't right. You need to go to a hospital."

"I was *just at* the hospital." There's an edge to my voice. "It doesn't hurt and I'm not bleeding any more, so what's the point?"

"*What's the point*, Hunter?" He finally turns and jabs his finger at my leg.

I drop it into the water. Gabe looks away, and nobody says anything for a minute.

In the silence, my eyes fall to my chest. There's not even a scratch. Just the healing scars that had already been there, and a thin cluster of hair on my sternum. I close my fingers around the howlite stone around my neck and take a shaking breath.

"I think Dad is supposed to get back on Wednesday," I finally say. "I mean, if I start foaming at the mouth, that's different, but I can't do a hospital by myself. I *can't*. I'll do urgent care with my dad, but…not before then, okay?"

I don't know where exactly my apprehension stems from, only that it's not from one specific place. It's the knowledge that I would be walking into a hospital while transgender, a terrifying game of chance I try to avoid as much as possible. The memory of the receptionist who called me *she* when I signed in for my surgery is still fresh. Less fresh but no less impactful is the memory of the *years* I spent going through female puberty.

My dad has dragged his feet for every moment of my transition; he might kill me if I rack up another thousand-dollar hospital bill for wounds that have already stopped bleeding.

Gabe doesn't say anything. He keeps his arms crossed over his chest and his eyes trained on the floor. The longer it goes, the more my skin burns with discomfort.

I'm a man. I have a man's chest now. This still isn't exactly how I expected to show Gabe what it looked like.

"I thought you were dead," Gabe finally says, voice unsteady.

I look up at him. He's chewing on his top lip, which is usually the first sign that something's pissed him off. For a second, I wonder if he's mad at *me*.

"I'm not," I offer, nervously crossing my arms over my chest.

Gabe's smile is tight and unamused. "Seriously. I thought..."

Then it clicks. He's mad at himself.

"I didn't even hear you," Gabe adds. "I went to the bathroom and when I came back, I thought it was too cold, so I went to see if you still had the door open for Norman."

That hangs in the air. I'd be dead if I'd remembered to shut the door behind me.

Instead of doing something as simple as saying *thank you*, I swallow down the lump in my throat and wrap my arms tighter around my chest. "How did you know where that pepper spray was?"

"It's been there for, like, the entire time we've known each other."

"Where?"

"Kitchen. Same drawer your dad keeps the gas money in."

Gabe's nickname on the ice is *Momma Bear*. Sometimes I forget how thoroughly he's earned that. I glance at my arm. "You think there's gauze in there?"

Gabe shrugs. "I can check."

He steps out, leaving me somehow feeling worse than I already did. I carefully open my hand and look at the howlite. The white-and-black stone is smeared with dried blood.

I wince and lower my arms, sinking down until only my head is above water. I stare at the wobbly image of my body. My chest almost looks perfect like this. Or, at least, it looks exactly as distorted as the rest of me.

There's a world where that *thing* killed me. There's also a world in which I came out of it with this horrible, mangled chest, and somehow that scares me more.

Somehow, this is a best-case scenario.

When I wake up, my head feels like it's sealed in twenty layers of cellophane. I'm thirsty and *hot*. I kick at the covers until they're bunched at the end of the bed. Blindly, I reach for my phone on the nightstand. A phone that isn't there.

My hand goes still. Details come back to me one at a time.

I lie there for a second and listen to the sound of total silence. Norman was an extremely lazy dog, but he always knew the moment I woke up and would always come running. The bottom strip of my door is covered in tiny scratches.

Grief scuttles under my skin, although I'm barely conscious enough to know what to do with it. I don't hear anything.

I press my face into my pillow and try to repeat this to myself until the sob dislodges itself from the back of my throat. Norman is kdead. There's nothing I can do about it. He's dead; I'm not.

Finally, I force myself to sit up and look at my injuries. Gabe helped me wrap my arm and leg in gauze last night. I slowly flex my arm back and forth. Nothing *hurts* beyond a faint, distant sense of soreness.

Gabe is asleep in the bed beside me, smooshed up against the wall. I don't remember when *I* fell asleep, so I have no clue when he finally stopped pacing around like a worried mother hen. I'm careful to be quiet as I get up. I catch a glimpse of myself in the mirror that hangs from the back of my door: I'm pale, maybe, but otherwise fine. I slip out into the hall.

Then it occurs to me how easy that was. I can put full weight on my leg without issue.

I make a quick detour to the bathroom, pulling my shirt over my head before I'm even in front of the mirror. As if I might have missed something. There's a bruise on the back of my shoulder, which is tender to the touch, but my chest remains clean. I can't help but smile at myself in the mirror. *You lucky son of a bitch.*

I unwrap the bandage on my arm. In the light of day, it's easier to imagine teeth making these wounds. A film has formed over the puncture marks, skin bruised in shades of pink and purple. Not too bad, considering.

To balance things out, I pull the gauze on my leg down and see the same chunk of *extremely* visible bone. My whole body flashes cold before I'm able to hurriedly yank the bandage back up. I don't move again until my stomach stops doing flips.

So, my leg stays wrapped up, but I leave my arm out to breathe before pulling my shirt on again and stepping into the hall. I find Dad's jacket on the floor, and between the blood and the fact that one sleeve has been torn completely to shreds, I end up shoving it into the garbage. If I'm lucky, he'll think he left it behind in some airport somewhere. Wouldn't be the first time.

Then there's the mudroom. Little chunks of wood and plaster litter the floor. The door doesn't shut fully any more, and that's to say nothing of the few bits of mesh that used to be the screen. I carefully slip into my boots before I step outside.

Once I've stepped through the broken fence, the first sign of myself I can find is my sneaker, sticking straight up out of the snow. I don't find the second shoe right away, so I sort of shuffle around until I feel it bump against my leg. I find my phone the same way.

Amazingly, it still has a little bit of a charge left. I have several unread texts waiting for me, some of them from my father. I linger, a sneaker tucked under each arm, as I read them.

(YESTERDAY 6:16 AM) DAD

Hey kiddo. Snowed in at MN.
Hoping to be home Saturday
at the latest.
Please try to cook something.
Don't just eat pizza.

He's snowed in.

I should call him. Even if it takes him a few days to get here, he should know that something like *this* happened.

But I don't. I hurry back inside, shivering by the time I shut the door. Only then does something in my brain nag at me. I look at my phone again to confirm. *Yesterday?*

The date on my phone reads Wednesday, January 11, 7:05 AM.

There's no way I slept through an entire day. And yet that's what the calendar tells me. I fell asleep Monday night, and now it's Wednesday morning. I still have twenty minutes to make it to school on time.

I go straight back to my room and shake Gabe by the shoulder. He bolts upright, but as soon as he recognizes me, he lies back down and groans.

"Why is it Wednesday?" I ask him.

"Why—what?"

"It's Wednesday," I repeat. "How long was I asleep for?"

Gabe runs a hand over his face and blinks heavily. "Um, a day. Figured you needed it."

My head fills with so many questions that I swear the room starts to spin. I can't even think of the last time I slept past nine or ten in the morning. A full day. *Twenty-four hours.*

"Did you go to school yesterday?" I manage. It's not an important question, but it's the only one I can stomach asking.

Gabe sits up slower this time and stretches. "No. I told Mom you had food poisoning, and that I was keeping an eye on you. I didn't want to..."

He doesn't say *leave and have you immediately die*, but I fill in the blanks. I nod, still trying to process everything else. "Thanks."

Gabe's eyes search mine. "How are you feeling?"

"Fine. I guess. Thirsty."

It takes a minute to realize what he's talking about. I hold my arm out and Gabe swings his legs over the side of the bed. His touch is light, gently turning my arm from side to side. "This is *impossible*," he finally says.

"I feel okay," I insist. "Sore, but not, like, festering with rabies."

"It looks like it's already healing," Gabe clarifies. His fingers dance around each puncture mark, though he never touches them. A small wave of goosebumps forms on my skin.

I try to play it casual. "Yeah, they were healing Monday night, too. Pretty standard."

The expression on Gabe's face makes it clear he doesn't agree, but he doesn't push it. He shakes his head. "What *was* that, anyway?"

I shrug. "I don't know. Some…pissed-off dog? I figured you got a better look."

Gabe finally lets me have my arm back. "Not really. That'd be *big* for a dog, but I don't know what else it would've been."

I don't know either, and I don't know what difference it makes. An animal like that is gonna get shot by somebody by the end of the week. It'll end up on the news, and they'll interview Annie Searchwell so she can go on about how horrible it is, and nobody will ever think about it again.

Gabe follows me as I go into the kitchen, probably waiting for me to keel over and start seizing. Except I'm really *fine*. I have more energy than I know what to do with. The only real problem is that I'm starving.

Cold pizza is disgusting, but I don't have the patience to throw anything in the microwave. I fold up a slice that's gone in two bites.

"So…you're good, then, Bambi?" Gabe's eyes stick to me.

My hands are already folding up a second slice. "I literally couldn't be better. You okay to drive?"

He frowns. "To school?"

I nod.

Gabe blinks. "What about your dad?"

"Snowed in at the airport in Minneapolis again."

He sighs. "Urgent care first, then school. Deal?"

I roll my eyes, but Gabe's not letting this go. If I really have to choose between the two of them, I'd rather do this with Gabe than with my dad.

When we walk outside to the car, Annie Searchwell is standing in her driveway, scraping the ice off her windshield. One of her cats, an orange one, is sitting in what I think is the kitchen window, watching her.

At the sound of Gabe unlocking the car, she glances over at us. She waves and shouts, "Good morning, honey!"

I cringe at the pet name. Not because there's anything *wrong* with it, but because Annie only stopped calling me by my deadname maybe six months ago. At most. Every time she shouts hello to me from across the street, I tense with horrible anticipation.

Gabe, for his part, politely waves back. I smile tightly and nod in Annie's general direction before I pull myself into the passenger seat. My leg feels no discomfort in the movement.

"That's the chick who's always on Channel 17, right?" Gabe asks, sitting down behind the wheel.

"The very same."

"I forgot she lives around here."

"Don't worry," I sigh, "I haven't. Every time she loses one of her cats, I'm up all night hearing her scream after 'em."

At the mention of them, I glance back at Annie's house. I have no idea how many animals she has at any given moment; half of her Channel 17 appearances are about the joys of fostering. And though her house is technically on another street, it's not any larger than mine. I'm still not expecting the number of cats suddenly looking through the kitchen window.

Their heads are all cocked in the same direction: at me.

4

Urgent care is an hour of wasted time. Gabe and I spend most of it in the waiting room, awkwardly avoiding eye contact with the few other people there at eight in the morning. When my name is called, I go in alone. This is mostly so I can avoid the weight of Gabe's judgement when I lie about being a cisgender boy, bitten by a friend's dog and definitely not able to see part of his leg bone. I show the doctor the bite on my wrist and ask if she thinks I have rabies.

She inspects the injury with a frown. "Any reason to believe your friend's dog *hasn't* been vaccinated?"

I slowly shake my head. Obviously, I don't know for sure whether that thing was rabid or just pissed off. But from what I was able to Google in the waiting room, I'm not symptomatic, and neither was it.

"Have *you* been vaccinated for rabies within the last year?"

I think I surprise her when I say I have. "My dad travels a lot," I explain, "and we live right next to the preserve."

The doctor marks something on my chart and makes a contemplative *hm*. "Well then, if you so much as get a head cold over the next month, I want you to come right back in. Otherwise, I don't think you'll have more than a little scarring." She takes one more look at the bite on my arm. "Can't imagine the size of that dog."

The only other notable thing that happens all week comes on Friday. I open my gym locker to another paper: a black-and-white printout of the cover of *Irreversible Damage: The Transgender Craze Seducing Our Daughters*. Ethan must've used all his artistic ability on the first attempt. Or, at least, all his colour ink. I roll my eyes and stuff it into my bag before Gabe can see it, and nothing comes of it.

Beyond that, everything is almost normal again. The bites are still hell to look at, but they don't hurt, and I can almost pretend they aren't there. The hardest part is waking up and not hearing Norman come running for breakfast.

Also on Friday, I shoot a text to my manager, Natalie, since I ended up sleeping through my first shift back. I make up a vague medical emergency, and she asks if I'm okay to come in tomorrow.

When Saturday morning rolls around, I wake up to a text from Dad. He's still snowed in, and even though he thinks he'll be able to get home soon, the weather is rougher up there than it is down here. I tell him not to worry. I don't mention Norman or the door.

I will eventually; I *have to*. But he's stranded in another state, and I'm still healing fine on my own, so I tell myself that it can wait.

Normally, when we're scheduled for similar shifts, Mars will drive me to and from work at the Bolingbrook Regal, the cinema a few minutes down the road. I decide to walk today instead. It hasn't snowed since Monday night, so I'm mostly sidestepping puddles of blackened slush. At no point does my leg buckle on me. In fact, I have a slightly optimistic spring to my step the whole time.

The weekends are always nightmarishly busy, so there's no time for Mars and me to talk once I finally clock in. I get behind the snack counter, let Mars handle the talking, and become a cog in the machine. There's no clock for me to watch, but I'd still swear that half my shift goes by before the line finally dies down for more than a minute.

By the time it does, my back's started to ache. A part of my brain buzzes with overstimulation, but at a level that's manageable. I'm in the middle of restocking cups when Mars suddenly slams her hands down on the counter next to me.

"I thought you were fucking dead." She stares at me so hard she might as well be looking straight through my skull. Now that she's not wearing a hat, I can see how much her brunette roots have grown out.

"Sorry." I awkwardly smile. "Shit happened."

"Shit better have. Are you good?"

"Fine now." I push the plastic wrap into the trash. "I gotta replace our back door before my dad gets home, though."

Mars frowns. "What'd you do?"

I glance around the lobby. Tammy Spangler, the girl with the dead corgi, is sweeping the lobby with a broom, and there's a group of people chatting at the ticket counter, so we've only got a minute. I crouch down beneath the counter and Mars follows my lead.

"I think it was a dog," I say as I pull my sleeve up. My leg will remain bandaged until I stop seeing bone, but I've continued to let this lesser wound breathe.

Her eyes widen. "Holy *shit*," she whispers, grabbing my arm and yanking it towards her.

"It killed Norman," I add, wincing when my voice buckles.

Mars's expression becomes an entirely different kind of horrified. "Oh my God, Hunter. Seriously, are you okay?"

I clear my throat and take my arm back. "Yeah. That's what's weird, though. I'm fine. I mean, everything's healing."

Becoming *emotionally fine* about all this might take a couple weeks longer.

"Did you go to a hospital? What did they say?"

I shake my head. "No, no hospital."

Mars frowns. "Why the hell not?"

"Because my dad just paid ten grand for me to have a

normal chest. I didn't want to be responsible for— Anyway, I'm fine. Urgent care said I was fine."

Mars makes a face but doesn't argue.

She gets back to her feet, and the next thing I hear is her customer service voice, pitched significantly higher than she normally speaks. "Hi! Welcome to Regal, dude, what can I get ya?"

I pop up, too, and come face to face with Ethan Adams.

My recognition of him is instantaneous, but I watch his recognition of *me* slowly light his eyes. His mouth curls into a smile. "No shit. How long have you worked here, man?"

It takes me a moment to find my voice. "Two years."

My eyes focus on movement over his shoulder. There's a girl taking a box of Cookie Dough Bites down from the shelf. Green eyes make contact with mine.

Riley.

"Oh, well I sound like a dick now." Ethan's snigger punches me back down to earth. "In that case: a large popcorn, two Cokes and whatever she wants."

He jabs a thumb back at Riley, and my eyes helplessly follow.

This time, Riley avoids looking straight at me. Her shoulders shake with what I think is laughter. My stomach twists impossibly tighter.

"Perfect. Let me take you over here." Mars's customer service voice doesn't slip an inch.

I glance at her. I've never told her anything about Ethan or Riley, but I notice that when she smiles at them, it doesn't reach the rest of her face. She walks down to the register. Riley follows her, but Ethan stays with me.

My heart is jackhammering so hard it's *embarrassing*. I hate it. The hate clogs my throat.

"You got my message, right?" Ethan whispers.

I could punch him. He wouldn't have the time to dodge it if I were to swing right now.

"Great seeing you," I manage.

I take a popcorn bucket and turn my back to him as I fill it. I can feel his eyes burning into the back of my skull even when his voice moves to Mars's end of the counter. Another wave of sudden nausea nearly makes me curl in on myself.

Then Mars is beside me, silently taking the popcorn from my hands. In a matter of seconds, it's over. Ethan and Riley are gone by the time I can bring myself to look up.

Embarrassment comes flooding in immediately. I go outside of my body and visualize myself against Ethan, and I wonder how anybody has *ever* seen me as a guy. Pathetic, whimpering, small. What is *wrong* with me?

"You good?" Mars is here again. I don't know how she manages to look more serious now than when I showed her the bite on my arm.

I nod. "Yeah. Good."

"Because you look like you're gonna throw up."

"I'm *fine*."

We get busy after that, so Mars doesn't get to keep poking at it. I try to retreat inside my head, but my anxiety keeps pulling me right back out again. I'm hyperaware of every part of myself, every move I make. A cis guy wouldn't stand like me, wouldn't walk like me, wouldn't smile like me.

It takes me way too long to realize that I'm spiralling.

Once we slow down again, I volunteer for trash duty and I'm gone before Mars can try and tag along.

It must be close to freezing outside, but I'm sweating so much that I take off my jacket and hang it from the handle of the trash chute. There's a small parking lot out here for employees and a thin wooden fence that separates us from the closest residential neighbourhood. Most importantly, I'm alone.

I try to slow my breathing, but each time it comes out as a frantic hiccup. It takes a minute for me to finally give up and sit on the ground, my head in my hands. My heart feels like it's managed to beat its way to the top of my throat.

Am I having a heart attack?

No. That'd be even more ridiculous than the panic attack I know this to be.

I'm fine.

As soon as I tell myself this, a stabbing sensation flashes through my stomach. My body's answer of *no, you aren't*.

I wince and grind my teeth together. It's not that I want to go back, but the longer I sit here, the more it feels like someone is ripping at my insides. I grab my jacket, lock the chute, and hurry inside. Thankfully, no one is in the halls, which means no screens have emptied recently and I don't have to elbow my way into the singular stall in the men's room.

I sit down and curl up on myself, one hand pressing into my stomach, trying to alleviate the pressure – the cramping.

It takes an embarrassingly long time for my brain to make the connection between the hot flashes and the pain. It's been *years* since I've had to. Because that'd be impossible.

I don't think there's a dignified way to check if you've started your period. Dread and shame are both thick in my mouth as I pop the button on my jeans and stick my hand inside my briefs.

My fingers come back red.

5

Mars finds me in the women's restroom.

I threw an Out of Order sign on the door before locking myself inside a stall to cry in peace, so the sound of squeaking hinges and footsteps against the tile makes me go rigid. At least until I look down and recognize the bright yellow Docs on the opposite side of the door. Neither of us says anything at first. The only thing that breaks the silence is my sniffling.

"Wanna talk about it?" Mars finally asks, more serious than I'm ready for.

All of a sudden, I *wish* Ethan was the worst of my night. "I got my period," I mumble.

There's a beat. Just as I'm gearing up to say it again, Mars goes, "Oh!"

Then, "*Oh.*"

Her Docs abruptly pivot and walk away. I have no idea what she's doing until I hear the jangle of her key ring and then metal violently clanking together. It's loud enough to get me out of my head. I wipe my eyes and take a look down at myself. By some miracle, I realized what was happening before I could bleed through any of my clothes, though that still leaves me with the indignity of sitting with wads of toilet paper shoved down my pants.

Mars comes back and sits down on the floor. She sticks her arm underneath the stall door, a fistful of tampons in her hand.

I'm really not in the mood to laugh, but something about the absurd sincerity of a tampon bouquet breaks me. I snort, wipe the lingering tears out of my eyes, and lean forward to pluck a tampon from between her fingers.

"Thanks," I breathe.

Mars steps away from the door while I clean myself up. Once I'm feeling closer to human again, I force myself to stand and step out. Mars is sitting on the counter, feet dangling several inches off the ground. A couple of feet to our left, the tampon dispenser is hanging open, thoroughly looted.

She smiles and gives me a little wave. The air between us isn't tense, but it's skittish.

Finally, though, Mars exhales and opens her arms. "Get over here."

I shuffle forward until I'm close enough for Mars to drag me into a hug, her chin coming to rest on my shoulder. Something in my chest constricts.

"God, you're really getting perfect marks this week, huh?"

She sighs, one hand rubbing up and down my back.

She doesn't know the half of it.

Later that night, after Mars has dropped me off at home, I stick my phone inside a Ziploc so I can take it with me into the shower. I need to figure out what the hell is wrong with me as badly as I need to feel *clean* again.

My period was the first thing to go away when I started testosterone. Since then, it hasn't been uncommon for a little spotting here and there. Bodies are weird, I still have a uterus, shit happens. But it's never *come back*. Not like this. My brain jumps straight to the worst: there's not enough testosterone in my body. Some part of me is rejecting my hormones. I'm gonna die; I'm *already* dying.

I Google a few different phrases. Official medical sites can sometimes be helpful, but I only click on old forum websites. They're the only places where real trans people get specific and honest. All I need to know is that I'm not a singular, freakish anomaly, and I get that confirmation back in spades.

u/transinquisator

stress on the body definitely can make a difference, so it might be to do with that. Top surgery might also have messed with your hormone levels slightly as breast tissue produces a small amount of oestrogen

[deleted]

Sometimes periods can have that "comeback" moment once in a blue moon on T. Also stress can counteract your testosterone levels. Cortisol blocks testosterone production, so if you're stressing, try to find ways to calm down.

u/yes_its_jane86

breasts create a lot of hormones normally & a lot of ppl report feeling sad after top bc of the sudden loss of those hormones! its completely normal 2 feel this way, its just the chemicals

u/HenryDeer5

It'll stop like it did before. I just went through this for three weeks. Give it time brother

It's hardly professional medical advice, but it makes sense. Top surgery + animal attack + my typical high levels of stress = a uterus in revolt.

I make it through the rest of the weekend alone. Gabe seems uneasy about not being with me, but as long as I respond to the memes he sends me in a timely manner, he doesn't bombard me with questions about how I'm doing and what he can bring me and am I *sure* I don't want him to swing by?

There are some positives to being alone. I take plenty of showers and find the heated blanket Mom bought for me when I was a kid and watch a bunch of ice hockey. When the texture of my shirt starts to overstimulate me, I can take it off and not get nauseous with dysphoria. But despite the positives, I'm certainly not having a good time. My team the Penguins lose, I can't find a door that costs less than two grand, and as my wound continues scabbing over, my arm starts itching like crazy. I can't eat and I can barely sleep.

I keep catching myself staring at my chest, too. It's weird to be able to see something when it's still too numb to properly feel. I press my thumbnail into the skin, watching the colours shift from white to pink to red to convince myself there's still blood flowing under there.

I read online that it takes years for some people to regain total feeling in their chest. I try to imagine that. *Years*.

Then it's Monday. My period hasn't gotten any better, which means Gabe has to drive me to the corner store down the road from school first thing in the morning.

It feels like every car that drives by is homed in on me. Everybody at school, half a mile away, is watching me grab a box of Tampax off the shelf. The cashier who rings me up knows that I'm buying these for myself. He knows they're for me; he might as well be staring right through my clothes at my horrible, disgusting, traitorous body.

There's a part of my brain that knows I'm tripping, but

knowing that doesn't make my skin stop crawling. It only serves to make me feel like even more of an idiot. I want to cry. I feel hyper-visible, overexposed and overstimulated even when nothing happens.

I get back into Gabe's car and cram the box of tampons into the bottom of my bag, and he gets us to school in one piece.

"You know I can drop you back at home," Gabe offers, after he's put the car into park.

I shake my head. Despite the paranoia buzzing between my ears, I haven't *seriously* considered going home. I'm already here, at the daily limit of pain meds and still getting hot flushes, but I'm here. "Appreciate it, but no thanks."

I pull my bag into my lap and check inside. There's not a chance in hell I'm gonna risk anybody seeing the box of tampons there, not for any reason.

"What are you trying to prove?" Gabe suddenly asks.

Startled, I look at him. "What?"

Gabe shrugs, hands lingering on the wheel. His hair is matted to his forehead the way it does after he's taken his helmet off, and it occurs to me that he must've had one of his awful five-in-the-morning hockey practices today. We both hate them, but he doesn't go to them *without me*.

"I don't know," he finally says. "I mean, half the girls I know skip school when they're on their period. It's not a big deal."

Fire ignites under my skin. "Well, I'm not a *girl*, Gabe, first of all."

He shoots me a dark look. "I *know that*. My point is that you look like hell, and what are you proving by torturing yourself?"

I answer him by zipping my bag shut and getting out of the car.

Dick move. I know. I'm also entirely focused on not bleeding through the last shitty tampon Mars gave me from the bathroom machine, so I literally don't have the time to be truly angry at Gabe. I slip into the men's room and change out tampons, and for this I'm granted about five seconds of relief.

Then the pain resumes.

I know Gabe's trying to be helpful. In his never-had-a-uterus way. But just like I don't know how to describe dysphoria, I don't know how to explain a period to somebody who's never had one. If I stayed home every time my body does something it isn't supposed to, I'd never leave the house.

Things are fine for the first hour. Paranoia continues to hang in the back of my mind, but I force myself to accept its familiarity. It's the same paranoia I've been trying to beat since I was twelve: the idea that everyone knows, everyone can *smell it*, they're all gonna laugh at me, etc.

Nobody here cares about me that much. Every time I become too aware of the blood my body is trying to expel, I repeat this to myself over and over again. Nobody here cares.

I change my tampon before second period to get an idea of how bad the flow is. The answer is still *bad*. Which, admittedly, is weird, but maybe this is just my body's way of making up for not having a menstrual cycle in nearly two years.

It's only after third period that I see Gabe again. We walk from the B wing to the E wing. I apologize for being a dick, and Gabe apologizes for calling me a girl, and I tell him I know he didn't mean it like that. It's fast – apologies between men always seem to be, I've learned – and it's settled before we make it to the locker room.

As we walk onto the football field, it occurs to me that I could tell Ms Bailey that I'm on my period. If I tell her, the thought goes, maybe she'll take a little pity on me.

But then I would have to say, out loud, that I'm on my period.

I keep my mouth shut and start walking my laps.

I remember when I first got my period. I was twelve years old, and the first thing I did was hysterically call my mom, who was already living in Texas by then. She told me that I needed to *listen* to my body. The cramps, the mood swings, the back pain; all these things were my body's way of trying to warn me. Listen to what it tells me. Because my body was meant to do this horrible purging every month for the rest of my life.

From the moment she said it, I hated the idea that my body was a thing *I* had to listen to. It's *my* body. It listens to *me*.

Gabe's female friends might skip class and retreat to a little cushioned pile of heated blankets and chocolate at the first sign of cramps, but I don't. I never have, even when my cramps used to be so bad that I'd run out of class to throw up. I've always done what I'm doing right now: grit my teeth and push forward, until my body takes the hint.

I'm in charge of my body. My body is not in charge of me.

A quick glance at my phone tells me that I've only been doing this for about five minutes. One lap. Twenty-five minutes left to kill. I stop and sigh. This is a self-imposed death march, but out of all my options, it's the one I hate the least.

When I go to take my next step, the inside of my pant leg is suddenly wet.

I freeze, and I know. As innately as I know how to breathe, I know the feeling of blood on my thigh. Time freezes, my body locks up, everything around me screeches to an instant halt.

Then, idiotically, I think: *maybe if I don't move, it won't get worse.*

The cold, sticky feeling is all I can focus on as I turn back to where the class is huddled. Ms Bailey is going over proper throwing form or something, pointing at her elbow as she addresses the group. I try to find Gabe in the crowd, before quickly deciding there's no point. Still focused on the bleeding, worst part of me, I stalk over and stand at the back of the group, where only a couple of heads twist at my arrival.

I wait through Ms Bailey's entire spiel about proper finger placement and the importance of follow-through. I don't make a scene. Each breath I take is slow, conscious, measured. I wait patiently, and I don't look down at myself.

Dark clouds above seem to signal a storm. A gust of wind whips past me. The blood has reached my ankle. It has gone down my entire leg to my ankle, where it tickles the bone. I want to throw up.

Ms Bailey's whistle chirps. The class moves forward seamlessly, half of them grabbing footballs from a cart and the other half chattering among themselves. As soon as they've gone, I push forward into Ms Bailey's line of sight.

"Wakesfield?" She frowns. "What's up?"

"Can I go back inside?" I ask. My voice breaks, and I want to die all over again.

"Something wrong?"

My mouth opens for the words – *please, I just need to go clean up* – when another voice cuts through the air like a missile. "Yo, Frankentits, is your dick okay?"

That's Damien Hulme. When I look up, Ethan is standing right beside him, and there are plenty more guys staring at me and openly cackling. I know what they're laughing at, and yet I lower my gaze anyway.

The inside of my left pant leg has a blood trail going all the way down to my shoe. So visible. So much worse than I thought. My face burns hot with embarrassment.

Ms Bailey gives a short, sharp blow to her whistle. That doesn't stop Gabe from suddenly shooting through the crowd like a knife, right up to Damien. He doesn't hit him. He gets nose-to-nose with him and says something. The mood of the laughter shifts just as quickly as Damien, all five feet nine of him, suddenly gets in Gabe's face, too. Everybody frenzies at the promise of blood.

"*Hey!*" Ms Bailey blows her whistle again and starts towards them, but not before remembering that I'm there. "Oh, yes, go ahead inside, honey. *Boys—*"

I don't run. Somehow, running feels like it would be the final indignity atop the mountain already suffocating me. As Ms Bailey's voice comes down over the field, I walk to the locker room as quickly as my legs can take me. Above, snow begins to fall. The flakes sharply prick my face where they land.

It's not until I'm inside that I realize the horrible, wounded sound I'm hearing is coming from my own throat. I don't know if there's a difference between a panic attack and hyperventilating. In the middle of all the noise, though, one thought repeats itself with clarity:

Something is deeply, seriously wrong with me.

The nurse's assistant doesn't believe me when I tell her why I'm not in class. I have to argue with her about why I'm *really* there until the nurse, Mrs Hearst, pokes her head out from the supply cabinet and recognizes me. "They're – transgender, Stefanie, they're not messing with you," she explains, sounding exasperated.

My jaw clenches. Whether it's insisting on using my last name or using they/them pronouns, everybody's *continued* inability to deal with me digs deeper under my skin. Stefanie at least has the decency to look embarrassed, face flushed red as she checks the lost and found box. They don't have any spare pants that would fit me.

Then she asks me if I want to contact either of my parents, and the thing is I *do*, except my dad is still in Minnesota and my mom is in Texas. Even if I wanted their help, I couldn't have it. I tuck my hands into my armpits to keep from anxiously flapping them. Tension coils around my bones until I can feel my fingers shaking.

Gabe comes while we're trying to figure out what to do with me, his face red from the cold and both of our bags slung over his shoulder. He tells me we're going. I don't ask questions. I just follow him as quickly as I can.

We don't talk in the car. The atmosphere is thick. I can only describe it as a heavy sense of defeat, though I can tell that Gabe is still thrumming with adrenaline. Then his mom calls. I can hear her shouting through the phone speaker. Gabe hardly reacts beyond chewing on his lip and the occasional "yes, Ma".

He's still taking the heat when we park, so I go inside without him. The house is freezing. On my way to the bathroom, I notice that snow has started to build up around the back door frame, where the broken door flops around uselessly.

I don't attempt to salvage any of my clothes; anything with blood on it goes straight in the garbage. I trash the bandage on my leg, too, horrified at the thought of whatever cross-contamination I could've been exposed to. In the shower, I scrub myself clean around the wounds, waiting for the water to stop stinging before I sit down and take a really good look at the bite on my leg.

At last, there seems to be some kind of film building up over the bone. It's barely visible now. A small relief. The bruises, though, have turned almost black. And I know that's how bruises work: they get dark before they get light. It's just that mine only appear to be getting darker and darker.

Damien's voice rattles around in my head. Helplessly, I put one hand over my chest. Flat, but numb. I trace a finger over one of the incision scars, tiny flickers of prickly discomfort shooting up as I do. Some reminders of maleness despite the womanhood still stubbornly leaking down my legs. *Something.*

There's a knock on the bathroom door, which I realize I've left open. "You good?"

I jump. My voice comes out wobbly. "Yeah."

I rest my head against my knees and try to breathe. The

worst of it is over. For now, at least. I try to repeat this to myself until it hurts to think.

"When was the last time you even had a period?" Gabe's voice is a little closer now.

I take one last deep breath before I turn the shower off. "Two years ago."

A moment passes in silence. Then I hear him whisper, "Jesus."

I manage to smile, grab the towel from the rack, and dry myself off. There's a part of me that wonders if I should be more modest around Gabe, but he's my straight best friend and, more importantly, I am a transgender void where things like attraction go to die. I have bigger priorities right now, anyway.

I wrap the towel around my waist before I pull the curtain back and find Gabe sitting on the counter, spinning his phone in his hands. "Was it always that intense?" he asks.

My laugh is dry. I sit on the counter beside him, gripping the edge so I don't fidget. "I think something might be wrong with me," I finally admit.

Gabe sighs. "I've been trying to tell you that."

I glare up at him. "This isn't because of the animal thing."

"How is it *not?*"

"I don't know! But my uterus isn't connected to a bite on my arm!" I push my palms against the counter and huff. "This is hormones," I insist. As if doing so will make it true. "My body's freaking out, and it'll calm down, I— This week *sucks*."

This is my body failing me for the umpteenth time. Like that's all it knows how to do.

Something suddenly occurs to me. I look up at Gabe. "Did you get suspended?"

He frowns. "No."

At least there's that. I exhale. "What did you even say to him?"

Gabe doesn't answer straight away, which is the first sign of something bad. He sighs and glares at the wall in front of us. "Told him to shut up," he finally says.

I don't believe him for a moment. "Uh-huh?"

More silence. At last, he says, "I told him to shut up, and that if he ever did anything like that again, I'd fucking kill him."

My stomach drops. "Gabe—"

"Hey, it's done." He quickly hops down and stands in front of me. "Also, not the point."

I clench my jaw. I hate how he treats me sometimes, like I'm too small or stupid to know how to take care of myself. I hate knowing he'd *never* act like this for any of his other buddies.

My hair drips onto my shoulders. Gabe is staring at me like my face is the only safe part of my body. I don't know whether having his eyes on me is comforting, or if it makes me a lab rat under observation. I hate how this feels, too.

"That was a lot of blood," Gabe finally whispers. "This is starting to freak me out."

An understatement. I look away and nod.

"Have you called your dad yet?" he asks.

I can't help laughing. Dad hasn't even told me if the weather up in Minnesota has cleared. "I'm not calling him because I got my period."

"Also the—"

"If I tell him about the animal thing, he's just gonna freak out." I make sure my towel is secure before I climb down. "I need us – *both of us*, seriously – to not get suspended over a bunch of meathead jocks."

Gabe frowns. "Am I not also a meathead jock?"

I scoff. "No, you're a dork in skates. Move, before I start bleeding on everything."

Gabe stays for the rest of the night. I imagine it's mostly to delay facing his mom's wrath, but I'm quietly relieved that I'm not alone. We pick at some takeout I ordered over the weekend (though my stomach is so knotted I barely eat anything) and the Penguins win in overtime, which earns me about five minutes of bragging rights before Gabe chirps back at me: "Okay, Bambi, you beat *the Ducks*."

An hour later, Gabe falls asleep on the opposite end of the couch. I let the *Smiling Friends* episode finish before I shut the TV off. Gabe's slow breathing is suddenly the only sound in the room. I glance at him. His cheek is smooshed against his shoulder.

I understand completely why I used to have a crush on

him. Plenty of men are hot, or objectively attractive, but Gabe is one of the few where I'm like: That is a *beautiful* guy.

This is one of those moments where I almost wish I were a girl. These moments come rarely, but they do come. If I were a girl, I could ask Gabe to hold me and tell me that I'm not going to die.

Sometimes I worry about these flashes of longing. I try to tell myself that it's one of those human urges, to miss a time that wasn't *happy*, exactly, but familiar. I don't know what the "right" language is – if I'm a girl who became a guy, or if I was a guy from the beginning – but I still spent years *trying* to be a girl, even if it never worked. No matter how rigorously I tried to mirror their behaviour, I was always one step out of sync, failing each of their strange social tests.

Men, in that way, are simpler. At least in my experience, teenage guys aren't playing 4D chess to try and catch you in a contradiction. You punch each other in the stomach and carry on. But I've found no ease in their company, either. I still feel like a funny puzzle piece that the factory made wrong and that'll never fit no matter who or *what* I am.

I sit there in the dark for a long time, thinking about tomorrow. There's no way I can show up at school. Not with my body like *this*. *This* shit doesn't happen to boys. But I can't just skip class until whenever this period decides to end, either. Gabe *definitely* can't.

Eventually, I pull out my phone. I haven't had a consistent

period in years; maybe I've forgotten how bad they can be. Maybe I'm blowing this all out of proportion without meaning to. Or maybe this is exactly as bad as I'm afraid it is. Maybe something's wrong with me in ways I'm not even aware of yet.

Either way, Gabe's not exactly an expert on these things. As much as he might want to, I don't think he'll actually be able to help me through this.

Mars, on the other hand, might.

hey, you awake?

MARS BAR

wazzuppp

a lot lol.

need you to be the voice of reason

can you come over tomorrow?

totally dude

everything okay?

i'm technically alive,

if that's what you mean

so not okay

yeah i'll come over and see you
in the morning before school babe
love you

love you too

6

I started having weird dreams when I began taking testosterone. Dreams where I whale on Ethan even though the physics are all wrong and I never manage to hurt him. Dreams where I'm a girl, tugging at the neckline of a dress that keeps trying to choke me. Dreams where I'm unquestionably, totally, physically male.

The first solid image of this particular dream is Norman. He's peeing on the tree in the corner of the yard. I'm standing on the other side of the fence. I don't appear to have a body, insofar as I can't see anything when I look down at myself. I'm a consciousness, a pair of eyes floating in the dark.

hungry

I step closer until I'm pressing against the chain link. Norman's head whips towards the sound and stares at me. He growls, first, before he puts his leg down and starts barking.

hungry

Norman keeps barking like he isn't only slightly bigger than a football. He seems especially small in this dream.

Everything suddenly seems small to me. A tiny dog, behind nothing but a thin, frail little fence.

hungry

The voice is not my own, although it echoes inside my head as if it were. I lunge for the fence and tear through it.

hungryhungryhungryhungryhungry

I wake up to the sound of somebody's thumb on the doorbell.

The ringing persists for several long seconds before it cuts out. Then I hear voices at the front of the house. As soon as the shock of being awake fades, I slump back into bed and shut my eyes. My jaw aches, like I've been clenching it all night. I'm sweaty. So, so incredibly sweaty.

I check my phone. No texts from my dad, so I can't imagine the voice outside is him. Which means it's Mars, or there's some random person at the door that Gabe is stuck having to talk to. Maybe it's Annie Searchwell; does she have a sixth sense for when a pet gets eaten?

No matter who it is, though, it's also a school day. I sit up.

Now, I haven't seen *The Godfather*. Mars has already yelled at me for this, like, a million times. But I have watched the scene with the guy who wakes up with the dead horse's head in his bed. You see the guy's hand first, already stained with blood when he pulls it out from under the sheets. Then he pushes the covers back, revealing more and more blood and gore until he finally finds the horse's head. This bloody, *real* horse head that some production assistant got from a slaughterhouse, staring up at this tough Italian mobster while he screams and screams.

Yeah. Pulling the covers off myself and seeing the blood is something like that.

I don't scream. Instead, I slam myself up against the wall and freeze there, trying to process what I'm looking at. This doesn't seem like it's another dream. I *think* I'm awake. Which means all this blood on the sheets came from *me*.

The voices are suddenly coming down the hall. Before I can even get out of bed, the door opens. Mars's hair swings freshly cut at her shoulders, dyed bright pink.

I don't know which she sees first – my face, or the crime scene in front of me – but she comes to a sharp stop in the doorway. Several feet back, I can see Gabe come to an equally sudden stop, his face pinched with confusion and concern. To Mars's credit, she doesn't run out screaming. Her look of shock goes away quickly behind a steeled expression of determination.

"*Okay*," Mars exhales. Thinks for a moment. "Shower. Tampon. Laundry. Talk."

It doesn't occur to me until I'm cramming my sheets into the washer that *this* is how Mars and Gabe finally meet. It almost makes this whole situation perversely funny. Like meeting your best friend's *other* best friend isn't already weird enough.

After we clean up – after I shower and get another tampon and get everything that'll fit into the washer – we end up in my living room. Gabe and I sit on the couch while Mars paces in a small semicircle in front of us. Her backpack is lying on the ground, as if she'd been planning on going to school after this.

"Okay," she finally says. "From the beginning."

I do most of the talking, although Gabe makes a point to fill in the details I avoid. I tell Mars again about Norman and whatever it was that attacked me. Gabe talks about how I slept for a full day and how quickly my bites have healed. We look down at my arm, at the bruises that've only gotten worse. I explain how my period came back, more intensely than any I've ever had in my life. I don't mention the nightmare.

Mars takes a minute to absorb it all. I have no idea how she does. But once she has, she puts her hands on her hips and sighs. "Okay. I think there are three options. Option one is that I take your legs, and Gabe here takes your arms, and we get you to a hospital."

I open my mouth, but Mars keeps going. "I know you don't want that. And I think we should respect that. *For now*."

Relief. However, as the tension in my shoulders starts to unwind, Gabe pipes up from beside me. "Okay, so is the second option waiting for him to bleed out?"

I shoot him a glare. "Dude."

"Hey, I appreciate that you're trying to help. Seriously."

He looks at Mars, who nods, before he turns back to me. "But she's not a doctor! What's she gonna tell us that we don't already know?"

Mars tilts her head to the side. "Are you someone who has periods?"

Gabe frowns. "No."

"Cool. I think I'm here to tell you that's not how periods work. Can I explain what option two *actually* is?"

Gabe puts his hands up in surrender.

I catch the ghost of a grin on Mars's lips. Her eyes linger on him for a moment before she continues: "Option two. This is an infection or whatever. Some reason your hormones are going all out of whack."

"Like rabies?" I ask sarcastically.

"Nah, you're too coherent for rabies."

"*To you*," Gabe says to himself.

Mars ignores him. "There's not a whole lot of exotic wildlife around here, I think our options are pretty limited. Did either of you manage to get a good look at this thing?"

I look at Gabe, who shrugs. "Some kind of dog," he says. "I don't know. It was big."

"Wolves are usually pretty big."

"I *know that* – I mean I've never seen a wolf out here, and the coyotes are terrified of people. This chased us."

Mars shrugs. "Grumpy wolf. Point is, we need to start somewhere. If we can find some kind of connection between whatever attacked you guys and whatever's happening with Hunter, maybe we can find a good antibiotic and knock this out over the weekend."

I doubt this, and yet I nod along. "What's option three?"

The grin that spreads across her face is like a shark's. "I'm so glad you asked."

Mars picks up her backpack and turns it over, dumping its contents at our feet. Gabe and I both peer down at a whole bunch of DVDs. "Option three is werewolves," she declares.

Gabe snorts, then puts both of his hands up again. "Sorry."

"No, it's supposed to be a joke. I didn't have a real third." Mars shrugs. "But you guys *did* get jumped by a wolf-adjacent animal, and now Hunter's all twitchy. So, let's say 49-49-2."

I pick up a few cases. There's a Blu-ray of *Ginger Snaps*. A DVD of *Silver Bullet* with the ninety-nine-cent price sticker on the cover. I think the *American Werewolf in London* disc is some kind of bootleg.

Werewolves. It's ridiculous to say out loud, even as a joke. What's more embarrassing is that for about five seconds, I almost treat it seriously.

"Hey." I look up to find Mars crouching in front of me. "You wanna know what I think, for real? You're *still* healing from surgery. That's trauma. Then you got *more* trauma with Cujo. Your body is probably really, *really* pissed at you right now. Doesn't mean you're dying. It just means you need to chill for a minute, okay? Gabe and I'll keep an eye on you. You get better? Great. You get worse? We drag you to a doc, kicking and screaming. How's that sound?"

Like everything about this situation, it doesn't sound ideal. But I nod because I can't imagine having another day like I had yesterday. I can't imagine going to class and having to look at any of those people, knowing what they must think of me.

Mars smiles and stands up. "Sweet! You weren't gonna go to school today, were you?"

Gabe answers for us both. "*No.*"

"Cool. Same. Here's another thought." Mars takes the DVDs I'm holding and puts them back in her bag. "It's *freezing* in here, and my parents won't bug us if we stay in my room. Let's go to mine and watch a bunch of stupid movies, and by next week, the only things we're gonna remember from this whole shebang are a bunch of shitty synth scores and bad puns. How's that sound?"

Even though Mars is on a first-name basis with my dad, I have met her parents exactly once. Her mom owns a hair salon on South Washington Street, and her dad is a short, nerdy-looking white guy who Mars gets her nose from. They live in a two-bedroom apartment not too far from my house, though I've only been inside as many times as I've met her parents.

"*Hi, Mom! Company, Mom!*" Mars shouts into the kitchen as she enters, pushing Gabe ahead of her and pulling me behind.

I don't hear a response before we're herded down a little hallway and into Mars's bedroom. I wonder if Mars skips school often, or if she'd just texted her mom: *hey, I have to have my weird friends over*, and her mom was like, *cool, have fun, don't get pregnant*.

Mars basically has her own little living space, her bedroom and bathroom tucked away in the corner of the apartment. Her room is dark, curtains drawn, and lit by red LED lights. There are a ton of posters on the walls, although I only know what a few of them are: namely the Waterparks one over her bed, and the *Brain Damage* one near her window.

"All right. Welcome to Casa de la Calico." Mars does a little spin before she unzips her bag and starts stacking DVDs on the shelf where her TV sits. "Now, we aren't limited to whatever I happen to own physically. We are only limited by my credit card and the fact that I have to work a closing shift tomorrow."

I sit down in the tiny lounge chair that Mars has at the foot of her bed. Gabe sits on the bed itself while Mars empties her bag and even takes a few more cases off her shelf. I count at least ten. When she's done, Mars steps back and sits next to Gabe.

Then it's the three of us, staring at a blank TV and a stack of DVDs that are supposed to be a joke, even though none of us are laughing. We're here because my body is tweaking out. Something might be seriously wrong with me, and we're… just hoping that isn't the case.

I don't realize Mars is on her phone until she suddenly speaks. "According to this, orange juice is good for boosting natural testosterone levels."

That's how I end up with a giant glass of orange juice that Mars instructs me to drink before she hits *play* on *Howling II: Your Sister Is a Werewolf*.

Howling II is silly and stupid, and it sets a silly and stupid mood. Although it takes a while for the unease to melt away, the movie is so nonsensical that I can't do anything *but* laugh. Even Gabe, who's been dead silent since we all piled into Mars's car, starts laughing at Mars's Christopher Lee impression. In between the jokes, I listen to them talk. At first, it's only about the movie, and then it's Gabe asking Mars about one of the posters on the wall, and before long Mars is explaining exactly why it is so, *so* obvious that Gabe is a Capricorn.

The only problem is that *Howling II* is genuinely too bad for me to make any direct comparisons to whatever it is I'm going through. Once we move on to better movies, the shared connective tissue becomes more apparent.

Mars and I have talked about this before: monster movies have always been about The Other. Like, vampires – or

Dracula, more specifically – started out as an anti-immigration metaphor, and then over time they've also become symbolic of sexual deviance. That's why most vampires still have heavy foreign accents, why the female vampires especially *love* making out with their female victims. That way, when the British nobleman comes running and stabs the vampire through the heart, the audience feels like proper balance has been restored. Your average white guy sees himself in Van Helsing, not Dracula, after all.

I've never thought much about werewolves. They're easier to make fun of, with the bad latex masks and the *Twilight* of it all, but I guess they're like any monster: you're born one or you become one, but everybody agrees you need to be destroyed.

"Okay, I am so disappointed *neither* of you have seen this one," Mars says as she pulls the *Ginger Snaps* Blu-ray from the pile. "It's the last great werewolf movie with practical effects, the first werewolf movie truly about girls, and the *only* werewolf movie about girls that's worth a shit."

"I thought *Werewolves on Wheels* was worth a couple shits," Gabe pipes up.

Mars seems to weigh the risks and benefits of chucking the case at Gabe's head before she sighs and pops the disc into the player. "Sure, wiseass. Anyway, Hunter, if you were turning into anything, it'd be one of these guys."

I frown. "Elaborate?"

"Well, if you were attacked by a real, bona fide werewolf, you would've gotten bitten during the full moon on the sixth, not on the ninth." Mars sits on the bed with a bounce. "The dates are all wrong. So even if it *was* a werewolf, it's not changing based on the phase of the moon."

"And in this movie, they don't?" Gabe asks for both of us.

Mars stops, then makes a face and a *so-so* motion with her hand. "Kind of? It's more the change isn't like flipping a light switch on and off. You get bitten, you turn, and then you're wolfed-out for ever. Moon ain't got much to do with it."

The orange juice has been making me nauseous from the moment I sat down with it. All of a sudden, though, it seems to worsen. "So I'm not a werewolf," I summarize, "but if I were, I'd be the *Ginger Snaps* kind."

"Exactly." Mars grins at me. "Hey, it's better than the *American Werewolf in London* kind. That'd hurt to do once a month for the rest of your life."

Ginger Snaps is more than a movie about girl werewolves. It's a movie specifically about how messed up menstrual cycles are. The main girl, Ginger, gets her period right before a werewolf attacks her, so her period is directly linked to her monstrous transformation. She gets hairy, bleeds everywhere, and gets a taste for killing that she can't stop. Becoming a woman is literally the start of the end of her life. When Ginger's sister, Brigitte, infects herself with the lycanthropic virus, the wound takes on the appearance of a vagina.

I know that Mars is joking with all this werewolf stuff. It's a distraction, but the anxiety of *what if?* still gnaws at the edge of my thoughts.

Also, during her rampage, Ginger eats a tiny little dog named Norman. Mars must've completely forgotten about that little detail, based on the look of absolute mortification that comes over her face when it happens. I don't say anything, but I do clench my jaw and stare at the posters on the wall until the urge to cry finally retreats.

The werewolf dies in *Ginger Snaps*. That's the other common thread between all these movies: the monster always has to die. Even if there's a moment of hesitation, a slight bit of humanity clearly there, their monstrous urges win out. Then they die.

After the credits roll on *Ginger Snaps*, Gabe calls for a bathroom break.

I shut my eyes and rest my head on the foot of the bed. My glass is still full enough to be heavy, and I'm so nauseous my mouth is dry.

As soon as I hear Gabe shut the door, Mars scrambles down to me. "I like him."

I snort. "Good. Gabe's very likable."

"And he's—?" She doesn't finish the thought, so I lift my head. Mars has both hands out in front of her, limp wristed.

I burst out laughing. "Oh God, no. He's straight. Crazy straight."

Her eyes narrow. "You're sure?"

"I'm— He's been my best friend since we were twelve, *yes*, I'm sure!"

"He's said that to you? Explicitly?"

I frown. Of course Gabe is straight. He dated Kylee Welch for a few weeks in junior year, and he's only ever talked about girls. He's going to play ice hockey for the rest of his life. Of course he's straight. But I suddenly find myself unable to vocalize this.

Mars shrugs and puts her hands up, like she's suddenly decided to accept my answer. For now. "Okay," she sighs. "Am I allowed to ask a second stupid question?"

I look at her from the corner of my eye as Gabe comes back into the room. "Depends."

She shrugs, *fair enough*, and waits for Gabe to sit on the bed beside her before she asks: "Who was the guy that freaked you out on Saturday?"

I don't know how she's found a worse thing than probing Gabe's sexuality. I twist in the chair so I can better face them, because this isn't going to be brief. "Ethan."

As expected, Gabe freezes and stares at me. "What?"

"He and Riley saw a movie. Nothing happened."

"Well, thanks for telling me."

"Nothing happened, okay? And you threatened to kill Damien for giving me shit; I don't want to worry about you babysitting me at work, too!"

Mars quietly raises her hand. When neither Gabe nor I go on, she asks, "Who's Riley?"

I shrug, like it's nothing, even as my hand instinctively finds the stone around my neck and grips it. "The girl he was with. Old friend."

"*Oh*. Tea?"

I shrug and tell her what I tell everybody: "We were best friends since we were kids. In the middle of eighth grade, she changed schools, and then we both ended up at Asena in ninth grade, and she was a normal teenage girl, and I was this weird transgender freak, and she hates that we ever used to be connected to each other."

I do believe that's partially the truth. It's the truth as everybody knows it. Riley is beautiful, I'm *me*, and people like me aren't friends with people like Riley. But the full truth is a little more complicated.

Riley and Ethan started dating over the summer before high school began. The three of us wound up sharing a civics class. I didn't like him, but my friendship with Riley had already changed so much in the time we spent apart that I didn't want to crack the glass any further. Then we had a field trip to Chicago, which resulted in me being stuck in a seat next to Ethan for the hour-long ride home.

There, in the middle of the bus, Ethan started asking me a bunch of questions about what testosterone was gonna do to my body. He swore it was just curiosity, but he kept talking even after I stopped giving him curt answers. He laughed at the concept of top surgery. Even if I sounded like a boy, even if I began to look like one, *it's still a girl's body. Nothing wrong with a girl's body. It'd be fucked if you ruined yours.*

The whole time, he had his hand on my thigh, slowly moving his touch higher and higher and smiling like the whole thing was hysterical. I never moved. Never screamed for the teacher. I sat there, tight with tension and mortification, staring at the back of Riley's head where she sat with her girlfriends at the front of the bus.

It took me a month to finally work up the nerve to tell Riley that her boyfriend was a creep. She told me I was a liar, that she couldn't believe I would even accuse her of associating with somebody like that, and it's been nearly three years since we've said a word to each other besides that.

Gabe is the only one who knows the whole story, and he doesn't do anything but pick at a hangnail as I tell Mars my sanitized version of events. The whole truth is a bummer. I like the half-truth because I think it's what everybody already assumes, and it's the version where I don't feel like everything is my fault.

Mars watches Gabe for a moment, before she sums the whole thing up pretty well: "That's some bullshit."

7

My dream doesn't last long. There are only a few fractured images. I'm running through my house, a sense of urgency propelling me as if I'm looking for something I can't find, something that's supposed to be here but isn't. Something I *need*. I throw the cushions off the couch, I tear open the kitchen cabinets, desperate for something that just *isn't here*.

Then I'm awake, and something in the back of my mouth is throbbing.

After a moment, I'm able to unclench my jaw. I push my hair out of my face before I carefully run my tongue along the inside of my mouth. It's not until I reach the upper-left corner that I find the sensitive spot. As soon as my tongue hits it, my body jolts. As if I'm something I can recoil away from.

I sit up and blink the sleep out of my eyes. Mars's room is dark, morning sunlight beginning to creep through the drawn curtains. Taking up the other half of the bed is Mars. She's dead to the world, one hand gripping the bottom of my T-shirt. Gabe is asleep on the lounge chair. The room is still. I try to be quiet as I catch my breath and strain to remember my dream before it can fade. I let my mouth fully shut, and the subsequent stab of pain makes my eyes prick with tears.

I carefully pull myself out of Mars's grasp before stumbling out of bed and locking myself in the bathroom.

Maybe it should be comforting that my reflection looks just as bad as I feel. I'm visibly damp and several shades whiter than usual. There's a zit trying to push its way out from the corner of my mouth, where a few pathetically wispy hairs are clinging to life.

I pull my shirt up to my shoulders. My chest still seems fine. I give my left nipple a testing, gentle scrape, and the last of the scab chips off against my thumb. At least there's that. I let my shirt fall down and change out my tampon before I focus again on the ache in my mouth.

I lean over the counter, getting as close to the mirror as I can, and hook my finger into my cheek. I bare my teeth and examine the right side of my mouth first, then the left.

It's my molar, the second tooth from the back. The slightest scrape of my finger against the inflamed gums brings tears to my eyes. I turn a little, trying to get more light into my mouth. It has to be this tooth. The black, rotten molar.

bad

I recoil from the mirror. Then I lean back in and take another look, as if I might be seeing things. As if my tooth is not visibly *black*.

bad out

The thought echoes in my head, sluggish and heavy. I get onto my knees and open the cabinet under the sink, as if Mars might be hiding a secret arsenal of dental tools. The closest thing she has to pliers is a pair of tiny tweezers. I stand up and stare at myself in the mirror again.

The bite on my arm is pulsating, like a second heartbeat.

out

I need to get this tooth out. It's rotting inside me. I open my mouth right when somebody gently raps on the door. "Hunter?" It's Mars. "Good in there?"

I don't answer. There's a part of me that wants to be careful, but as soon as I take my tooth between my thumb and index finger, the pain is a reminder that this is going to suck no matter how I go about it.

When I was a kid, I pulled out my own baby teeth. Neither of my parents would ever know that a tooth had become loose until after I'd wiggled and yanked it free. Sometimes it took minutes, sometimes hours. I just flat-out refused to deal with any extended discomfort. Same concept here, I guess.

My grip, though, is non-existent, and my knuckles smack against the mirror when I give my first pull. The throbbing in my mouth overtakes the pulsating of the bite on my arm. I press my lips together and groan until the pain ebbs away.

Mars rattles the doorknob. "Hey. Dude. Open up."

I ignore her and brace my other hand on the counter. This

time, my grip doesn't immediately slide off the tooth. It's not out yet, but on my second pull, there's real movement. The hot salt of blood hits my tongue a moment later.

out out out outoutoutout

My palms are sweating so heavily that I have to wipe them on my pants before I can continue. The tooth still refuses to break free on the third pull. A tear falls down my cheek as the pain spikes again. I'm trying to ignore it. I'm so close. I know it.

The next knock on the door is harder. I know it's Gabe before he speaks. "Hunter?"

Deep breath. I spit into the sink, and my saliva is bright red.

The door suddenly shudders with a sharp *BAM!* I whip towards it. That sounded like somebody trying to kick the door in.

"*Hey!*" Mars snaps. "Jesus Christ, dude, there's a key, let me find it—"

I spin back to the mirror and catch my own eye. Under the harsh lights, my blue irises seem darker than they ever have. There's blood on my chin.

Three, two—

The tooth pops loose and I can hear it skitter across the countertop. I slam my hand down over the plughole instinctively, even as I gasp and wheeze in pain. In disbelief. *I got it.*

The door flies open and slams into the wall behind me.

I flinch, but my eyes don't move from the tooth, pressed against the side of my hand in the sink. A small sliver of it is white, but the rest of the tooth is black from every angle. There even appears to be a small hole in the middle of it, where the rot was eating away at the enamel.

"Holy shit."

I look up. Mars has one hand against the door, and in the mirror, I can see her staring at my face. The blood in my mouth burns as it trickles down my throat.

Behind her, Gabe's eyes are fixed on the sink. On the tooth.

The molar sits on a napkin at the centre of Mars's dining room table. The three of us stand around it. Mars has her arms crossed over her chest, skin white where her fingers grip her arms.

There's a dull pain at the back of my mouth now, but it actually hurts less than it did before. My tongue roves over the new gap in my teeth, over and over until the gum goes numb. I'm beyond knowing how to process this. Mostly, I'm focused on the fact that I just pulled a tooth out of my mouth. A tooth that wasn't black with rot yesterday.

The longer we stand there, the more I start to pick apart how my voice sounds in my head. It's crisp and it sounds like me, and it doesn't echo into the far corners of my skull.

Not like it did in the bathroom.

"Hunter," Mars finally breathes out, "do you have any tooth fillings?"

Gabe frowns. "What does that have to do with anything?"

She ignores him. "Hunter, do you?"

I have to think about it. "Uh, maybe one?"

"In *that* tooth?"

"What does it matter, Marcy?" Gabe asks.

Mars stares at the tooth again. Her throat bobs with a heavy swallow. "Silver fillings."

Silence follows. Then Gabe smiles and huffs.

"Funny," he sighs. "Really funny."

Mars and I lock eyes. Maybe *terrified* isn't the right word, but I've never seen her look like this before. She didn't look this scared when they got the bathroom door open. Dread falls on me like a heavy curtain. I reach for my necklace and grip the stone nervously.

When neither of us joins in the laughter, the smile finally drops from Gabe's face. "Are you serious? I thought you were joking with the werewolf crap."

"I *was!* But how do you explain *that?*" Mars points at the tooth, her linchpin.

Gabe opens his mouth, but I speak first. "That's a *rotten tooth*, Gabe."

He finally looks at me. "Yeah, I can see that."

"Well, it wasn't rotten last night!"

"What do you want me to say?" he demands. "I'm not your

dentist! You have one bad tooth and it's werewolves now?"

"Explain the tooth then, genius." Mars's voice is finally sharp.

"I don't *know* what it is," Gabe snaps back. "I just know it doesn't mean Hunter's *a werewolf*."

My phone buzzes on the table, and everybody shuts up. It's only a text, but the name lighting up the centre of the screen is DAD.

Come home now.

Without argument, Mars drives us back to my house as quickly as she can.

Neither of them linger before driving off in their respective cars, and nobody says anything else about the tooth, which I appreciate, since it's the last thing on my mind once I get inside and see the state of my house.

The couch cushions have been strewn about the living room. Most of the kitchen cabinets are knocked off their hinges, hanging limply in the air. The cop that shows up a minute after I do almost immediately declares that it was an animal, not a burglar; there are dirty paw prints tracked up and down the hallway. Nothing valuable is missing. The cop tells us that whatever it was, it probably forced its way inside through the back door, freaked out, and left on its own.

I wonder if it was – *it*. The possible-however-unlikely werewolf. If it came back for me last night to finish the job.

The silver lining of this horrible realization is that my dad doesn't bring up his jacket. He doesn't even ask about where Norman is. As far as he knows, this all happened last night and had nothing to do with me.

After the officer leaves, though, my dad tells me to grab a coat and get in the car. It's then that I remember I'm *supposed* to be at school right now, and my silver lining is really too thin to save me in any meaningful way.

Thankfully, everybody's still in first period by the time we pull up to the school. I'm mortified enough as it is to be walking beside my dad like a twenty-first-century Carrie White. The longer I'm on my feet, the more my cramps worsen. The more I wonder what this is all about. I've overslept before; all *this* isn't necessary for coming in late.

Then I see Damien Hulme leaving the front office.

We lock eyes for the briefest moment. It'd be wrong to say that he glares at me; his face barely twists as he holds the door open for himself and a man I assume to be his father. But I can feel the heat that flashes behind his eyes when we pass each other.

My stomach twists. Is *that* what this is about?

The door shuts behind us, and it's just me, Dad and the front desk secretary, Mrs Cressotti. I nervously push my hands into my pockets and look at the chairs lined along the wall—

Which is when I see Riley.

I freeze. She's not looking at me, but very pointedly so.

Despite the size of the school, it's a small office. There are only four chairs: empty, empty, Riley, empty. Before I can catch my breath and take the only seat that doesn't put me elbow to elbow with her, Dad sits down in that exact spot with a belaboured exhale.

Dad, empty, Riley, empty.

That leaves me with two options, and I've already stood in the middle of the room for long enough. I take a breath and sit between Dad and Riley.

Nobody says a word until Mrs Cressotti peeps up from behind her desk, asking my dad to fill out a form for the day and a half of school I've missed. I stare at the floor as he gets up.

That leaves Riley and me alone. Inches apart. The plan is to continue staring at the tiles and ignore her as easily as she's ignoring me. But almost as soon as Dad walks away, my eyes flick back up so I can steal a look at her.

Everybody had figured out that Riley was gonna be the pretty one by the time we were seven years old. Her auburn hair hangs at her shoulders, choppy bangs stylishly cut across her forehead. Her eyes are lime green, like freshly trimmed grass at the height of spring, and they have yet to so much as twitch in my direction.

"What are you doing here?" I finally ask, voice low.

Riley continues staring down the nook where the deans' offices are. "Support," she answers a moment later.

This catches me so off guard that a laugh bursts out of me.

Riley turns to me then, eyebrows raised. "This is funny to you?"

The silver chain around my neck seems to tingle against my skin. "Hysterical."

She stares at me for a heavy moment. My stomach feels like it's burning a hole in itself, the acid climbing into my throat.

At last, she shakes her head and turns away. "Ethan didn't even say anything to you."

I hate that she's technically right. He was there laughing with Damien, but he didn't actually say anything *(this time)*. Before I can try to point that out to her, a door opens and shuts, and Ethan walks out from the nook. I recognize his dad from a few school events; same square jaw and near-black hair.

The senior dean, Mr Fitzgerald, stops behind them. "Wakesfield," he sighs. "Good. Come on in."

Ethan stares at me, and I catch the same venom I saw with Damien. Riley quickly gets up and follows the men out without a backwards glance in my direction.

The moment we step into Mr Fitzgerald's office, my eyes lock on to a small collection of incident reports on his desk. My stomach does an uneasy flip as I sit down. I don't want to be here. On the long, *long* list of things I don't want to think about, what happened on Monday is close to the top.

"All right. Wakesfield, Wakesfield..." Mr Fitzgerald sighs as he shuts the door and takes a seat on the opposite side of his desk. My jaw twitches. "Leaving campus without permission and a subsequent unexcused absence."

"I can explain—" I begin.

Mr Fitzgerald puts his hand up before he looks at my dad. "I apologize for contacting you on such short notice, but I'm glad to see the weather didn't delay your arrival. I appreciate you being involved like this."

Dad nods, face unreadable. "Right. Well, the woman I spoke to never explained *what* the incident was."

Mr Fitzgerald glances at me, like it's weird that I haven't told my dad all about my public humiliation. "Oh. Well, your son was involved in an altercation with some other students. There was, uh..."

I swear to God, I watch a bead of sweat break down the side of his face.

"I bled through my pants and Gabe took me home," I quietly mutter, but Dad's head still snaps towards me. "Wasn't a big deal."

Dad frowns before turning to Mr Fitzgerald. "You're telling me he's in trouble for—"

"*No.*" Mr Fitzgerald laughs uncomfortably. "God, no. I have already spoken with the gym instructor and our nurse, and both are willing to provide documentation to excuse his absences in this instance. We are extremely concerned with making sure your child does not feel persecuted."

Oh, *that's* nice of him. I'm aware that I didn't do anything wrong, but my jaw twitches with the implication that he's doing me a favour when he can't even say *my name*.

"You were in a fight?" Dad asks *me* this.

I blink. "There wasn't a fight."

"Other students were fighting," Mr Fitzgerald unhelpfully interjects, "apparently in relation to comments made about—"

"Am I in trouble?" I quickly cut him off. "For anything?"

Mr Fitzgerald sighs, honestly seeming relieved that I've asked. "No. Now—"

Good enough for me. I scoot my chair back and start to stand, but Dad grabs me by the arm before I can try and get us out of here. I do make a point, though, to stay standing.

Mr Fitzgerald starts again: "Any further unexcused absences or attempts to leave campus without permission absolutely will not be tolerated. Understood?"

I nod, skin crawling with impatience.

A metal drawer grinds as Mr Fitzgerald pulls it open. "Is this the first time these students have made comments towards you?"

At once, everything going through my brain comes to a halt. I frown. "What?"

Mr Fitzgerald sets a manila envelope on his desk. "Well,

it was brought to my attention that there was another unreported incident from this same class earlier last week."

He opens the envelope, and I freeze up even before I see Boris Karloff's crumpled face grimly staring up at me again. The stains of jelly have hardened the paper into a disfigured, funhouse-mirror version of itself.

"A member of our custodial staff recovered this." Mr Fitzgerald pushes the poster to the edge of the desk. I flinch and hope he doesn't notice. "Was this put in your locker?"

I want to grab it and cram it down his throat. Instead, I force myself to answer as evenly as I can. "I don't know who made it, if that's what you're trying to ask."

A long stretch of silence passes. "There's nobody you can think of who might've done this?" Mr Fitzgerald prods.

Oh, yeah, hundreds of guys, probably. I'm not an idiot: I understand exactly what he's trying to get me to say. If I say Damien and Ethan put this poster in my locker, then Monday's outburst wasn't a one-off. Bullying is one of the few things I've seen people actually expelled for.

I could ruin Damien's life. More than that, I could ruin *Ethan's.*

But I don't have any proof. Nobody believed me the last time it was my word against Ethan's. Why would it be any different now?

"No," I finally grind out.

Mr Fitzgerald nods. "All right. Well, thank you for coming

in and talking to me about this. I'll see you first thing tomorrow morning, Wakesfield."

Dad and I don't talk for the entire drive home. I sit there and hold Riley's face in my mind. The first time she speaks to me in three years, and it's to admonish me for *her* boyfriend being a dick.

I'm angry because it's easier to be angry than anything else. It's easier than acknowledging that I've been fighting back tears from the moment I saw her because at one point, *that* was my best friend. Before Mars, before Gabe, before I was Hunter. Riley was the first person I ever *told* that I was Hunter.

She looks at me like I'm nothing. I press my tongue into the gap at the back of my mouth and try to will away the nausea that comes with it.

Dad parks in the driveway and I'm fast to get out of the car. I want to go straight to my room and crawl into bed.

I don't even make it to the front door before I hear Dad behind me. "Hunter."

He doesn't shout, but I come to a stop as if he had.

"Is everything good?" he asks.

I glance at him. His face is impossible to read. No grief that Norman is gone, no relief that I'm not, nothing. That impenetrable distance doesn't usually bother me so badly, but for some reason, today it strikes a nerve.

“I’m good,” I answer.

The bite on my arm throbs. My fingers twitch with the urge to start scratching.

At last, Dad shakes his head and steps up beside me to unlock the front door. “If you skip class again—”

“What? You’ll ground me?”

I think I shock us both by saying it, even though I know we were both thinking it. How’s he supposed to ground me when he’s never around? And how is *that* what he’s mad about?

Dad and I look the same when we get angry. Our faces get red, and it always starts at our nose. “Hunter—”

“I’m sorry,” I rush to say, “I’m just upset about Norman.”

I’m not expecting this to save me, but it throws a little water onto the fire. Dad’s face *ticks* more than it winces. He probably forgot about Norman. To be fair, I try to consider what coming home was like for him: back door torn to pieces, house in shambles, *me* nowhere to be found.

Hell, with everything going on, *I* keep almost forgetting that Norman’s dead, which makes the inevitable remembering even worse. It feels as fresh as it did when it happened.

Dad sighs and finally sticks the key into the lock. “Somebody might find him.”

“I don’t think he’s lost, Dad.”

Silence. “No, probably not.”

We step inside and take our coats off in the silence of an empty, Norman-less house. I wonder if he wants to say more.

Because dads are supposed to comfort their daughters and to tell their sons to chin up, *man up*. So far, he's given me neither.

"Let Gabe know I'll be driving you to school in the morning," is what he finally says. "Work, too. And we'll see where we go from there."

"I picked up a shift tonight—"

"Tell them you aren't coming in."

My mouth opens to argue even though there isn't anything ready in my throat to say. I stand there and flounder.

"I want you catching up on whatever you missed at school this week," Dad continues, "and if you finish that, you can help me fix the fence."

He walks towards the back, presumably to figure out what he's gonna have to buy from the hardware store later. Anger simmers under my skin as I go to my room and find my backpack on the floor. I pick it up and empty it onto the bed, and it's only then that I remember Ethan's second poster, somehow jammed in the pages of a sociology textbook. I hesitate before I pull it out and give it another look.

Irreversible Damage: The Transgender Craze Seducing Our Daughters.

If I were in a better mood, I might be able to find some humour in how much weight those words are supposed to carry. The *drama* of the title. But there's too much frothing inside my brain for me to find the poster more than cruel. A childish dig that gets deeper under my skin than it ever should.

Just as my hand starts to close around it, I realize that there's text on the back. A double-sided poster; Ethan's not out of ideas yet. I flip it over. It's a cheap scan of one of the pages from *Irreversible Damage*. My eyes jump around the words in front of me, trying to take in what Ethan has done, crudely underlining sections about breasts and top surgery and scars.

The risks of deformities.

The detail.

The disgust.

I don't realize I've stopped breathing until I reach the end.

I crush the paper into a ball and surge through the house, straight through the front door and towards the trash can outside. The sound the lid makes as I slam it shut is like a thunderclap.

I linger for a moment, shaking.

The sun is out but my skin still stings with the January cold. It takes another moment for me to realize that there's a different, distinct tingling sensation around my neck. I reach down and pull my shirt collar away from my chest. It's a bad angle, but it'd be hard to miss the red, irritated rash that's formed where the necklace chain hangs.

Silver chain, I think, before a delirious giggle escapes my mouth.

8

The next day, Ms Bailey is waiting for me outside the locker room. She tells me that until I'm clear to actually participate in class, it'll be easier for me if I spend this period in the library. She doesn't mention anything about what happened on Monday, and I find myself grateful for it. Then I have to watch Gabe continue into the locker room without me, and that brief moment of relief fades into dread.

I pray to a God I don't entirely believe in that Gabe doesn't do anything stupid without me there.

The school's library is nice, at least. The centre of the room is filled with cushioned chairs and couches, and shelves of books fill out the edges. I go straight to the wall of computers and try to catch up on some of the homework I've fallen behind on in the two and a half days since I was last in class.

Frustratingly, my brain keeps pulling me back to the bite on my arm. The dull but constant throbbing that reverberates through my bones is like an echo to the cramps, which have only just begun to diminish alongside the blood flow. My necklace sits heavy in my pocket.

After twenty minutes, I've gotten nothing done. It feels stupid to be writing out linear equations when my body is in revolt of its own existence. I finally abandon the effort and take out my phone instead. A couple of taps bring me to Riley's Instagram account. There are a lot of selfies, family reunions populated with faces I half remember. Her oldest post is a photo reel from her thirteenth birthday. My face is only half there, but she still has my old account tagged.

I click on it. I am the only follower on my old account, which I made private and scrubbed my deadname from years ago. Going through these posts, I fixate on two things: how strange I used to look as a girl, and how both of our smiles nearly reached our ears.

The throb on my arm steadily becomes a burn and distracts me from my pity party. Before the class period ends, I actually log onto one of the computers. It takes a couple of extra steps to get around the school's filters and onto one of the forums I was looking at a few days earlier, but within a couple of minutes, I have a burner account made up.

posted by u/ThrowAway111

(ADVICE) Unusual Post-Op Changes?

hi, 17 years old, about one month post-op. long story

short, an animal bit me recently. it wasn't mine, my friends think it was some kind of wolf or dog. i didn't need to go to the hospital, but it did gnaw on me pretty good. since then, my period has come back and all these other weird things have been happening. at first i thought this was just a hormonal issue and maybe it was related to the top surgery, but i'm less sure of that now.

not seeking medical advice. i just need to know i'm not alone. has this happened to anyone else???

I don't get to check the post again until after school. There's a little banner posted at the bottom, where any replies would normally be.

This post has been removed by the moderators. Please refer to Rule 6 of the FtM Sub, namely *No trolling or reposting trolling/transphobic content.*

After Dad drops me off at work, I clock in and find my name scribbled onto the schedule for the ticket booth. It's not my favourite position, but it's a slow Thursday, at least, and I get to be alone.

The irritated ring around my neck has faded a little more. In the long stretches between customers, I take the necklace out of my pocket and wrap the silver chain around my hand. I squeeze my fist rhythmically, feeling the metal flex against my skin.

Before long, the skin under the chain starts to tingle. I wind it tighter around my palm. Ethan's posters flutter through my mind.

I flinch out of my head when the door of the ticket booth opens. It's Mars who slides into the chair next to me. She's somehow found a sweater that's the same shade of pink as her hair, which is pulled back into space buns.

"Natalie'll kill you if the snack counter's empty," I say, resting my chin in my good hand.

"It's not empty. The new guy can handle himself for five minutes."

I frown and glance back. Through a tiny window, I watch this new guy fill a cup with Coke, look around to be sure he's in the clear, and take a long drink.

"*Anyway.*" Mars brings her legs onto the chair and crosses them. "How are you feeling?"

I face her and shrug. "Okay. All things considered."

"Your dad?"

"Mad that I skipped school. Didn't really seem interested why."

We sit there in silence. I can tell this isn't what Mars came to talk about, but her eyebrows have knitted together with concern anyway. "You didn't tell him, did you?"

I shake my head.

Mars doesn't ask *why not?* or otherwise interrogate me, which is something of a surprise. She simply nods and reaches into her pocket, pulling out a folded piece of notebook paper that she smooths out and places on the table between us.

The first word I read is *werewolf*, and I can't help but groan and put my face in my hands. "Neither of us is crazy enough to believe in this," I mutter.

"Your tooth rotted out of your mouth, I'm ready to believe in pretty much anything."

I drop my hands. "How about something that's *real?*"

Mars frowns and grabs the paper back. "Have you been experiencing any changes in appetite? Increased agitation? Hair loss? Hair *growth?*"

The joke comes too easily. "Yeah. It's called being trans. It'd be weird if any of that *wasn't* happening to me."

Mars glares. "Can you take this seriously?"

"I'm taking this very seriously."

"If this was some hormonal funk, you'd know that. All of *this* would've been in your little post-care packet. But we both know this is something else. Right?"

Here's the thing: if it were *just* my period or *just* my tooth, I could find more grounded explanations for them. But as outlandish as it feels to think, let alone say out loud, *werewolf* is the only one that covers everything that's happened to me over the last two weeks.

"I don't *want* this to be the answer," she goes on, "but if it is, we need to figure it out as fast as possible. Because you weren't attacked during the full moon. Which means you're not on a lunar cycle, which means we don't know how fast this is gonna progress."

I stare at my partial reflection in the glass. I'm having a hard enough time wrapping my head around the fact that a *werewolf* made me into a chew toy. No full moon means no calendar for when this is gonna go from bad to worse.

"A hormonal funk doesn't come back a week later and tear up the house," I finally agree.

Mars's expression is troubled. "I don't think you got bit by a giant hormone, Hunter."

Not a hormone. *Lycanthrope*. And now I'm becoming one, too.

"So, what do we do?" I quietly ask.

Mars scoots closer and grabs a pen from the desk. "Can't cure a giant hormone. But, if it's lycanthropy, we have a chance."

She circles something on her paper. I look down and read:

1. silver

"You think *werewolf*, you think *silver bullet*." Mars looks up at me. "It shows up in all the movies – it's the first solution anybody goes for, right?"

My fingers twitch against my silver chain. "Right."

"Except I can't find *anything* about a silver filling causing what happened to your mouth," she says. "Some people have allergies, but the worst thing a silver allergy ever did to anybody was give 'em dry eye. It's actually *really* hard to be hurt by silver in most instances."

Carefully, I move the chain around my hand to glimpse the skin underneath. Mars follows my line of sight, and we both observe the angry red stripe that's formed there.

She reaches over and takes my hand, never quite touching the mark but getting really close to it. I watch her jaw clench as she thinks. She's careful but firm when she unwraps the chain completely to study it more closely. I wait for a joke about *howl*ite that never comes.

"How long have you had this?" she asks.

"Since I was thirteen," I answer.

"Hm. Well, unless your body spontaneously decided to gift you the worst silver allergy I've ever seen, *clearly* this is having an effect on you. But I don't know how we make a cure out of that."

Mars hands the necklace back to me and I tuck it into my pocket. She stays close enough that I can smell the butter from the popcorn machine on her. We go down to the next line:

2. monkshood

"Option two is monkshood. Remember *Ginger Snaps*?"

I have to think about it for a minute. "The flower?"

Mars grins. "Exactly. Otherwise known as wolfsbane, the blue rocket, or my personal favourite, *the devil's helmet*. Brigitte jams a syringe full of monkshood into that kid's neck and his lycanthropy clears up immediately. Insta-cure."

Something about the way she says this makes me uneasy. "What's the downside?"

Her smile twists into a grimace. "In real life, that kid would be fucking *dead*. Monkshood is pure poison. It's literally been boiled down and used to go whale hunting. Some lady died last year because she grabbed a bunch without gloves on. People die from *touching it*."

Great. My options for a cure are silver, which isn't exactly helping me, or monkshood, which might kill me the moment I so much as look at it. I slump down and curl my hand against my chest.

"Now, you *can* ingest a tiny amount of monkshood safely, but I have no idea how we figure out where that line is. And Google didn't love my questions about poisoning proportions." Mars circles *monkshood* and puts a question mark beside it. "I think it's a better idea than silver, but there's still a lot of risk involved."

Which brings us to the final line:

3. kill it

I don't mean to laugh as loud as I do. "So silver, monkshood, or I can kill myself."

Mars punches me in the arm. "Not suicide, jackass—"

A knocking sound makes us both whirl around. Natalie is already glaring when she opens the door. She's somewhere in her thirties, arms covered in tattoos and voice a nasally high pitch. "I wasn't interrupting social hour, was I?" Natalie asks, looking between the two of us.

Mars sits up, and it's only then I realize how close she'd been. "Sorry, I had a question about the schedule." She quickly flashes her paper before tucking it away. "I'll be right out."

"You're not out in the next sixty seconds—"

"—and you can totally fire me this time, okay? Thanks."

Natalie smiles like there's nothing she'd rather do before her eyes move to me. "Good, Wakesfield?"

I nod and try to ignore the twitch of my jaw. More non-gendering.

After Natalie's shut the door, Mars rolls her eyes and turns back to me. "Not suicide," she repeats, just above a whisper. "We don't have time to go into all the hypotheticals, but it's this idea that if lycanthropy's spread like a virus, it can be cured like a virus. Because, you know, there are the two kinds of werewolves: the ones who go back and forth, and the ones who *become wolves*—"

"Mars."

She shakes her head. "Basically, it's a viral hivemind: you

kill the queen, and the workers aren't controlled by anything any more. If we can manage to find what bit you and kill it—"

"You wanna trust the internet about this?" I raise an eyebrow.

"It's either the internet or it's *Ginger Snaps*, and their idea of a cure was to inject you with poison that would literally, instantly kill you in real life. What do you think?"

I think I want to cry. But that's not a real, viable solution to the massive problem at hand.

I swallow and nod.

At last, a real smile breaks across her face. We're close enough that I can smell the spearmint gum on her breath. "When's the next time your dad leaves?"

"Uh, Saturday. I think."

"Cool. Text me Gabe's number, and I'll see you Saturday."

Mars takes my hand and squeezes it before she jumps up and rushes back to her station. My hand continues to tingle where she held it long after she's gone.

Dad picks me up at the end of the shift. I send Gabe's contact to Mars. By the time I've showered and gotten into bed, there are already messages waiting for me.

MARS BAR added YOU

MARS BAR added GABE

MARS BAR changed the chat name to
🐺STIRBA SLAYERS🐺

MARS BAR

alright boys here's the plan

we meet at hunter's house.

saturday night at sunset.

that should be 5pm

be there or be 🔪😵

9

Friday evening, I have a dream about Riley. We're twelve years old again, crammed onto the same chair and clicking through Photobooth filters and screaming with laughter. The walls of Riley's bedroom are the same terrible shade of green she's always loved. When I wake up on Saturday morning, my throat hurts like I've been holding back a sob all night.

The sun has barely risen above the rooftops when I stumble out of bed, but Dad is already gone. It's nothing unusual, but something about finding myself truly *alone* for the first time in days makes my chest feel funny.

I try to shake it off. It's not like Dad could help me if I tried to explain what's wrong with me. It's better that he's gone.

I run a cold shower for myself. Testosterone makes me run hot even in the dead of winter, but there's something especially stifling about the sweat that's clung to my skin ever since the attack. In the shower, I look down at myself and try to think positively. The silver burns have both mostly faded. A scab has formed over the bite on my leg, and, after perhaps the longest week of my life, my period has *finally* ended.

Then, I run my hand down my sternum, and what little hair had grown back on my chest falls away and clings to my palms. Like it was never a part of me to begin with.

When I try to swallow the tears, the burning at the back of my throat hits me again at full force. The pain alone is enough to push me into actually crying.

There are texts waiting for me when I recompose myself and step out of the shower. Gabe has practice scheduled for tonight, so whatever meeting Mars wants to have will have to be at the rink. Mars has already lashed him enough for, quote, *not checking his calendar like a functional adult*, so I just send a thumbs up and Mars promises she'll swing by to pick me up later. That means I have more than a few hours to kill, me and my empty house.

Dad replaced the mudroom door sometime while I was at school, and I helped him scrub the paw prints out of the carpet, but there's still noticeable discolouration where they used to be. I can easily follow its rampage through the house.

I wonder what would've happened if I'd been home, and I quickly realize I don't want to be here by myself.

It's not hard to find an excuse to leave. My box of tampons is nearly empty, and even though my period seems to be over, I don't exactly trust my body at the moment. So, I get dressed and start walking towards the corner store near school.

As I do, I go through the rest of my unread text messages,

since I haven't exactly been attentive to them recently. A boba store sent me a buy-one-get-one coupon that expired yesterday. There's nothing from Dad or Mom.

My thumb hovers over my last message with Mom, which was that article about Texas. Maybe I should've thought about texting her sooner, but it's not like she's especially active in my life. I have my summer visit, and that's about the extent of it. I chose to live with Dad, and neither of us harbours any hard feelings about it.

Still, there's a little voice in the back of my head that wishes she'd decided to tackle the whole "proud parent of a trans kid" thing a little closer to *me*.

Thankfully, there are only a few people milling around when I step inside the store. An Olivia Rodrigo song plays faintly over tinny speakers, nearly drowned out by the conversation the pharmacist is having with an old woman through the glass. I tuck my hands into my pockets and wander the aisles for a minute, like going straight for the feminine care section isn't an option. Anxiety rattles around my ribcage. I grab a small bag of throat lozenges.

Nobody here cares about you, I tell myself. *Just get it over with.*

It's a decent sentiment until I actually step into the aisle. Of course there's somebody standing in front of the wall of pads and tampons. But it's not until I've already come closer that I recognize the curve of Riley's mouth. She looks up and meets my eye before I can backpedal.

Three years, and all of a sudden, she's everywhere I go.

Riley seems like she's just woken up, freckles fully visible on her cheeks and hair falling out of its ponytail. She has no immediate reaction to me, and I attempt to mirror her. I nod in acknowledgement and face the shelves.

A moment goes by. Riley pulls an AirPod out of her ear. "What are you looking for?"

"What?"

"I mean which—what brand do you use?"

Heat spreads under my skin. I grab the first box I can reach and have already started to turn when Riley puts her hand out and stops me. I freeze.

She takes the box from me and smiles. "I don't think you want the junior size."

Correct. But maybe I *do* want them. Maybe I *love* kid-sized tampons. Riley doesn't know me any more, I remind myself with some indignation. I still let her put the box back on the shelf before she scans the rows.

"Here." Riley takes a box from the bottom and hands it to me. "These ones are organic."

I don't know what the difference is, but I take the box and immediately turn on my heel out of there, heartbeat pounding between my ears. I don't even say *thank you*.

There are four people in line ahead of me. I've only been standing there for a couple of seconds before I hear Riley's shoes slowly tap against the tiles, until they come to a stop behind me. We're both quiet for the length of two transactions, and then it's too much for me to handle.

I turn around and ask, hushed, "Do you want something?"

It comes out harder than it sounded in my head. Riley blinks, then sets her shoulders. "Yeah. You look really sick."

"Thanks. It's cramps."

I face forward. One more person between me and the register.

"Heard you got top surgery," Riley says.

I don't turn around again, but I nod. "Yeah."

"Congrats."

"Thanks."

"I just— I wanted you to know that Ethan would never—"

I whirl around. Whatever's on my face is enough to stop that sentence dead. "Don't."

Riley's gaze hardens. "Don't? You got him *suspended*."

I blink. "What?"

"Next in line?"

We both turn. The cashier doesn't seem especially rushed, but he *is* staring at us. Face hot, I step up and place my tampons and lozenges on the counter.

I look over at Riley and, after a moment, she steps up to my side. Her basket consists of the same tampons, a can of Arizona green tea and a box of Plan B.

"What do you mean he got suspended?" I ask, as the cashier bags my things.

At first, Riley glares at me like I'm making fun of her. I

watch her expression slowly shift as she realizes I have no idea what she's talking about. "You told Fitzgerald that he put some poster in your gym locker," she answers. "He got suspended for a week. Damien, too."

Hearing her say that should automatically be the second-best moment of my life. But then I hear the card reader beeping at me, and I realize I've been standing there in horrified silence. I quickly yank my card out, decline a receipt, and hurry outside. A few moments later, Riley joins me, shivering as the frigid air hits her skin.

I jam my free hand into my pocket and find the necklace, gripping it until I feel the chain link digging sharply into my palm. "I didn't tell Fitzgerald shit," I say.

As soon as I do, I realize it doesn't matter. Ethan saw me in that office, he knows I *talked* to Mr Fitzgerald. He thinks I got him suspended.

Riley tucks her hands under her arms and sighs. "You didn't?"

"No! I want him to leave me alone, why would I do that?"

"I don't know! Why wouldn't you?"

As she says it, the answer clicks in my brain. *Gabe.*

I never saw him in the office, but he was the one who got up in Damien's face. He cut school with me. Mr Fitzgerald would've *had* to talk to him.

I'm gonna kill him.

In the meantime, what Riley's said sinks in. She still thinks I'm a liar.

"Great seeing you, Ri," I grit out, my fist tightening around the necklace chain as I turn to go.

"Hunter."

Against my better judgement, I stop and look back at her.

"Seriously. Are you okay?"

For a moment, I consider the possibility that she might care if I weren't. Then the absurdity of such a thought quickly follows, and I keep walking, gripping the necklace the entire way home until I've got another burn sizzling across the face of my palm.

That night, it's Gabe's car that pulls up to my house. Mars is sitting in the passenger seat.

It really shouldn't be such a strange sight, except for an instant feeling of *bad* that seizes my chest. I catch a glimpse of myself in the window's reflection: my face is pinched in a frown.

I blink and quickly get into the back seat. Mars and Gabe have always been aware of each other. It's been less than a week since they've started hanging out in the same space. Why is the thought of them together, without me, an instant bad taste in my mouth?

"Hi!" Mars twists herself around to grin at me. "We got supplies. Look in my bag."

Her backpack is in the seat beside me, laid on top of Gabe's hockey gear. I pull her bag into my lap and look inside. It's a unique haul: flashlights, a notebook, a first-aid kit and a massive bottle of extra-strength painkillers.

"I still can't believe they let us buy all this at the same time," Gabe says.

"I don't think they flag you unless you're buying, like, shovels and concrete." Mars shrugs. "But anyway, Hunter, we do have one small problem."

I look up and frown. "What problem?"

Gabe takes a right turn a little hard; both Mars and I brace ourselves on his seat.

Mars shoots him a glare before she exhales. "Monkshood is only in bloom for a few months, and January ain't one of 'em. Now, between here and Chicago, there's, like, a dozen nurseries and botanic gardens. Gabe and I were talking, and we figured that we could go and check some of them out tomorrow. Get our hands on something as soon as possible."

It's strange to have confirmation that Gabe and Mars have had their own conversations together. Stranger still that *that* is what my brain lingers on. But it does. Jealousy makes my mouth feel numb.

"Just you two?" I ask.

"Well, yeah." Mars shrugs like she hadn't even thought about it. "You are actively dealing with lycanthropy. Sleep in or something."

I blink. "Then what are we doing tonight?"

“We’re forming a game plan,” Gabe answers, with a confidence that pushes my jealousy into something else entirely.

They’ve talked about this, a voice in my head whispers, *they’ve been talking about* you.

“Mighty Duck is gonna fulfil his sport obligation, and you and me are gonna make sure we’re on the same page with the cure plan,” Mars says. “Once he’s done, we’ll head back to your house and finish up there.”

Ice hockey practice is held at the south end of town at Canlan Sportsplex, a brown brick building so big that it’s hard to believe it’s only ever been a sports complex. Having to prepare to be around other people helps shrink my knot of nerves into something more manageable. Something I can swallow down. I watch Gabe tie his hair back before he grabs his bag. He shoots me a smile and goes inside.

It’s a Saturday night, so the halls are mostly filled with younger kids. Mars and I walk past them all to reach the rink in the far back of the building, which is always where the team holds their practices. Mars takes note of where we are, then offloads her coat onto me and promises to grab us dinner from the food court.

Gabe hits the ice as I take a seat on the bleachers. Compared to the rest of the building, it’s quiet back here. A few guys notice me, which quickly leads to *everybody* waving at me. I smile and wave back, though my eyes stick to Gabe as he skates around the rink.

Of course he'd get called into Mr Fitzgerald's office. He was the one actually involved in the almost-fight. I can imagine the exchange: *You can't suspend me, sir, I was standing up for my friend. Maybe it was wrong, but what those guys did was worse. Didn't you hear about the poster we found in his locker?*

What pisses me off is that I've made it so, *so* clear that I didn't want this. I just want to get through these last few months, graduate and never think about Ethan again. And what did Gabe do? He went behind my back, got Ethan *suspended*, and didn't say *a word* to me about it. Hasn't even brought up being called into Fitzgerald's office in the first place.

My train of thought takes me further back. I've been to countless hockey games over the years, and true fights are few and far between. The fight between Ethan and Gabe remains the only time I've ever seen somebody bleed. That splash of red looked other-worldly on the ice.

Gabe skates by and softly slaps the glass in front of me. I force a smile as he passes.

Mars comes back with a hot dog in each hand and grumbling about a nine-year-old's birthday party happening at the other rink. The pink dye in her hair has already begun to fade, but it seems vibrant against the funeral grey colour of her Grounded Gardening shirt.

"Okay." Mars has barely sat before she unzips her bag and fishes her notebook from it. "I got a little more reading done last night, and I realized what we talked about on Thursday wasn't three plans. Silver and monkshood aren't *plans*. They're *weapons*. Lycanthropy as a communicable disease with a source – *that's* the plan."

"Uh-huh." I take a bite of hot dog. It's cold at the centre and the ketchup is watery. Between us, Mars's phone buzzes violently against the metal bench.

Mars ignores it to flip through her notebook. "Now, *finding* our source is probably going to be the hardest part of this. I haven't exactly heard anybody talking about a wolf wandering down residential roads. But maybe that's a good thing, y'know? You said it got into your house a week *after* it bit you."

I swear I'm *trying* to listen to her. But louder than her voice is the sound of sticks thwacking against the ice. I watch Gabe glide to the back of the line, a grin lighting up his face.

Gabe moves like he was born to be on the ice. Effortless, not a thing weighing on his shoulders. It's not that he's especially hulking or clumsy on solid ground, but when he's on a rink, he's…lighter.

I'm suddenly filled with the childish urge to walk out there and shove him down.

"You never told me you have a crush on him."

Already frowning, I look at Mars. She's resting her chin in her hand, her expression bored. When a few seconds go by without my answer, she cocks an eyebrow. "Are we pretending you're *not* ogling him?"

"What? No." My skin burns with embarrassment. "I'm not— I'm *glaring at him*."

She looks at Gabe, clearly unsatisfied with her unanswered question, but she takes my bait. "Why are we glaring at him?"

I sigh. "You remember Ethan?"

Mars nods.

"He started leaving transphobic shit in my locker. Gabe told the dean, so now Ethan's suspended *and* he thinks *I* did it."

I don't think Mars understands the extent of why this is *so bad*, but she understands enough. "Oh. Yikes."

I face the rink again. The team is gathered around Coach Ryan, this tall, buff guy with a scraggly beard. I find the back of Gabe's head and glare at it again. "He keeps...*pushing it*. Ethan would get bored and stop if we left it alone, but Gabe won't do it."

Mars clicks her pen. "That's not usually how you stop bullies, but I get your point."

I glare at her. Her phone buzzes again between us.

She shrugs, unfazed by both things. "Any smart bully would never leave evidence, so he's a moron. If he doesn't respond to getting suspended, then you pop him in the nose and show him who's boss."

"Gabe already tried that," I tell her. "*He* nearly got suspended, and nothing changed."

Impressed is not the reaction I was expecting, but that's the look Mars gives me.

I roll my eyes. Sure, if punching Ethan between the eyes had knocked the transphobia out of him, of course it would've been cool. But it didn't, it nearly ruined Gabe's life, and it only happened because of *me*.

"Have we thought about going out, getting a gun, and shooting this werewolf?" I ask.

Mars sighs heavily. "Okay, *Gabe*, that *might* be an option if any of our parents had shotguns lying around, but they don't. It also takes, like, three months for those Firearm Owner's ID cards to get approved, the ones none of us are old enough to apply for anyway, so *buying* a shotgun is *also* out of the question."

I'm not surprised Gabe suggested this same idea. I also get Mars's point: short of doing something *extremely* illegal, guns aren't on the table. "Beating it with a hockey stick worked pretty well," I add.

Mars smiles before getting serious again. "We aren't trying to beat up and kill some random animal, though, this is a *werewolf*." She scoots closer, picking up her notebook before reading from it. "*Historically, lycanthropes were eliminated with the silver bullet. However, many believed that monkshood had the power not only to protect the innocent but calmed those afflicted to a restored self.*"

She sets the notebook down on her leg and mine. "Look, Gabe and I were talking about it earlier: silver is supposed to be a purifier. But between your tooth and your necklace..."

I nod, trying to ignore the twist in my chest that comes with *Gabe and I*. "Yeah, it'd be cool if that didn't happen to the rest of me."

"Agreed. But besides that, pure silver weapons are impossible to find, and none of us have the budget to *bedazzle* a werewolf to death. Monkshood will at least knock *anything* on its ass. We can use it raw, or we can do like the ancient hunters did and boil it down, make a liquid poison of it."

My necklace starts to feel like it's burning a hole in my pocket. "That assumes we can find the lycanthrope again."

"Yeah, well, I've got a few ideas." Mars sighs and finally takes a bite of her hot dog. "Like I said while you were *ogling*, it got into your house a week *after* it bit you. Are you gonna finish that?"

She nods to my own abandoned dinner.

"Yeah, sorry." I pick my hot dog up even though my body baulks at the thought. "You think it's still hanging around?"

Mars shrugs. "I don't know. That's what we need to find out."

Her voice is even, but her jaw is clenched with thought. It feels somewhat hollow to have a plan with no guarantee its most pivotal aspect is even still in the same state as us, but I guess it's better than sitting on my hands and hoping I've got some generations-old lycanthropic immunity somewhere in my blood.

"All right, I'm aware I sound like my mother here, but you're sick. *Eat*."

She takes my arm and gently shakes me, which is enough to make me break a smile. We leave the werewolf talk there, but Mars never scoots away, so our legs remain pressed together as she picks up her phone and responds to whoever has been blowing her up. The closeness is comforting, albeit distantly. There's still too much for me to be worried about: Riley and Ethan, Mars and Gabe, Dad's apparent newfound desire to try parenting by grounding me, the giant bites still lingering on my body. Each thing is as unapproachable as the one before it.

Silently, I run my tongue along the back of my mouth. It bumps against something hard, and it takes a moment for me to figure out what it is.

It's a new tooth, growing where my molar rotted out.

10

After an hour of watching drills, I have the worst headache in the world. The pressure has been building behind my eyes, taking the rest of my appetite and a good chunk of my patience with it. On top of that, the corner of my mouth is numb from roving my tongue over it again and again.

Once the team breaks from their final huddle, I follow Mars to the exit gate, hoping to get us home as fast as possible. But while the guys grab their stuff, Coach Ryan is the one who skates up to me. He sticks his fist out. "Good to see you, kid. How've you been?"

I shrug and complete the fist bump. "Staying alive."

A moment later, the team bottlenecks at the gate. Taylor is the first through. He grins at me, all teeth. "Hi, Bambi."

I can feel my face go as red as Taylor's hair. I wave at him as he passes, then press my fingers into my temple. It's not enough to keep Mars's voice from exacerbating my headache as she leans into my space. "*Bambi?*"

"Bad skater," I explain, voice tight, "and it was one time,

but they think it's cute."

"It's *adorable*," she corrects me. "Does Gabe have a nickname?"

Everybody on the team has a nickname. Taylor, for example, is *Taser*. Eugene, who also smiles at me as he passes by, has been *GG* for as long as I've been *Bambi*. "Team calls him Momma Bear," I finally answer. Then, a little quieter, "Everybody else calls him Haymaker."

Mars's eyebrows knit together, so I make a soft punching motion. She mouths *oh*, and then turns to Gabe as he glides up to the gate. "Hey, what would my hockey nickname be?"

Gabe blinks, exhales dramatically, and starts rattling some off: "Spark Plug. Loudmouth. Crazy Calico."

Mars puts a hand over her heart. "All so *mean*."

I roll my eyes at both of them before my focus wanders. I watch the rest of the guys waddle to the side to get their skates off, shoving each other the whole way, and my heart takes a funny beat. That's it; ideal boyhood. Playful shoves and incessant chirping and stupid nicknames that don't make any sense. As easy and effortless as breathing.

Clenching my teeth is not helping the headache. I rub my jaw and sigh.

In the car, I take two of the painkillers and rest my head against the window, trying to relax within the empty void of space behind my eyes. It doesn't take long for me to realize that I can't because I'm still mad. Still trying to piece together why my skull feels like it's throbbing whenever Gabe makes a comment and Mars giggles from the front seat. Trying to understand who, exactly, I'm jealous of. That it's not clear is worrying.

Once we're back at my house, Mars and Gabe sequester themselves in Dad's office with his computer. I go straight for my room and flop face-down onto my bed. While I wait for my head to stop pounding in time with my heartbeat, I try and get my ducks in a row.

Gabe is straight. I'm not a girl, ergo it would be incredibly stupid of me to *redevelop* a crush on him. Which I haven't. Mars, at least, is bisexual like I am. It causes less of a dysphoric crisis to consider that my jealousy is a craving for *her* attention, not Gabe's. But it's not accurate. Trying to choose one doesn't alleviate the hurt in my chest; it just makes it feel uneven.

I'm aware how incredibly stupid it is to be worrying about this right now.

Eventually, my headache becomes less of a *pounding* than it does a gentle *squeeze* of my skull, and I need to think about something that isn't related to my current situation. I lift my head in search of my phone, only to find it's nowhere in sight. I groan, but I put my feet on the floor and force myself to walk. It feels like somebody's stuck a whisk in my brain and made scrambled eggs out of it.

Dad's office is directly down the hall from my room, so it's impossible to pass by the half-open door without catching a bit of the chatter. Somebody is clacking away on the keyboard, Gabe starts spelling out Elgin, Illinois, and Mars cuts him off: "*I know how to spell it.*"

I find my phone in my coat, which I dropped on the kitchen table on top of everybody's bags. I'm vaguely aware that I should sleep. But with all the dreams I've been having recently, I'd much rather put that off for as long as I can. So, I take my phone back with me and try to rub the exhaustion out of my eyes.

Just as I'm about to pass the doorway to Dad's office, I hear Mars's voice as clear as ever: "Can I ask you something about Hunter?"

I stop.

Gabe answers, "Uh-huh?"

"He told me that you punched that Ethan guy."

A pause. Gabe snorts. "Yeah. A million years ago, but yeah."

"Why'd you do it?" Mars asks.

"I don't know. He's a piece of shit who had it coming."

"Okay, sure, that's why *anybody* would punch this guy. But why did *you?*"

I linger there, even though my brain screams at me to keep walking. Gabe is silent for the longest time before he finally answers. "You've known him for, like, two years, right?"

"Yeah," Mars says.

"Then you know what he's like. About...conflict."

"Sure."

I imagine Gabe's shrug. "I don't know. He just *takes it*. Doesn't stand up for himself but he gets mad if you try to stand up for him." He sighs. "I know I can't make him do something, but if I end up on the ice with the asshole that hurt my friend...shit happens."

I dig my nails into my palm until the sweat stings at the broken skin.

Gabe didn't find out about what Ethan did to me until after Riley and I fell out. I only remember caring that he didn't also call me a liar. I wasn't thinking about how Gabe's anger builds quietly. I didn't have the space in my brain to think about what would happen when Gabe's team inevitably met Ethan's on the ice.

What happened, ultimately, went fast. Gabe slammed Ethan into the boards, and before the ref could even signal the penalty, Gabe had ripped Ethan's helmet off and begun whaling on him until Eugene and Josh were able to pull him off. Done in thirty seconds.

But to watch it unfold in real time, it seemed like it'd never end.

I nearly rush into the room to tell Gabe to *shut the hell up, don't act like that was ever something I* wanted *you to do*. It's only by some miracle of restraint that I don't.

Mars makes a contemplative noise. "Sounds like I should be impressed that you're going along with the lycanthrope theory."

“What do you mean?” Gabe asks.

“I mean you’re…well, you haven’t called me outright crazy since Wednesday, but I don’t think you’re the kind of guy to go along with something just ’cause.”

Gabe’s quiet for a moment. “Well, *no*, none of this makes me go straight to *werewolf*.”

“Hunter’s tooth rotted out of his head. What’s the other option?”

“I don’t know! Anything that isn’t *this*.”

Quiet again.

Finally, Mars exhales. “Just throwing our hands up won’t help him.”

“It’d be honest.”

“We *are* being honest. Even if we don’t know what this is, we know what it isn’t. This isn’t a hormonal imbalance, it isn’t a botched surgery, it’s not a bad dentist. I would say it’s not even him being a Taurus!”

Gabe’s laugh is a quiet, strained huff.

Mars goes on, “Look, I *know* how crazy this sounds. This is a fundamentally unbelievable situation, but it all makes a strange kind of sense, too, don’t you think? Either way, Hunter needs help, and this is the only way I can think of to help him. I don’t have an answer that isn’t *this*.”

I can’t handle this any more. I take a few steps back, enough to build up believable momentum and pretend like I haven’t been standing there, and push the door fully open.

Gabe and Mars look up, both wearing that nervous, guilty expression that people get when they're not sure if they've been caught (but suspect they probably have been). Mars is in my dad's chair, while Gabe sits on the desk, arms resting on his legs. Gabe shuts his mouth, canning whatever response he was about to give.

"Hey." I lean against the door frame. "Making progress?"

Mars nods. "Yeah, c'mere."

I walk over and Mars slides her papers closer. On top is a map of northern Illinois, a few circles marked seemingly at random. She taps the end of her pen against one of the circles. "These are all reported missing or mutilated animals from the last six months."

I frown and push the paper aside. There's a map of Minnesota underneath, with its own assortment of circles. "There's no way this is all one animal."

"No, probably not," Mars agrees. "But remember how Tammy's dog went missing?" She flips through the papers until she finds a recognizable map of Naperville and jabs her pen at a mark that I suppose is meant to indicate my house. She drags it westward until she hits another circle, not far from here. "Tammy lives right down the road, and her dog went missing less than a week before you got bitten."

Gabe takes the pen and taps the Minnesota map. "We think it came down from the north. Minnesota, probably."

I bite down on a snarky *thanks, asshole, I do have eyes*.

"I mean, obviously nobody's gonna go to the news and say that werewolves ate their dog," Mars goes on. "But *normal* wolf attacks are rare, and people flip their shit when they happen. So, if we can figure out how this thing got here in the first place, maybe we can get one step ahead and figure out where it's gone."

I nod, though my chest is tight. Even if we manage to perfectly predict where this werewolf would go, it's got a four-day head start on us on top of the million other obstacles between us and it. All I can hear are *ifs* and *maybes*.

"I'm gonna lie back down. Still have a headache," I mumble.

It's more of an excuse than an outright lie but Mars and Gabe nod understandingly, like they aren't waiting for me to leave so they can keep talking about how crazy I am. It takes everything in me to walk from the room rather than run.

Eventually, Mars comes to collect me from my room, where I've been doomscrolling and continuing to rub my tongue raw against the new tooth.

Together, the three of us go over all of the maps and news articles Mars has pulled together and organized. If Mars is right, the lycanthrope that bit me began its rampage in Dassel, Minnesota. Last August, two people were attacked near a lake, but the only thing it actually killed was their hunting dog. No human injuries. It seemed to travel south along the

Mississippi River for a while, picking off pets as it went, before suddenly veering east and ending up here. We all think it's unlikely it'd keep going east into Chicago, but we don't know where it might've gone otherwise. *A Minnesotan Werewolf in Bloomington, Indiana* doesn't exactly roll off the tongue, but I keep my cynical jokes to myself.

We make it all the way to midnight before finally calling it quits. Mars volunteers herself for the couch, which means that Gabe and I will share my bed again. It shouldn't be a big deal. But as soon as we're alone, I find the anger bubbling up to the surface. I'm still pissed at him.

Maybe I shouldn't be. Priorities, after all. But I am.

Gabe should know better. He even said it. He's known me longer than Mars has. He knows what Ethan did to me, he knows how it obliterated my relationship with Riley, he should know better than to keep doing *any* of what he's done.

I get into bed and lie there, staring at the ceiling and stewing in my anger until Gabe hits the lights. The mattress jostles as he scoots in between me and the wall.

"Aren't you cold?" Gabe asks, muffled by the blanket he's pulled partially over his face.

I shrug. "I keep waking up all sweaty."

After a beat, I slip under the comforter anyway. My bed isn't small, but there's not a whole lot of room between us. I can't tell if I'm imagining the tension in the air.

We're just two guys in bed. Gabe is straight.

I think, anyway.

"Why did you break up with Kylee Welch?" I ask before I can think any better of it.

Gabe lifts his head up, and even in the darkness I can see the confused expression on his face. "Why did I break up with *Kylee?*"

My face is already alight with embarrassment. "Yeah. I don't know why I asked that."

I roll onto my side. I can feel Gabe's eyes on me. Of all the questions, why *that one?*

"She was nice." He sighs, and the mattress shifts. I cringe. "That was it. I mean, it's high school. Doesn't always have to be serious."

"Well, I wouldn't know. That's not exactly my wheelhouse."

"What's stopping you?"

I look back at him over my shoulder. Gabe's propped himself up on his forearm. "What do you mean, what's stopping me?"

He shrugs. "You can date. That's a thing you can do. You and Mars seem pretty close."

A strange emotion flutters in my chest. It's not relief, but it's not disappointment, either. I don't know what I expected him to say. "I'm not— No, I'm not dating anybody while I'm half finished."

"Half finished?"

"You wouldn't get it, Gabe."

"Don't tell me what I wouldn't understand—" Gabe's hand comes to rest on my bicep, hot and painful like a flame.

I whip around to face him fully. "You know the only person who's been attracted to me since I came out? *Ethan*. Thanks for getting him suspended by the way, because everybody thinks *I* did that."

He frowns. "They deserved—"

"*Riley* thinks I did that." I cut him off. "So not only am I still dealing with my body *mutating*, I have to deal with them now, too."

I turn my back to him and glare into the darkness. The silence is a knife's edge. Then, there's the unmistakable sound of Gabe sucking at his lip.

I wait for him to yell back at me. I want him to scream in my face and I want to punch him in the teeth like two men would. *Come on*, I think, *let's have some conflict*.

He doesn't, and I don't. The bed jostles. When I finally work up the courage to check, I see that Gabe has turned his back on me as well. There isn't a single justification for the anguish that blocks up my throat. I press my face into my pillow in a vain effort to fall asleep faster.

When I wake up, it's still dark. Sweat glues my shirt to the back of my neck. My throat aches horribly. And I can hear something outside.

After a moment, my eyes adjust to the low light. Gabe is asleep next to me, face pressed against his own arm. I stare at him for a moment, an anchor of familiarity in the void. I stare at him until my brain settles into the fact of being awake.

home

I look past Gabe, now, at the wall behind him. It's hard to figure out how a voice in my head can be coming from any one direction. But I know it as innately as I know that I am lying in my bed. I know that the voice is coming from outside.

I slip out of bed and tiptoe through the hall, only stopping to get into my sneakers before stepping outside. Right away, the cold is like getting smacked by a wave. I wince, then pull the door shut and walk down to the street. Every house on the block is dark. Half of the street lights are out. Ours works, at least, and it illuminates each breath I exhale. I wrap my arms around my chest, wondering what the hell I'm even looking for.

you

My head whips towards the forest preserve to my right.

I see it. As plainly as the moonlight and distance allows, I can see the animal standing in the open field on the opposite side of the road. It matches my memory: large, wolf-like, white-and-brown fur that allows it to blend in with the snowy treeline. When the moonlight hits its eyes, I would swear the two orbs are staring back at me. I hear the voice again:

you

I walk towards it slowly, as if I might startle it with any sudden movement. A magnetic feeling tugs me forward, warmth expanding inside my chest. It's a sensation that I can't name, but I know it instinctively.

It's the comfort of coming back to Chicago after spending the summer with my mom and seeing Gabe again. It's the burning at the back of my throat that comes at the end of scream-singing "deathwish" for the first time in weeks.

My shoes crunch against the asphalt of the road.

home

It's the feeling of seeing an old friend. It's coming home.

home come you home you come home hunter come—

A horn suddenly blares from my right, and I don't even have time to move before the car swerves around me. I jerk backwards and my heel slips off the road.

I land in a pile of cold that's thankfully more snow than ice. The car that nearly hit me snaps back into its lane and never slows down. I watch the tail lights until they make a left and disappear. Only then do I finally turn back to the preserve.

The eyes have vanished. The voice in my head has gone silent, too. Its absence is suddenly palpable. There's not just nothing there, there's an absence of *something*. It makes me feel sick to my stomach.

Then coldness starts to leak in, and I realize I'm sitting in snow. Wearing a T-shirt and underwear and sneakers and literally nothing else. For the first time in weeks, I'm freezing.

I hurry back to the house, where I kick off my shoes and stumble blindly back to my room. Considering it's pitch black, it's impressive that I don't wake Gabe up until I've gotten under the covers. I hear him move around. His hand brushes against mine.

"Why are you freezing?" His voice is rough with half consciousness.

"Bad dream," I answer, trying not to shiver.

I don't know if Gabe is awake in any meaningful way. He barely reacts to what I said.

Then, just as I'm about to roll away from him, Gabe's hand finds mine again.

There are some calluses on his palm, but Gabe's hand is softer than you'd expect a lifelong ice hockey player's to be. Without thinking about it, I let my fingers close around his. As the minutes tick by, I realize neither of us is letting go. Gabe's breathing slowly evens out. He falls asleep holding my hand.

I stare at his face and try not to move. This terrifies me, as everything involving Gabe does on some level. I'm terrified of my reliance on him. I'm terrified of how little he seems to rely on me. I'm terrified of him realizing the depth of this disparity and recoiling from me for good.

I'm also exhausted, and the warmth of his hand thaws out the tension in my shoulders. It feels like I've only just gotten used to the feeling of his hand around mine when an unsteady, dreamless sleep takes me away.

11

When I wake up in the morning, Gabe is facing the wall, breathing slow and heavy. I'm almost positive that I didn't dream all of that. There are scratches on my palms that tell me at least *some* of it was real.

I hope holding Gabe's hand was real, too.

I put on trousers before I tiptoe into the hallway and find Mars sitting at the kitchen table, her maps and a bowl of cereal spread out in front of her. She looks like she's just woken up, eyes bleary and arms showing imprints from the couch pattern.

We give each other small waves of acknowledgement. I pop some waffles into the toaster and drown them in syrup, but after just one bite, a wave of nausea hits me with such force that I get goosebumps from it.

"I don't think I've ever seen somebody this *sad* about waffles," Mars comments, and her sincerity almost makes me crack a smile.

Gabe emerges from the bedroom not long after I let Mars

finish off my plate. I can't gauge if we're still mad at each other, but I'm used to him spending the night. I'm used to the sight of the raggedy muscle shirt he wears to bed, hair matted against the side of his forehead.

Mars is decidedly not. While Gabe pokes through the fridge, Mars turns to me and mouths *oh my God*.

Either she still thinks he's gay and is doing that for my sake, or she's ogling for the sake of it. Both remind me of the scab I've only half pulled off that old wound.

Mars waits for Gabe to sit down with his own bowl of cereal before she speaks. "So, Gabe and I are gonna go plant hunting. Hunter, is there anything we can help you with? Anything we can get while we're out?"

I cross my arms on the table and rest my head on them. I'm almost positive I wasn't dreaming last night. But not enough to say it out loud. I'm already a werewolf. The last thing I need is to be a werewolf with no sense of what's real and what isn't.

"I'm fine," I say instead, voice ragged. I try to clear my throat. "You guys do that; I'll do my shot and try to relax."

Gabe looks at me and frowns. "You do your shots on Monday."

"Uh-huh."

"It's Sunday."

I shrug. "Yeah, and I forgot to do it last week. Which might explain a few things."

What I mean by that is the slight emotional instability. It's not even close to an apology.

Gabe still nods, even if it seems hesitant. "Okay. You need anything, you call us."

From here to downtown Chicago is an hour's drive on a good day. It's a nice thought, but while Mars and Gabe are gone, I'll be on my own.

After we finish eating, Mars and Gabe change for colder weather. I sit back in the living room and watch them, zipping up and down the hall and talking to each other as they do. There's no sense of awkwardness. It's familiar, comfortable, almost to a degree that's unsettling.

I'm used to having that dynamic with Gabe. I'm used to having that dynamic with Mars. But seeing it between the two of them is *weird*. It feels like I'm watching my life play out in front of me. Without me.

Then, Mars pokes her head into the living room and holds up my faded Cubs crew neck. "Mind if I borrow this?"

I come back to the moment and nod. Mars grins and pulls it on over her shirt.

"Hey, you want me to drive?" she asks, glancing over her shoulder as Gabe comes out of the bathroom.

His eyes narrow. "I'll drive."

Mars cocks an eyebrow. "Right, my bad for thinking we wanted to be *fast*. Don't worry, Bambi, if you need us, we'll come screaming to the rescue on a Jeep Patriot."

She walks over and gives me a hug, which thankfully hides the blush that creeps into my face. "Seriously, though," she whispers, "try to relax, and call us if you need anything."

"It'll be two hours, not two weeks." I pat her shoulder before she lets me go.

Gabe's goodbye is a quiet nod, and I don't press him for anything more than that, no matter how much I might want to.

As soon as the door shuts behind them, a heavy silence settles over the house. Somehow worse than the silence I've been forced to sit in since Norman died. It makes the house feel small and stretched thin. I stick my hands in my pockets and walk quickly into my bedroom, where at least the silence is *mine*.

All my needles and syringes and alcohol wipes are in a plastic organizer in the bottom drawer of my nightstand. I've got all this time to kill, I might as well try to get my hormones back to normal. I grab each individual bit one by one, more from habit than conscious thought.

No Band-Aids, though.

I frown and pull the drawer open a little further, and that's when I hear the voice again.

come

I freeze.

Until now, every time I've heard this voice, I've been half asleep and could excuse it: an intrusive thought, a misremembered nightmare, *something*. This is the first time I've been wide awake, and there's nothing hazy about it. It's distinct, heavy against the inside of my ear. Close enough to itch.

comenowcomenowcomenowcomenow

I wince at the sudden escalation and nearly drop the bottle of testosterone. The voice is sharp and painful, but it's also gone as fast as it came. Then the room is suddenly silent, save for the sound of my breathing.

Maybe it's a bad idea to try and stab myself with a needle right now. I take a few deep breaths until my heart stops jackhammering against my ribs.

Band-Aids are a decent enough excuse. I can't stand the indoor silence any more. So, I leave the supplies for my shot on my nightstand and hurry into the hall, as if the inside of my head is something I can get away from.

I comb through the drawers in the kitchen, including the one that's full of gas money and pepper spray. No Band-Aids. Add it to the list of things that have fallen to the wayside in the wake of the bite. I finally give up and grab my coat, not bothering to change out of the clothes I fell asleep in. I'm too skittish to care much about how I look or what I smell like.

The silence in my head no longer feels like the silence of being alone. It's *too* silent now. The total quiet you only ever hear in horror movies.

Thankfully, stepping outside provides me with a small

amount of white noise: a faint breeze, the crunch of my boots against frozen concrete, the occasional rumble of a car driving by on the main road. Whatever amount of relief I start to feel, though, dissipates once I come down the driveway and look out at Springbrook in the distance.

The field is dead and dry and uninteresting. I still stop and stare at the empty space, trying to imagine a monster there.

I wonder if I've started seeing things. After all, I *am* hearing voices.

Across the street, I catch movement through the windows on the side of Annie Searchwell's house. Ordinarily, I'd be thrilled to hurry past and avoid any interaction with her. But Annie's house is also a hell of a lot closer than the corner store. So, after a couple of seconds to really think about how *weird* my day-to-day life has gotten, I walk across the street and press my thumb against her doorbell.

Annie comes to the door less than thirty seconds later, her hair pushed back by a pink-spotted headband. "Yes?"

I weakly smile. "Hi, Annie. Uh, I need…Band-Aids."

Her eyebrows knit together. "Is everything okay?"

"Yeah, I just—" I falter. My tongue trips over the easy explanation of being a trans kid who just needs to do one lousy shot. "We're out."

Annie blessedly accepts this. "Oh. Well, goodness, get inside before you catch your death."

Annie pulls her door open all the way and ushers me

inside. She must have her thermostat cranked up as high as it can go. By the time she gets me to her kitchen, there's a thin layer of sweat on the back of my neck. I shrug my coat off and hold it nervously over my chest, lingering on the other side of the kitchen island.

It's not a dirty house, but there's clutter on nearly every flat surface able to hold something larger than a coaster. Unopened mail and crumpled receipts and news articles printed from a variety of websites. I glance over my shoulder into the living room, right as one of her cats scrambles under the couch.

"Can I get you anything to drink?" Annie asks. When I turn back to her, she's going through her cabinets. "Got plenty of tea. Decaf coffee."

"No thank you." I take a breath and rest my arms on the kitchen island, nervously fiddling with a button on my coat sleeve.

At last, Annie pulls a plastic box out of the tiny cabinet above her fridge and makes a small, triumphant noise. There's a grin on her face as she hands it to me. "Is your dad out of town again?" she asks.

"Uh-huh." I nod as I check the box. It's been opened, but it's mostly full so I don't really care. "Yeah, he's— Work, you know."

Annie *mm-hms* and rests her arms on the island. "Well, I know you've got your boyfriend over most days, but I'm always here if you need me. Miko *loves* visitors."

Behind us, the cat under the couch makes a quiet, uneasy *yowl* sound that makes Annie frown and crane her neck to get a look.

"Miko," she tuts, "they're a *friend*."

In the interest of getting out of here as quickly as possible, I try to ignore the misgendering. And the *boyfriend* comment.

"Right, uh," I clear my throat and pull back.

As I do, my eyes catch on one of the dozens of papers laid out on the island. A splash of pixelated yellow. It's a literal stock photo of a wolf. I frown and pull it out from the pile. Above the wolf are several different websites and phone numbers, all crammed under a bolded title: **DO YOU KNOW WHERE YOUR PETS ARE?**

"What's this?" I ask.

"Oh, good grief, did I forget to give you one of those?" Annie sighs. "A girl's dog went missing down the road."

It takes me a moment to realize she's talking about Tammy. "Oh?"

"Rangers think it might've been a wolf. Please, take that one. I know you keep Norman inside, but just in case you see something, you can call the right people."

I flinch at the mention of Norman before what she says actually processes. I look up at her. "Wolf? Like, someone saw it?"

Someone else?

"No." She shakes her head. "They found some tracks.

Too big for the coyotes we've got."

I blink as the slight surge of hope poofs out of existence. Even still, I can't help but soften at the mention of Norman. "Right." I fold the paper in my hands. "Thanks."

Annie beams. "You're a smart kid. I'm not too worried about you."

Behind me, the collar of the cat jangles. I look back and watch it scurry down the hall like its tail is on fire. Annie notices and makes a confused tut, but she doesn't think enough of it to say anything.

"Well...you sure I can't do anything else for you?" she asks.

"No, but thank you for this." I give the box a little shake.

The smile returns to Annie's face, and she ushers me to follow her into the hallway. I have to make a conscious effort to keep off her heels.

"Is your dad coming home soon at least?" Annie takes the latch off the front door and looks back at me.

"Soon." *I think.*

She moves aside and lets me step through the doorway. "You need anything else, you come right over, understand?"

I nod. "For sure."

"All right. Don't be a stranger, Ha—*honey*."

I spin back around, but Annie's already shut the door with a gentle *click*. I stand there for a second, frozen by the first syllable of a name that hasn't been mine since I was thirteen.

Then, I stomp across the street and dunk the flyer into my trash can.

I'm nowhere near the right headspace to think about needles, but I'm not doing myself any favours if I skip my shot for a second week in a row. I clearly *still* don't look enough like a guy to have earned my own name. I grind my teeth as I get my jacket off and sit down on the edge of my bed.

The curve of my upper thigh is covered in pockmarks. Little rust-coloured reminders of two years of previous shots. My fingers are still a little stiff from the cold as I grab a fistful of leg fat and squeeze it until the skin goes white. I give a testing press of the needle tip to my thigh. A sharp prick webs out from the spot, and again from every other spot I try.

I take a deep breath. This is why Gabe started helping me in the first place. A part of me is frustrated that Gabe left with Mars without so much as offering to help me do this. Another part of me is horribly embarrassed that I want him to do this for me. Like, seriously, the *real man* has to do my shots.

A real man would get it done on his own.

I grab a handful of skin and exhale.

don't

I tense up, before another wave of shame curdles rapidly into anger.

Fuck this voice.

I grit my teeth, heartbeat reverberating up through my jawbone, and shove the needle into my leg. Sometimes the skin resists, especially on this side of my body, where I've built up a lot of scar tissue. But I'm not expecting the needle to make it only halfway in before coming to a sharp halt.

Instead of pain, there's a sudden sense of numbness. As if I'd hit a button to put my leg to sleep. As if I'd hit *something*.

If I were smart, I'd force it the rest of the way, push down on the plunger, and be done with it. Instead, I panic and pull back, taking the needle with me.

The first pulse of blood is instantaneous. I don't even get to react before a second *spurt* comes and I finally remember how to move. I slap my hand down over the injection spot and run for the bathroom, paranoia surging as fast as the blood leaks through my fingers. I grab a wad of toilet tissue and shove it over the puncture.

For whatever reason, *that* is what snaps me out of the panic. I pricked myself. That's all. The fear that felt rational five seconds ago is suddenly so *childish*.

I carefully lift the wad of tissue off my leg. The skin is red, but there's now only a slight, delayed dribble of blood. I exhale and sit on the edge of the tub, dabbing at the spot until the bleeding finally stops. The embarrassment lingers for a while longer before finally turning into something like relief. I'm fine.

My fingers, though, stay on my leg where the other pockmarks sit. I know I'm calling 'em pockmarks, but they're discolourations at best. Ugly little spots that only I can see.

Except right now, I *can* feel them. A tangible hardness like when a zit starts to form under the skin.

I twist until I can get a better look and grab a fistful of skin at random. I pinch the skin between my nails and squeeze.

It doesn't pop. Instead, whatever's built up under my skin is pushed out slowly. Like squeezing toothpaste from the tube. I keep pinching until the build-up collapses against the side of my thumb, and then I bring my hand up to my face.

There's a slight transparency to the substance. I don't think it's pus, but I don't know what it could be otherwise. I quickly wipe my hand against my shirt and then press my nail into my leg again. This time, only blood dribbles out.

I lose myself in the monotony of finding a bump and squeezing it until I draw blood. The longer I go, the tougher my skin gets. The harder I have to pinch it between my nails. The darker red it all becomes.

Somewhere in the middle of it all, twisting myself in half to get the angle right, I break the skin and the residue I squeeze out is inexplicably *yellow*. Like mucus, suddenly much less solid as it leaks across the side of my finger.

I startle, and, at last, stop. My leg pulsates from how much I've been pinching at it. I bring my hand up and nervously start chewing at my nail bed, brain scrambling for any sort of explanation for what's happening. That's when my knuckle brushes against my cheek.

The skin feels wrong there, too.

My skin feels wrong all over.

Here's the thing about zits: people have come up with a million different ways to pop or extract them. Riley's bathroom is probably still crowded with cleansers, exfoliating serums, patches and lancets. I only have a lancet myself, but that's all I need. A small piece of metal filed down to a singular, dangerously sharp point.

There's no voice in my head. I don't have that excuse when I scramble to my feet and pick up the lancet from its spot beside the sink. I lean so far over the counter that my nose scrapes the mirror. I feel out my cheek until I find a solid bump, and then I press the end of the lancet into my skin. Harder and harder until it finally pierces through.

Only a small bead of blood rises to the surface.

On the second strike, pus, the colour of pea soup, runs down the side of my face. The noise of disgust that comes out of me is completely involuntary. As is the slight whimper that I make next. Because as I wipe the pus away, I see there's something else. Something under my skin. I reach into the wound and carefully pull it out.

Hair. It's hair, maybe two inches in length, but longer than any hair I've ever been able to grow on my face. I stare at it in bewilderment.

The sound of the front door opening comes first. Then, Mars's voice rings out: "Hunter!"

Shit. I rip off another wad of toilet paper and press it against the bleeding gash on my face. The hair goes into the sink, where I run the water and rinse it down the drain. Everything in my chest feels tight. Anger and discomfort each have a boot on the back of my brain, pressing and pressing and there's nothing I can do about it.

"So, we've got good news and bad—" Mars comes running from around the corner, gets her first look at me, and falters at the doorway. "Uh, are you okay?"

I nod, even as my eyes lock on the countertop. "I'm fine."

"Cool. Explain why you're bleeding?"

My whole body aches with stiffness. *How long was I picking at myself?*

"I was trying to do my shot," I manage.

"You do your shots in your face?"

"*Marcy*," I snap.

The air leaves the room. I have never, in all the time we've been friends, called her by her full name. I open my eyes, and I can't place the look on Mars's face. Not anger, but nothing good.

I'm almost thankful Gabe comes around the corner to defuse the tension. His eyes land on my face and immediately a frown breaks across his own. "What the hell did you do to yourself?"

A laugh comes bubbling out of my mouth while my eyes prick with tears. "I didn't—"

Glass shatters.

We all freeze for a moment. It wasn't a small sound, as if something knocked over a cup. It sounded like what I can only imagine to be a window.

Gabe moves first, then Mars. I follow them to the door and watch them falter, before Gabe flings the door open and allows them to both rush out onto the porch. My eyes linger on the source of the shattering sound: a brick sitting on the carpet.

Outside, tyres squeal. I look up in time to catch a blue truck peeling out of the neighbourhood. Before it's gone, I catch its *EZBRZY* custom plate.

I've always had this half-serious fantasy about the fight that would someday break out between me and Ethan. I've had dreams about punching him and finally towering over him *once* in my life. I haven't really considered the fact that in a real fight, Ethan would kill me. Now there's a brick inside my house. Fear tastes like pennies in my mouth.

I barely realize that I'm just standing there until Gabe comes surging back inside. He puts a hand on my shoulder as he slips past me, and I turn to watch him snatch his keys from the kitchen counter.

"What are you doing?" I ask, though the answer is obvious.

Surprisingly, Gabe doesn't push past me again. He stops, anger palpable. "Do you want to call the cops?"

"What?"

"Either we call the cops, or I'm going and I'm handling this myself."

I don't mean to laugh. It just comes out of me. "He's doing this because we got him suspended, and you want to call the *cops?*"

Gabe could easily pick me up and move me out of the way. Instead, he pulls his lip between his teeth and exhales, like a rush of steam. "So you want to let him get away with this?"

"*I'm* letting him?"

"Yes! When is it gonna click that he's not gonna stop until somebody *makes* him stop?"

My stomach twists with something ugly. "When's it gonna click that you just keep making things worse?"

We both stand there for a moment, the air between us suddenly, terribly fragile. I break eye contact first, but Gabe is the one who moves. He disappears further inside the house. A moment later, I hear the brand-new back door slam shut. I realize that my nails have been digging into my palms hard enough to make my knuckles sore.

Then the porch creaks, and I remember that Mars has been here the whole time. I look back at her. Blessedly, she has the kindness to appear as uncomfortable as I feel.

"Uh..." My voice crumbles. I face forward again and clear my throat. "Sorry."

I nervously grab my arm, mostly trying to stop myself from having a complete meltdown.

"I'm gonna clean this up," I finally manage. "Then, I guess, um—"

"I can help with your shot," Mars offers.

She can't see my face, which is the only reason I let the emotion of the moment wash over me. "Thanks."

Mars ends up taking the broom from me and sweeping up the glass herself. I pick up the brick and walk out to the edge of the preserve, where I notice for the first time what's been scrawled on the bottom of it in Sharpie: *FRANKENTITS*.

I hurl it into the tall grass.

As I walk back inside, my brain cycles through the excuses I can give my dad for the window. Our neighbourhood is quiet. Never exactly overrun with stray baseballs or gangs of children with slingshots. But whatever I'm telling him, it won't be the truth. Of course it won't. I once alluded to the fact that somebody at school was giving me shit, and he told me two things: wait for them to hit me first, and then hit back twice as hard.

He'd be disgusted with how I've been handling this. Or, how I *haven't* been handling it. Letting Ethan press his heel further and further into my throat. A real man – somebody like Gabe – would have ended this years ago.

I grab my injection supplies and angrily set up at the kitchen table. Mars joins me a moment later, hanging her coat from the chair.

"What was the good news?" I ask.

She looks at me. "What?"

"You said you had good news and bad news."

"Oh. Yeah." Her jaw clenches and unclenches. "You want the good news first?"

I think about it as I unscrew and replace the needle head with a new one. "What's the bad news?"

Mars takes the syringe from me. "We're 0-for-2 on monkshood. There's maybe a chance I could find some online, but I don't know how long it takes to ship plants, if we can even find somebody selling enough for this to work." She takes the safety cap off and sighs. "Of course you couldn't get bitten during the summer."

I absently press my knuckle into the wound on my cheek. A little blood transfers to the back of my hand, but most of it has already dried. "What's the good news, then?"

Mars is staring very hard at the tip of the needle. "Maybe we can still try silver."

It's so bleak that I don't even know how to respond. I almost reflexively crack a joke – *you think* that's *bad? I'm hearing voices now!* – but I look at the clock on the wall instead and see that *two hours* have passed since I last looked at the time.

I just spent two hours picking myself apart, and I want her to believe that a voice inside my head is sentient?

Mars tears open an alcohol wipe with her teeth before she wipes my arm down, surprisingly gentle. I roll up my sleeve and stare vacantly at the table.

"Um, how do I…?" She makes a slightly dramatic stabbing motion at my arm.

"Oh." I blink, surprised by my own oversight. Mars has never done this before. "Just, uh, pinch the skin near my shoulder. Then you…stab me, I guess."

She nods. Her jaw clenches again.

It's then that I realize she's not angry with me; she's nervous. Mars is a lot of things, but lacking in confidence has never been one of them. I turn back to the table, feeling like I owe her a second of privacy.

Except a few seconds go by and then Mars blurts out, "You know he loves you, right?"

I look at her, bewildered.

She blinks, looking horrified. "I mean – ignore me, holy shit that was bad phrasing. He— *We* both love you, this whole thing is scary, and I think we're all a little freaked out."

I exhale. "He's got a hell of a way of showing it."

"No offence, but so do you."

My eyes snap to her. "Excuse me?"

Mars hesitates. In the silence, I visualize her and Gabe in the car together, talking about me for the whole drive to Chicago and back. "It's not that you don't have a good reason," she finally says, "but you've been a *little* short recently."

"Yeah," I bite, "I wonder why."

Mars glares at me, grip tightening on my arm, before she looks down and jabs the needle in. I deserved that. I still wince and turn away, trying not to focus on the syringe jostling as Mars's thumb pushes down on the plunger.

We're quiet, and her grip eventually softens.

"Sorry," she whispers. "You and Gabe have known each other way longer than I've known either of you, so maybe I'm just an asshole who doesn't know when to stop talking. But you guys clearly care about each other. You both just show it like men who've never experienced an emotion before."

I allow myself a small, half-felt smile. "Right. Thanks."

Mars sighs and pulls the needle out. She's too slow, but I'm thankful she doesn't rip it out and cause more bleeding. "Seriously! Like you know how Gabe, like, sucks his teeth?"

I nod.

"Well, on the drive out, we started talking a little about how you were gonna do your shot, and Gabe starts doing that, and you know me: I nag. Eventually, I nag him enough that he tells me he's been helping you with the shots whenever he can, and he tells me everything about how he practised with syringes to make sure he didn't hurt you. Which, first of all—"

"What do you mean he practised?" I cut her off as soon as that bit of information processes in my head.

Mars stops with the safety cap hovering over the needle. A smile tugs at her mouth. "Sorry, is that not something you rib him about constantly?"

I don't answer, because I don't know how to say *no*, and I watch the look of amusement on Mars's face shift to concern, then slight horror.

"Oh my God, I have the biggest fucking mouth." She shoves the cap fully onto the needle before she drops it on the table. "Well, he said that when you asked him, he didn't have any clue how to give somebody a shot. So, I guess he bought this pack of syringes and shit from Amazon, and he practised on oranges. He said his YouTube algorithm is still, like, mostly trans people giving injection tutorials. Gave his mom a total heart attack when he came out of his room with a mason jar full of needles."

Mars says it all like one detail will trigger a memory, and I'll remember that I *have* known all about this. Except it doesn't, I don't, and too much has happened today for me to be able to process any of the emotions that form because of that.

"So, I know that clearly none of this is any of my business, but...we all care about each other here." Mars nervously clears her throat. "I'd do anything for you, and Gabe would, too, he just shows it...differently. Like I'm rambling because I'm trying really hard to not make you feel worse and I don't know how to stop talking sometimes, and Gabe would probably go kill that asshole right now if you asked him to."

That's exactly what I'm trying to avoid. But for Mars's sake, I smile and nod.

Mars carefully places a Band-Aid on my arm before exhaling. "Okay. Uh, I am gonna go and make sure Gabe doesn't actually kill anybody. Just...let me think about what we can try with silver, okay?"

I nod, even though at this point, I think I'd let Ethan kill me if he came back.

Mars begins to stand, but before she does, she kisses the pad of her thumb and presses it against the Band-Aid. Then she leaves. My arm is covered in goosebumps.

Being alone again feels like being spat out of a hurricane. I put my hand over the Band-Aid and try to visualize the testosterone making its way through my body. There has to be *something* I can do. Figure out another possible cure or keep checking Channel 17's web page for any sort of sighting.

Instead, all I can do is think about all the time we wasted today. Time that I am increasingly aware I do not have.

12

The next morning, I wake up with such a bad sore throat that it takes me a moment to find my voice. Then, I realize the injection site on my arm is throbbing.

I shuffle towards the bathroom, the sound of my feet against the hardwood too loud in the otherwise ear-ringing silence of the empty house. I take the Band-Aid off my left arm; the skin underneath is red and swollen. I give it an exploratory press. The pain that jolts all the way down into my fingertips is enough to dissuade me from doing it again.

Then I check my other arm, and the sight of the bite turns my stomach. The black-and-blue bruises seem to be climbing up towards my shoulder. It makes me think of necrosis. It makes me run my finger along the spot on my leg where I used to be able to see bone, where the skin is also steadily turning purple, and think about what colour it's going to turn next.

I think it's that doom-tinged sense of certainty that pushes me to find Riley's number in my phone.

Can we talk? Today?

Sure. I'm free after my third period.

I'll meet you in the library?

Okay

I stare at the exchange and wonder if it's been that easy this whole time.

I suppose I never would've tried to find out. As much as I miss our friendship, she was pretty explicit with what she called me in our last big argument. I have no delusion that that's changed. On the other hand, there's still a tiny part of my fifteen-year-old heart that beats with the rest of me.

Either way, it still feels like someone's twisting a knife into already damaged ribs. I press a small Band-Aid over the scab that's formed on my cheek and try to tell myself I don't look overwhelmingly stupid.

Frigid air leaks into the house through the broken window in the living room. I spend a couple extra minutes rummaging around until I find a cardboard box in our garage that's big enough to cut apart and duct tape to the frame. It's not pretty, but it'll do in the short term. There's a new text from Dad that came in while I was sleeping that says have a good day at school.

I can read between the lines: don't cut class again.

Gabe and I don't talk during the drive to school. I pretend

my phone is the most interesting thing in the world, when all I'm doing is checking my face in the reflection of the glass. The bites have been easy enough to hide under the long sleeves and coats of wintertime, but now I get to worry about the Band-Aid awkwardly slapped on my cheek.

At school, though, nobody even bats an eye at me.

The only time someone gives me a double take is when Taylor catches me in the hall and makes a confused gesture towards the Band-Aid. I wave him off, mouth *I'm fine*, and we pass each other without actually speaking. The vocal minority of Ethan's ilk sometimes makes it hard to remember how little people notice me, let alone care about the horror show that my body is becoming.

A small part of me wishes they did notice. A part of me wishes somebody would look at me, see what's happening, and care about it as much as I do.

Once third period is over, I cut through the halls and pull open the library doors with shaking hands. I find a seat in the corner of the room, where the shelves and fluorescent lights make it feel like a completely different building.

Maybe she won't show up at all, I think. Maybe I'll sit here for an hour, and it'll be horribly depressing, but at least that would be the worst of it. I stick my hands into my pockets, where my right hand closes around the necklace. I may not be able to wear it right now, but I couldn't stand the thought of leaving it at home.

It takes several more minutes before I look up and see Riley walking down the aisle towards me. She's wearing a sweater of green and white stripes, hair flowing freely at her shoulders. She sits down in the chair next to me, and an awkward tension settles appropriately between us.

"So," she exhales. "What's up?"

I realize, suddenly, that I'd expected Riley to ghost me far more than I'd prepared to get this far. A thousand opening sentences generate in my brain. I scramble.

"Norman died," I blurt out, voice breaking at the end.

Riley visibly startles. "Oh. I'm sorry."

I nod, fixing my eyes to the floor. My face burns.

"He wasn't *that* old, was he?" she asks.

I shake my head. "An animal got him."

"Oh. That's terrible," she says. "I'm really sorry."

I nod and absent-mindedly scratch at the Band-Aid, wincing at the subsequent flash of pain.

Riley frowns. "Are you getting sick or something?"

I glance at her, and she makes a gesture to my throat. "Your voice is…weird."

My face burns even hotter, and I nod without giving any further elaboration.

I want to tell her about everything else. That not only is Norman dead, but it was a lycanthrope that killed him, and that there's now something really, seriously wrong with me. Instead, we both fall into awkward silence. I flex my fist around the necklace as I prepare to poke at the Ethan-shaped elephant in the room instead.

Riley speaks before I can. "Maybe this is crazy to ask, but how's Gabe doing?"

I look at her. Sometimes I forget that we were *all* friends, for however brief a time. "He's fine. Y'know, hockey all the time. Nothing new."

She smiles. "Is he going to college, or is he trying to go straight to pros?"

"College. Please, you know his mom." I smile back. "He'll be fine anywhere with flat roads, rocks and sticks."

For a moment, my grip around the necklace loosens.

"I'm probably staying local," Riley adds. "You?"

My next breath hurts to take. "I'm not saying this to be a dick. But even if I knew, I wouldn't tell you."

Riley blinks. "Oh. Cool. Glad you weren't saying that to be a dick."

I roll my eyes and slump into my chair. "I don't even know if I'm going to college," I admit. "I don't want to be where a whole bunch of people already know me."

Even though I'm not looking at her, I can still feel Riley's gaze on me. The heavy weight of surface-level sympathy. "You know, most people don't care that you're trans."

"That's bullshit and you know it."

"It's *not*, Hunter, people care whether or not you're an asshole."

I roll my eyes. "Yeah, plenty of people seem to like Ethan just fine."

It's like hitting a switch. Calling attention to the open, throbbing wound between us.

Riley sighs, sounding exhausted. "Is that why you wanted to talk to me?"

"It's not, but since we're here, he threw a brick through my window yesterday."

"Bullshit."

Her reply comes so quickly that it startles a laugh out of me. "You didn't even have to think about that, did you? I'm just forever a liar to you?"

"Did you watch him do it?" she asks.

I glare at her. "No, but I watched his *truck* speed out of my neighbourhood."

"Lots of people have blue trucks. Did you watch *him* do it?"

It doesn't matter that no other blue truck would have any business racing away from my house. "No," I grit out.

Riley *mm-hms*, mouth tight. "You always blame him for all these horrible things, and you never have any proof that he's done any of them."

"Except for what I *tell you* happened," I rebut, "but that's not good enough for you."

Riley's frowns have always looked like she's intentionally exaggerating them, but that's just how her mouth works. Two sharp, angular brushstrokes across the bottom of her face.

"Not when you accuse somebody of something like that, no. It's not."

My palm burns. I close my fist tighter, digging the jagged ends of the chain link into my skin. "Do you actually think I lied?" I ask. "About what Ethan said and did to me?"

To my surprise, Riley doesn't say anything right away. We sit there, the air simmering with unease, before she sighs and takes a sip from her water bottle.

"I don't know," she says.

Of all the possible answers, this confuses me. "You don't know—"

"*No*, I don't. Both of you are so immature, I don't think either of you would tell me the truth if I asked. I don't know if I believe what Ethan says, but I don't believe you, either."

"Why would I lie about something like that?"

"Because," Riley snaps, "how *incredibly* convenient that as soon as I get someone in my life that isn't you, you find the perfect excuse to get him out."

Somebody shushes us. It feels like getting hit with a cattle prod.

Riley and I both look at the librarian standing at the opposite end of the aisle. She gives us a warning glare before she continues pushing her cart of returned books.

Even once she's gone, the tense silence between Riley and me stretches on. Riley's words bounce around the inside of my head. She still thinks I'm a liar. She thinks I lie about everything.

Riley fiddles with the lid of her water bottle. "I thought about texting you after Saturday. But I assumed you had me blocked."

"I haven't had you blocked on anything for years," I answer.

She absorbs this. "So, why did you want to talk now?"

"I don't know." My voice is flat. "I figured you've been dating this guy for a while, maybe you could—"

"I didn't say *what*." Riley cuts me off. "I don't care *what* you wanted to talk about. I asked *why*. Why did you suddenly want to talk to me?"

Oh. That's trickier to articulate. I shut my mouth, trying to iron out the knot of emotion that suddenly sticks in my throat.

The problem is, I realize, that explaining *why* would put me at an unbearable risk of humiliation. It would require a level of vulnerability I can't reach with even Gabe or Mars. *Why* would involve unpacking why I still feel safe around her. Or, at least, why I *want* to still feel safe around her.

There are years between us, but I don't think either of us is unrecognizable. Riley's still Riley. I'm still me.

"I guess I'm just going through some shit," I finally whisper, feeling the silver burn my palm. "And...I don't know, I still want to talk to you about stuff. I want to trust you with it."

Even that feels like I've pulled the curtain back too far.

"You can trust me," Riley says, just as softly.

"I *want* to trust you," I reiterate. "I don't."

I finally look at her, and I think we both understand the

impasse we're at. Nothing moves with Ethan on the road.

"I wish you would," Riley whispers.

I don't trust my voice enough to answer. When neither of us says anything more, Riley slowly nods and pulls her bag into her lap. Whatever this was, it's over.

I watch her, and that's when her bag catches my eye. It's a tote with a cartoon Venus flytrap drawn on it. It's smiling as it opens its leaves up to the sky. A bunch of weird-looking flowers sprout at its base. I don't know why, but I know this from somewhere.

"Where'd you get that?" I ask.

Riley glances at the bag. "This? Um, I think it's off Boughton and...something, it's this flower shop—"

"Grounded Gardening?"

"Yeah! That's it." She frowns. "Why?"

I quickly shake my head. My mind races. "I just recognized the logo."

Riley gives me a look like this is the strangest part of the conversation. "Cool."

She stands and smooths out her jeans. Part of me is manic with the connection I've made. Another part of me is still here, horribly grounded, desperate for Riley to turn around and give some final word. Some signal that I might still mean *anything* to her.

The most I get is that she glances back and smiles at me before marching down the aisle.

The librarian gives me another displeased side-eye as I hurry past her. I flash her my best apologetic smile and push through the doors. I run to the closest bathroom, lock myself in the end stall, and call Mars.

She doesn't pick up the first time. Then, after a few rings on the second try, the call blessedly connects.

"Hi, are you okay?" Mars sounds like she's just stopped running, and I don't know how my brain forgot that we're both in the middle of a school day.

"Yeah, sorry. I'm all good." I take a deep breath. "What about Hazel?"

Mars is quiet for a minute. "Uh, what about her?"

"She works in a flower shop, right? Do you think she might be able to get monkshood?"

"Oh." Mars goes quiet again. "I didn't even think about that. Maybe?"

"Can we go find out?"

Another pause. "*Now?*"

I hold my phone in front of me and note the time: barely eleven o'clock. I also note the new red mark on my palm, crossing paths with the other burns that are only half faded.

There's no real reason it *has* to be now. But I put my phone back to my ear and nod. "Yeah. Now."

I don't know which part of this Mars isn't thrilled by (probably all of it), but with her sigh, I know I've got her. "Okay," she says. "Give me fifteen minutes and be ready to go."

* * *

I've met Hazel a handful of times. Like Mars, she's Filipino, although her skin is a little darker and she wears a septum ring with a tiny purple mushroom on the end of it. She seems nice, but she's also twenty, so I've never felt we had a whole lot to talk about. Her possible connection to monkshood is the first time I've felt a strong emotion towards her.

Mars pulls up to the concrete circle fifteen minutes after we hang up. I'm very aware that this will come back to bite me in the ass later. But in order for there to *be* a later for me to be in trouble in, I need this cure.

Mars is noticeably pale. She did not *actually* throw up, she tells me, but she made a good enough display of pretending she had that her English teacher allowed her to "call her mom" and get picked up. I'm sort of envious of how lax her school is, while also feeling guilty that I'm dragging her along with me.

Although Mars was the one who brought lycanthropes into this in the first place.

Grounded Gardening sits on the corner of Boughton and Ninety-Fifth Street. The red-brick building it occupies looks old, but in a cosy sort of way. We park up front, where there are normally a lot of vibrant flowers when the weather is right for it. At the moment, they have a few leftover Christmas wreaths still hanging from the planter boxes.

"Do you mind waiting in the car?" Mars asks.

She's still a little pale. I don't understand, but I nod and sink back into my seat.

Relief passes over her face. "Thanks." She smiles before she gets out.

I catch a glimpse of Hazel as she comes out of a supply closet, but there are too many plants inside for me to get a clear look at anything. So I sit back and try to relax, even though my fingers instinctively rise to my cheek to pick at the Band-Aid again.

About five seconds go by before my phone buzzes in my pocket. It's Gabe.

Please tell me you're just in the bathroom

I think we have a lead on monkshood

lots to explain. mars and I have it handled

The little three dots pop up for a moment, then go away.

I wish that I felt worse about closing my phone and slipping it back into my pocket. Whatever is happening to me isn't going away. It's progressing. If we keep sticking to the few free hours we have between school and work – well, either Gabe can have me in school, or he can have me *human*.

I grab a lozenge from my bag and pop it into my mouth before looking up. Hazel and Mars have come back into view, though I can see only Hazel's face. Her forehead is scrunched up, eyebrows nearly touching as she and Mars go back and forth.

Then she stops and stares at Mars for a very long time before her expression softens. I can't read their lips, so I only know the conversation is done when Mars comes out. Her face is vacant, eyes straight ahead. It's the first moment where I wonder if this was a bad idea.

She gets in the car and rubs her hands together over the vent before sighing. "She said she can rush order a shipment tonight. Unless there's a snowstorm or something, we'll have monkshood by Wednesday."

I feel a swell of relief, but it doesn't reach the height that it should. "I'll pay her back for whatever it costs," I promise.

"No, it's— You're fine, she didn't want to take our money." Mars nods, as if reiterating this to herself. She glances briefly at the rear-view mirror before pulling out of the spot.

We're both quiet until we get back on the street, without any stated destination. Thankfully, the first light we pull up to has just turned red.

"We— *She* ended things on Saturday," Mars blurts out. "Sorry."

I quickly shake my head. "Don't apologize. I'm sorry, I wouldn't have—"

"Hey, I would've said no if I had to. And it worked out; she can get us the monkshood." Mars sighs and glances at the radio. Her phone is playing a Baby Tate song that makes the mood a little weird until she turns the volume down. "I was gonna bring it up. It just seemed lame compared to everything else going on."

Well, most things probably pale in comparison to lycanthropy.

"Doesn't mean it sucks any less," I say instead. "Want to talk about it?"

She shakes her head. "Nothing to talk about. It wasn't that serious, and I've got way more important things going on in my life than her right now. I told her that and she threw a fit about it, but I mean, it's the truth."

The light turns green and the car jerks forward.

"Anyway." Mars clears her throat. "I told her if she did this, it'd be the last time I bugged her with anything. I'll Venmo her for the cost of shipping. I don't care."

So far, this werewolf has killed at least two dogs and one situationship. That last one really feels like it's my fault, though.

"I'm sorry," I say again.

Mars looks over, reads my expression, and frowns. "Don't apologize. In what world am I gonna look at my best friend having a fucking crisis and say *sorry, this girl I met at a house party over the summer wants to make out right now*? No way. You need me, I'm here."

She reaches over and grabs my hand to make a point, and then she doesn't let go.

For a few seconds, I watch her out of the corner of my eye. It hurts my head to think too hard about Mars choosing *me* over literally anybody. I've never expected her to, not when there's a whole world of other people out there. I've always been certain that I like Mars so much more than she might like me.

Except she likes me enough to choose me over an active intimate partner. Easily, from the sound of it. My thoughts redirect towards willing my hands to be as dry as possible.

At the next stop sign, Mars seems to realize that she doesn't know where she's driving. We idle there, the only car at the intersection.

I drag my thumb along the side of Mars's finger. "Can I ask you a stupid question?"

Mars looks over at me. "*Please.*"

My laugh is a huff. "Can we go home?"

That's the extent of the convincing that Mars needs. She nods, a big smile stretching across her face. As we cross through the intersection, I unlock her phone (the passcode is easy: 1006, her birthday) and find "deathwish" in her liked songs. I don't turn the volume up all the way, only enough that we can hear it over the rumble of the engine, but by the time we hit the chorus we've relaxed enough that we begin to sing along.

13

We park on the street outside my house, and my attention falls to the preserve. In the daylight, it barely seems like more than a collection of dead trees and, in the far distance, barren hills. As I step out of the car, though, I impose a monster onto the treeline. I try to imagine it under the glare of the midday sun. The juxtaposition of its white fur against the dirty snow.

"Whatcha looking at?" Mars shuts the car door behind her, one of our backpacks hanging off each shoulder.

I glance at her before I turn again to the preserve. "Nothing. Had a nightmare. I came out and thought I saw it there."

My nightmares have been weird recently. I'm hesitant to believe anything I think I see in the dead of night. Mars lingers at my side, though, looking out at the preserve with her eyes slightly squinted. I nervously check my phone. No new texts from Dad. I hope to God he's flying when the school calls him about my impromptu half-day.

Just when I'm getting ready to steer us both inside, she says, "Do you wanna go find out?"

I look at her. "Now?"

"Yeah? It's the perfect time to go poking around in the woods. Werewolf's not gonna attack us at noon on a Monday."

"What do you mean? It's a werewolf, not *Dracula*."

Mars shrugs before she wheels backwards towards the car. "Have you seen it in the light of day before? Think, Hunter, maybe all we *really* need is a fistful of garlic."

She throws our bags into the car again, and the matter is settled.

We enter the preserve on foot. It only takes a few minutes of walking before we come across one of the posted maps. There are four hiking trails, plus the Spring Brook that cuts through in a sideways S-shape, which the preserve takes its name from. In the north corner is marshland, mostly designated as a nesting site for endangered birds.

For a moment, I wonder if the lycanthrope has been hiding out there. But a closer look at the map dispels that thought: nesting season doesn't begin until mid-April.

Mars takes a photo of the map with her phone. "I'd say we should follow the river, but the trails don't really stick too close to it."

I glance at the trees and wait to feel something – to hear something – but if anything is out here, it's being quiet. "Let's try it anyway." I turn to Mars. "The worst we find is nothing, right?"

She nods and gives the map another look. "Then let's start

with the Henslow trail."

The Henslow trail is little more than a path of flattened weeds that cuts through a sea of tall grass. I think I catch a hawk flying overhead, but the trail is otherwise as barren of animals as it is of everything else.

Short of a flashing neon sign, I'm not sure what we could find out here that would confirm our lycanthrope is still here or has long since moved on.

"So." Mars starts kicking a rock down the path. "What made you think to ask Hazel?"

The rock tumbles in front of me. I softly nudge it back to her. "Uh…I was talking to Riley. She had one of their bags and it popped into my head."

Mars looks at me. "Ex-best friend Riley?"

"Yep."

"Oh. How'd that go?"

"Wasn't good. Could've been worse."

Mars kicks the rock, and it goes veering off into the weeds. She huffs and sticks her hands into her jacket pockets. "Gabe told me a bit about her," she suddenly says.

The feeling that grips my chest is like falling. Fear, then so much anger that it startles me even more. I try to swallow it back, but my voice is tight when I speak. "Like *what?*"

We both stop. Mars's eyes search mine, face pinched with what I think is concern.

Concern for you, or concern for herself?

"Not much," she finally answers, nearly at a whisper. "But he mentioned that you haven't really been friends since you were, like, fourteen. Sounds like it's a big deal that you guys met up and talked."

I take a deep breath and look away. "Yeah, it was... I don't know. She's really hard to avoid all of a sudden."

"Am I allowed to ask – did she start talking to you, or did you start talking to her?"

"I asked if she wanted to talk, and she said yes."

"Why?"

I make a face, but she's not asking to be judgemental. It's not the kind of *why?* that Gabe would come at me with. Because Gabe has seen the entire wound for what it is. For some reason, I'm trying to spare Mars the sight of it.

So, I do my best to consider a question I haven't even been able to answer for myself yet. Why now, when either of us could've reached out at any time before?

In the silence, Mars and I start walking again. Our boots crunch against the snow until the right combination of words comes together: "I didn't want the last things we said to each other to be the last things we said to each other."

That earns me a sideways look. "Okay, Sylvia Plath, you aren't terminally ill. Riley will still be here when you're back to normal."

Beneath us, the ground slopes. I can see the flat wooden bridge over the brook ahead.

About twenty feet out, the stench of rot suddenly pushes into my mouth.

I think it's only me until Mars comes to an equally sudden stop beside me. I turn to her, mouth already open to ask *what the hell is that?* when her expression shifts from confusion to bewilderment. She runs ahead. I follow, and I quickly realize what she's running towards.

We stop at the edge of the bridge and gaze down the slope.

I don't think it could be more than a few hours old. If the rangers have been especially lazy, maybe a day. Much of the sandy brown fur blends into the dirt, which makes the blood and bone appear as if they're bursting from the ground itself. It takes a second for me to figure out where the coyote begins and ends. A swarm of flies crawls over its torso.

"Hunter." Mars's voice makes me jump. I realize that I've taken a few steps closer, while she's hung back, holding her phone to her ear.

"What are you doing?" I ask.

"Calling somebody. That's disgusting."

I don't disagree. And yet, as somebody on the other line picks up and Mars introduces herself, I continue to get closer.

The coyote has no lower jaw, and its long, blackening tongue lies limp against the dirt. Its stomach has been ripped open and mostly eaten, either by the original killer or one of the hawks in the area. I try to give nature some credit – I've never seen what it looks like when one coyote kills another

– but I can't imagine another animal being this brutal and leaving so much behind. I can't imagine this being anything but our lycanthrope.

It makes me thankful that Norman was too small to be left behind like this. The image this thought conjures makes my throat burn. I force myself to keep staring at the gore until I'm no longer overwhelmed by the urge to scream.

I slowly sit down and lock eyes with the unseeing carcass. That could've been me. And it turns out that the creature that did this has lingered within a stone's throw of my front porch.

There are a lot of animals out here. There are a lot of people, too. If a person got attacked, it'd be all over the news, but there's been nothing. Nothing but a few missing pets, and now this.

Why am I the only human it's gone after?

In the corner of my eye, Mars sits down on the bridge, letting her feet dangle in the air. "Ranger guy said he'd come and check it out."

I nod, but I don't move.

"What are you thinking about?" Mars finally asks.

At last, I tear my eyes away from the carcass. "Did you read anywhere if there'd been attacks on anybody else? Or was it all animals?"

"Just animals, from what I could find."

I glance at the rib sticking out of the coyote's chest, bent 90 degrees in the wrong direction. The lycanthrope could've done that to me. But it didn't.

"Why am I the only thing it didn't kill?" I finally ask.

Mars stares at the coyote for a long time. When she finally looks at me, she's got the same expression that she had when she put the werewolf thing together for the first time.

"Okay. Stay with me." She takes a breath. "What's one thing we know about wolves?"

I frown. "Like…?"

"Yeah, my bad, that was too broad." Mars shakes her head and tries again. "What do we know about *solitary* wolves?"

My brain isn't exactly stuffed full of wolf facts, so I try to connect the dots between this question and the brutalized corpse. "It's…rare, right?"

"*Right.* Wolves are like humans, they want company. They build communities. I think they'll go off alone to hunt or whatever, but they're not supposed to *live alone*."

We turn back to the coyote at the same time.

"Do you think there's more of them?" I ask, the question almost sticking to my throat. I can't imagine *one* lycanthrope in my backyard, forget about a whole pack.

When I look at her, Mars is already watching me. "Or maybe it's making more."

The meaning of that suggestion takes a moment to sink in. When it does, my skin prickles with goosebumps. I didn't consider that any of this could be intentional. Could it be? Is the only reason it's sticking around because it's waiting for me to finish…*changing*?

A fly crawls over the coyote's milky cornea. I pull my knees into my chest. My nausea no longer stems from the gore. "Did Gabe tell you what Ethan did to me?"

I know she knows. I can hear it in her silence.

"Yeah," she finally says. "Not in detail, but yeah."

Anger twists in my chest, but I don't have the energy to *do anything* about it. Sitting here, staring at what I'm about to become capable of, I wonder how much of it mattered to begin with.

"Did you tell Riley about what's happening to you now?" Mars asks.

I shake my head. "She already thinks I'm a liar. But I wanted to."

I can tell that Mars wants to say something. Whether it's about Riley, or about how I shouldn't be angry at Gabe, or how this is all sure to work out in the end, I don't know. She never says it, and a moment later, I feel her hand on my shoulder.

She pulls me to my feet and walks us back to the bridge. We cross it and continue over in the direction we were headed before we stumbled across the coyote. The woods are no scarier than they were before, but our pace feels a little bit faster. Mars loops our arms together like she's afraid she'll lose me.

"Tell me something you want to do when this is over," Mars abruptly says.

I frown. "Why?"

She sighs. "I don't know. I think I just need something to

look forward to. So, tell me something you want to do, so we can do it once we're done with all this shit."

Mars's hand rests where our arms interlock, and despite our jackets, I can feel her thumb rubbing back and forth against my biceps. Mars has seemed more frazzled over the last two weeks than she has in the two years that I've known her. It's almost humanizing, but it also makes my sense of dread so much worse.

Before I can come up with anything, Mars suddenly offers, "What about prom?"

Startled, I begin to smile. "Are you asking me, or are you *asking me?*"

I wonder if it's self-absorbed of me to think there's a twinkle in her eye when she shrugs. "Why not both? Unless there's another chronically single, objectively hot bisexual werewolf slayer who is actively trying to save your life—"

"Shut up," I laugh.

We wobble in step with each other, arms locked like Dorothy and the Cowardly Lion. Her fingers clamp tighter around my arm.

"It doesn't have to be prom," she quickly goes on. "I could teach you how to drive or something. I was—"

"No, we can do prom."

She looks at me, expression guarded. "Yeah?"

My face feels too hot all of a sudden. "I mean, I should probably go to, like, one dance in my life."

"You haven't even been to *one*?"

"What about me *screams* enjoying extracurriculars with these people?"

Mars relents. "Point taken. But prom is actually kinda nice. My school holds it at this golf club and it's, like, *disgustingly* gaudy, but they do fireworks and there's always one couple that tries to bone on the green. I third-wheeled with some friends last year and we paid one of the club guys fifty bucks to turn on the sprinklers. Literally the most fun I've ever had. And they don't know your face, so we could totally do it again if you're the one bribing."

She continues to explain the intricacies of prom weekend, which she insists she does not believe in but feels I need to be informed of anyway. I think she must believe in them a little. We plan the weekend for the remainder of the trail, by which I mean Mars talks and plans and debates her options with herself, and I nod along and watch the sun illuminate the green speckles in her otherwise deep-brown eyes.

I'm sure of my feelings for Gabe. But the longer I spend with Mars's arm wrapped around mine, the more I can feel the fondness in my chest keeping me warm, and the more it starts to feel like two flames instead of one.

14

When Dad comes home Wednesday afternoon, I tell him that I found the window broken one day after school. If he can tell that I'm lying, he doesn't call me out on it. He just nods and has me grab measuring tape from the garage.

Mars has sent a photo to the group chat by the time I get back to my phone. She's standing in her bathroom, wearing oversized rubber gloves that go to her elbows. In one hand is her phone; in the other is a bundle of monkshood. A little limp, but *alive*. Usable.

STIRBA SLAYERS

MARS BAR

monkshood achieved :D

hunter, when does your dad leave again?

Friday, I think

cool cool cool

A couple of seconds go by, and instead of a response, I get a FaceTime request instead. I hesitate long enough to grab my clothes for work and run into the bathroom before hitting *accept*. Mars is in her bathroom as well; I can see the rubber gloves hanging off the edge of the sink. Gabe, it appears, has just arrived at the gym. He's sitting in his car, wearing a shirt that reads *I LOVE BASEBALL* above an action shot of a football player.

We still haven't talked a whole lot since Sunday. I get unreasonably skittish seeing him on my phone.

"Hi. Sorry." Mars grins sheepishly. "I thought a call would be easier. I wanted to talk scheduling."

I frown. "For Friday?"

Mars gives me a look. "Like, in general. Going forward. Now that we have monkshood."

"Well, the moon's bullshit, right?" Gabe offers.

I nod before stepping off-screen to change shirts. So they can't see the bruises crawling up my left arm and the infected injection site on my right.

"Perfect phrasing." Mars sighs. "But, yeah, the bite didn't happen during the full moon, so it wouldn't make sense to base a plan off the moon. So, without that built-in countdown, I was thinking we just go out and try to kill this thing as fast as possible?"

Gabe either laughs, or a short burst of static comes through the speakers. His hand is over his mouth when I look down at his corner of the screen.

Mars raises an eyebrow but continues on. "Look, we have the monkshood, and we think we know where this werewolf is. All we need to do is find the time to go out there again, and we can see whether or not killing this thing stops what's happening to Hunter."

"You're both *sure* it's still in the preserve?" Gabe asks.

I step in front of the camera once I've got my shirt on. "*I* think so."

"Ditto," Mars agrees. "It makes sense: big space, not a lot of people, and *something*'s clearly been feeding on the coyotes out there."

I don't think that Gabe is thrilled, but he's outvoted. He nods, and through all the pixels I'd swear that his jaw clenches. I catch myself digging my fingers into the rough edge of the bite mark on my arm and quickly place both hands on the countertop.

When the silence has gone on long enough, Mars nods. "Hunter, how does Friday sound?"

I shrug again. "Sounds fine. For what?"

Mars bares her teeth in a grin. "Stakeout, baby. I'll bring snacks."

The call ends shortly thereafter, with Mars promising to take care of all the details and neither Gabe nor I saying much else. I think we're all nervous, just showing it differently.

All I have to do is make it two more days and this might finally be over.

I tell myself this as if I haven't been telling myself that for my entire life. Just a few more years and I'll start testosterone; just a few more years and I'll have my perfect chest; just a few more years and I'll stop feeling like I've got *trans* branded on my forehead. Never *now*. Never *soon*. Always somewhere in that distant, unspecified future. It makes my skin crawl.

Before I leave the bathroom, I check myself. Even underneath the Band-Aid, I can see the skin on my cheek is still red and swollen.

I bare my teeth. The tooth coming in where my rotten molar was is more visible now. Nothing seems terribly wrong with it, not compared to the rest of my injuries. But I hesitate to say that it's normal, since I shouldn't have a tooth there *at all*.

Whatever it is, it's not mine.

Mars is off tonight. When I get in, I spend a moment looking over the schedule. Alicia and Bryan (the Coke kid from last week) are both scheduled for concessions; Billy, a college dropout in his twenties, is in the ticket booth tonight. That leaves me, Natalie and Tammy.

Tammy is a reasonably nice girl, though I wouldn't call us close by any stretch. She's a pretty brunette, with mousy features and hazel eyes she's always rolling at somebody. Every time I look at her, I think about her missing dog. The one

Mars told me about when all we could conceive of was a particularly nasty coyote.

A part of me wants to ask Tammy about her dog and what she might've seen, but the longer I think about it, the less useful it seems. What could she tell me that I don't already know?

So, although we're both on cleaning duty, we work in silence. She sweeps, I scrub at the pop stains. The smell of so much concentrated butter makes me light-headed. I wonder why she wasn't bitten instead and try to swallow the guilt that comes with such thoughts.

After an hour, we've cleaned enough to fill the big bin with garbage. I push it outside while Tammy lingers in the hall, the light from her phone turning her face a washed-out blue. When I push open the back doors and survey the sky, I see the same colour: the soft indigo between sunset and proper nightfall. I unlock the trash compactor and take my time dropping bags down the chute.

Behind me, an engine roars to life. I glance over my shoulder. There are a few cars scattered throughout the lot, but only one truck has its headlights on, illuminating me from the waist down. It takes a moment for me to make out the licence plate.

EZBRZY

It's a real specific sense of doom that seizes my chest. The same doom I felt when I *knew* something had happened to

Norman before I even reached the mudroom.

At the very least, Ethan is here to scare me with the *thought* of hurting me. Or maybe he's done teasing the concept. You don't usually *de*-escalate from bricks going through windows.

I stand there like a deer caught in headlights as the truck slowly creeps through the lot. Towards me.

"Yo, Natalie wants you." The sound of Tammy's voice makes me jump half a foot into the air. She frowns, then takes note of the truck pulling up. "You got friends?"

"*No*," I answer, and hope that that's enough as I rush past her.

I hurry through the hall as fast as I can and don't look back. But I *do* hear the door shut, and then the sound of the compactor keys jangling. I guess that's something to like about Tammy: she's kinda lazy when she can get away with it, but she doesn't leave you hanging. Or, at least, she won't let in the guys who might actively be trying to kill you.

Natalie is waiting for me in the front lobby. She looks up from her phone and smiles at me. "There you are, sweetheart. How are you doing?"

I briefly visualize myself. With every passing day, the ability to say *I'm fine* feels more and more far-fetched. "All right," I manage instead. "You needed me?"

The sound of my voice – broken, like I'm going through puberty for a *third* time – makes her face twitch, but it's gone before I can do more than notice it. She pats me on the shoulder. "Walk with me, the women's bathroom needs a shine."

Not what I was expecting, but, fine. I'm happy to be any place that doesn't have Ethan in it. I eyeball the back door while Natalie puts an Out of Order sign on the bathroom before handing me a bottle of Windex.

It's only when I've started wiping down the first mirror that I notice my hands are shaking. I don't know if it's the fear of what *almost* happened out there, or knowing that I've probably only delayed it.

"I didn't get to talk to you last week," Natalie comments from the other end of the sinks. "You seem like you're feeling better, though?"

I quietly press my hands together until they're a little steadier. "Yeah, I'm fine."

"Good. You had that surgery last month, right?"

In the corner of my eye, I can see her staring at me. I force myself to nod.

"That medical emergency—"

"Oh, that." Cutting her off feels beyond inappropriate, but as soon as she mentions the *emergency*, my stomach pitches. "It was just a fever, really. My dad wanted to be sure it wasn't an infection. And it wasn't, so. Y'know. All good."

Almost subconsciously, I press my tongue into the back of my mouth. Against the impossible tooth, which has grown *just* slightly bigger than the surrounding teeth. Not a visible mark of freakishness, just enough to make me constantly aware of it.

Natalie hums in agreement. "Well, keep an eye on it. Your voice is a little, uh, pitched."

She means high. Like a girl's.

"And, I mean, there are so many ways a surgery like that can go wrong," Natalie continues. "I've heard so much about the people who end up regretting the whole thing."

I falter. The heat of embarrassment (shame? anger?) rises in my throat.

"I was listening to a podcast the other day where this girl was talking about the rate of regret for those kinds of surgeries, and it blew my mind how easy it is to get doctors to do some of these things."

"I don't *regret it*," I blurt out.

Natalie turns to me. "Oh, no, I'm sure *you* don't, there's just—"

"You know more people regret having knee replacement surgery than trans people regret transitioning." My voice wavers on the final word.

A particular expression falls over Natalie's face. A condescending smile of superiority, of *knowing* she knows something I don't. I'm so angry I can feel it in my fingertips.

"Well, nobody's forcing children to have knee replacement surgery," she tells me.

"Nobody's forcing kids to be trans, either," I breathe.

It doesn't come out the way I want it to, as a thundering declaration of certainty. Instead, I sound like a kid. I sound like I'm thirteen years old, looking up at my dad and telling him for the first time that he has a son.

Natalie makes that face again. Pitiful patronization. "Of course, sweetheart."

She walks away towards the handicap stall, leaving me standing there, my ears *ringing* with rage.

It's not the worst thing anybody's ever said to me. But it's a breaking point. It's one more goddamn person telling me they know what I really need. What I really *am*.

A cold flash triggers an ache in every possible corner of my body. My fingernails actually, genuinely hurt.

"Do you even know any trans people besides me?" I ask.

In the mirror's reflection, I watch Natalie look up. "No, none that I'm aware of," she answers, still with far too much confidence.

I nod. "Okay, then maybe shut the fuck up about stuff you don't know *anything* about."

Saying that feels so, so good for about five seconds. Then Natalie's eyebrows knit together, and it occurs to me that that was maybe the worst thing I could have *ever* said.

"Excuse me?" Her voice is raised as she steps towards me, and I have no idea what she's planning to do – fire me? Scream at me?

Before I can find out, Tammy, completely oblivious to

what she's interrupting, opens the door and sticks her head inside. "Hey, Nat?"

Natalie stops and turns to Tammy with a glare. "What?"

"Can we call security to make a pass around the back? There's some creeps in a truck that're just sitting back there."

Natalie sighs. "What, *exactly*, does 'creep' mean?"

Tammy shrugs uselessly. "Creep. Being creepy. Hunter saw them."

Natalie turns to me. I nod. It feels like it takes years for her to exhale and jab a finger towards my face. "We'll talk later," she promises, voice low, before returning to Tammy. "Okay, show me *Mr Creepy*."

If Tammy knows what she's done, it doesn't show on her face. She just nods, holds the door open for Natalie, and lets it swing shut behind her. That leaves me alone, and I don't realize how heavily I'm breathing until it's the only sound I'm left with. A few more, and it turns into that wounded, horribly pathetic whimper that always precedes crying.

Before anything else can happen, I text my dad – natalie said i can go home, can you come pick me up? now? – and grab my things from the break room. I clock out, ignore the trilling noise the machine makes to warn me that I'm leaving too early, and wait out front. I can see how fast I'm breathing with each visible puff. I grab my injured arm and dig my nails in through the undershirt.

It takes fifteen agonizing minutes for my dad's car to come

rolling up. I don't realize how close I am to crying until I've gotten in and closed the door behind me. There's still this lump in my throat, and—

My hands really, really hurt.

"Everything okay?" Dad asks as he pulls away from the building.

I nod, although the question barely pings in my brain.

I turn my hands over in my lap. It's hard to tell at first, with the only light source being the street lights we pass, but I'm bleeding from vaguely crescent-shaped indents in my palms. I turn my hands back over and look at my nails.

They aren't as long as fake nails or anything that dramatic, but they're unquestionably longer than the last time I took notice of them. There's a new, unnatural downward curve to them. I place one of my nails between my fingers, and it's nearly as thick as a quarter.

"Yeah," I finally remember to answer as I slip my hands between my thighs.

If Dad's curious for details, he doesn't ask. He never asks.

It may only be the confrontation with Natalie fresh in my veins, but I find myself scrambling for the first loose thread I can grab. The scab that's still elevated above the skin.

"Can I ask you something?" My voice comes out stilted.

Dad glances at me. There's a Phoebe Bridgers song playing on the radio, her voice barely audible beyond the occasional willowy gasp rising above the purr of the engine. "Sure."

I fix my eyes on the dashboard. “If you could do it again, would you let me go on puberty blockers?”

God only knows what kind of answer I’m expecting. Maybe it’s remorse. Because maybe if I hadn’t spent so much of my life being seen as a girl, maybe it wouldn’t be so easy for my body to fall apart now. Because Riley thinks I’m a liar, and there’s this horrible itch in my brain that wonders how many people think of me in the same terms.

The silence that settles between us isn’t hostile, but it doesn’t feel *great*, either. Dad exhales through his mouth and flips his blinker on.

“I think we made the right choice,” he finally says. “This was something everybody had to think about—”

“But *I knew*—” I turn towards him.

“Hunter.” His tone shuts me up. “*We* didn’t *know*. Okay?”

He hasn’t taken his eyes off the road, so maybe he’s unaware of the daggers I’m glaring at him. *I knew*, I want to say. *I knew and I tried to tell you and* you *wouldn’t listen*.

Instead, I slump back into my seat and stare out the window. “Mom didn’t have to think about it.”

It’s a childishly low blow. I’m desperate for it to hurt.

If it does, it’s not obvious in Dad’s voice, which remains infuriatingly calm. “It wasn’t up to just your mom.”

We roll to a stop at an intersection. The car behind us has those impossibly bright headlights, which briefly blind me through the rear-view. I wince and hold my hand up to block the glare. When my eyes readjust, I can see that the car is a pickup truck, and it's blue.

I freeze, mind suddenly torn between this weirdly low-key argument with my dad and the realization that Ethan is sitting right behind us. He can't be following us to find out where I live; he already knows that. He's following us for the sake of it.

"It wasn't your mom who let you do this," Dad suddenly adds. When I look over, he's gesturing to my chest. "I told her you were way too young to make this kind of decision, but I let you do it anyway."

My throat is dry when I try to swallow. I want to say: *Dad, we're being followed*. But instead, I sink into myself and press my nails back into the indents in my palms.

I watch the truck, never riding our bumper but staying right behind us with every turn we make. Right, left, right. The tears that break over my cheeks feel cold.

Years must go by before we finally turn left into the neighbourhood. The truck keeps driving straight. As it passes, I catch a glimpse of the licence plate: *ZQN-225*.

Relief and embarrassment clash together in my throat. I'm an idiot. I'm alive.

Just as I go to wipe my eyes, the car jolts to a stop in the driveway. Dad turns the car off, but neither of us moves.

"If you'd let me get on puberty blockers, you wouldn't have had to deal with any of this in the first place," I mutter.

Dad sighs. "Hunter, that's something irreversible—"

That word lands like a backhand.

"Puberty is *irreversible*, too!" I snap. "That's my whole problem, that it's irreversible, and I'm going to spend the rest of my life trying to fix myself because *you* were scared!"

"You don't know that you wouldn't have regretted it."

"Maybe I *regret* not going to live with Mom!"

We stare at each other. Faces red, the air thick and heavy in the space between us.

I want him to scream at me. Hell, I think I'd be able to handle it if he started crying or something. I want him to do *something*.

Dad is silent for the longest time. Then he pulls the keys from the ignition and gets out, leaving me sitting there in the ear-ringing silence of no answer at all.

15

I call Mars the next morning to tell her about what happened with Natalie, and she laughs so hard she has to walk away from the phone. "I mean, obviously that's terrible, but I'm also so mad I wasn't there to see the look on her face," she says between giggles.

Quickly, though, Mars sobers up and insists that considering the content of our conversation, Natalie would be insane to try and fire me. Although when I check the digital schedule, I can't help but notice I'm no longer on it.

Maybe I shouldn't care, especially considering the looming lycanthrope issue, but I *did* like that job. It's the whole reason Mars and I know each other. Now it's just something else that being trans has fucked with, directly or not.

The rest of the day doesn't exactly get better from there. I speak *at* my dad once during the drive to school to ask if Gabe can come by later to help me catch up on homework. After an agonizing stretch of silence, I get a curt nod. Then there's Gabe himself. Things between us still feel strained when we see each other at lunch, but I must look as bad as I feel, since the tension isn't near what it's been all week.

Bigger problems, I guess. Like the fact that I cut my nails down to the beds, and now little jolts of pain shoot up my fingers every time I try and reach under the Band-Aid to scratch at my cheek.

It's during lunch that Gabe delivers his own bad news: Ethan and Damien are back.

"He really didn't say anything to you?" I ask.

When I bring it up again, we've been lying on my bed for the better part of two hours, watching hockey on my laptop. It's Blackhawks playing the Flames, but it's a blowout – Blackhawks ahead 4 to 1 – so it's barely a distraction. I haven't even touched my homework.

Gabe shakes his head, eyes fixed on the screen. "Bailey was watching us all pretty hard. Just a couple of dirty looks."

I chew on the end of my pencil and nod. The fact that I never crossed paths with either of them for the rest of the day feels more like blind luck than anything. I wonder how long it'll take for that luck to fail me. But I think my brain can handle exactly one crisis at a time, so I push the thought of Ethan into a box and promise myself I'll come back to it later. Instead, I start watching Gabe out of the corner of my eye.

His hair is tied into a tiny little ponytail at the base of his skull. A few strands hang loose at the sides of his face. I sigh. It's such a ridiculous time to have a crush. But of all the things

I have to think about, this is probably the only one that doesn't make me horribly miserable.

"Are you gonna keep growing out your hair?" I ask, taking the pencil out of my mouth.

Gabe glances over at me. "I don't know. Why?"

I shrug. "I like it long."

"Really?"

I look at him and nod.

Gabe makes a contemplative noise. "Ma says it makes me look like a girl."

"Your mom also thinks I'm cis."

Gabe snorts. It took us *months* to realize that Gabe's mom thinks I'm a completely different boy from the girl he was friends with before.

"Seriously," I add, "even pretending like butch girls aren't objectively hot, you're very clearly a buff guy who *barely* has a ponytail."

We settle into a comfortable silence. Out of the corner of my eye, I watch Gabe tuck some of the loose hair back behind his ear. His jaw clenches and unclenches.

"Do you…like butch girls?" Gabe suddenly asks.

Already frowning, I turn to face him. "What?"

"I don't know!" Gabe shrugs helplessly. "We've been friends for how long now and I still don't have a grasp on who or what you like. I mean, girls, boys, what?"

How about muscular hotheads who throw themselves into

danger for me when they aren't too pissed off to even talk to me. Know of any?

Instead of answering, I deflect. "Is this because I asked about Kylee?"

"What? No." Gabe's eyebrows furrow, but he's smiling. "Dude, I've barely thought about Kylee until you brought her up. She was…nice. And I dated her for five minutes."

The Blackhawks score again, and for a moment our attention turns to the screen. Considering the team's been shit for the last decade, 5 to 1 is a pretty good win.

"What about Mars?" I ask.

My eyes are locked on the screen, but I know Gabe turns. "What about her?"

I finally give him a look.

"Oh." Gabe gets quiet and thinks about it.

That, for me, is enough of an answer. If he thought the question was ridiculous, he would've laughed, and I'd never bring it up again. But he has to think about it. Jealousy makes me feel burning hot. Or it would if I hadn't spent the last two weeks burning hot as a baseline.

"I think she's probably insane," Gabe answers. "Smart. Pretty. But…I mean, I'm not really thinking about that stuff right now."

"Why not?" I tap my pencil against my paper. "She's a girl, and you're a guy—"

"And my best friend is going through a crisis, so I'm not

super occupied with being single." I look up, and he's glaring at me. "Can you give me a little more credit than that?"

A few different emotions clash in my chest. Embarrassment, obviously, but also a bit of indignation. *Obviously* that wasn't what I meant. I don't think that Gabe is so debilitatingly heterosexual that he's trying to hook up with my other best friend in the middle of all this.

But I stop, think about it, and realize I kind of implied it. The jealous heat turns into an embarrassed flush. "Sorry," I mumble, turning away.

A beat of silence. "It's fine, Bambi." Gabe's voice is already softer.

"I mean— Sorry for all of this. Sunday and...everything."

"Yeah, well. You're an asshole. I'm an asshole. Your excuse is better, at least."

I crack a smile, look over, and see that Gabe is smiling, too. I still don't understand it. You punch him, he punches you, and you're both fine.

Before I can think too hard about it, and because I don't know any better way to bring it up, I clear my throat. "Mars asked me to go to prom with her."

Maybe there's a small part of me that hopes to spark some jealousy in Gabe.

He cocks an eyebrow. "You said *yes*, right?"

I roll my eyes. "Yes, assuming I make it that far."

As expected, Gabe punches me in the shoulder for that,

but he's smiling. "That's…I'm happy for you, Bambi. You'll have fun." A moment passes. "I do like her."

I'm thankful he isn't looking at me. It makes it easier to pretend there isn't a part of me that's weirdly disappointed. "Are you gonna go?"

Gabe went last year – *with Kylee* – and a bunch of his hockey buddies. I stayed home, only to be woken up at two in the morning when Tanner dropped an unimaginably wasted Gabe off at my house. It's a funny memory, because Gabe is occasionally impulsive but rarely so stereotypically *teenaged*. We probably spent two hours sitting on the kitchen floor, with Gabe rambling absolute nonsense and me trying to keep him hydrated and upright.

That night was the only time Gabe ever asked me anything about being trans.

In between bursts of giggles, he asked me how I *knew*. How does a person *know* they're trans? My answer was something stupid – half awake and far too honest, about how my worst days as a boy were still leagues better than my best days as a girl – but Gabe was already half asleep by then, so I don't know if he even remembers that he asked me.

"Probably not," Gabe answers. The game ends, and he shuts the laptop. "Unless you'd wanna go with me."

I look up fast. Way too fast. "Like, going stag together?"

Gabe holds eye contact for a long moment. Then he shrugs and starts playing with the loose hair near his ear. "Yeah?"

"You think I'm gonna be able to survive prom with you and your drinking buddies?"

"Screw you," Gabe laughs. "*I'm* not gonna survive doing that again."

I grin. "Well, I can at least hold your hair back if you make yourself sick."

Gabe opens his mouth to say something else, but he's barely made a sound when my bedroom door suddenly swings open. Dad stands in the doorway, hand on the knob.

"You guys done in here?" he asks.

The only things I've added to my homework are a few pencil scratches. I fold my arms over the paper, nod, and do a very good job pretending like it doesn't hurt to look at him.

Dad nods back. "Good. Gabe, time for you to head home."

Gabe gathers his things without a word. My lingering anger at both of them briefly flares up. The rest of me is almost strangely calm.

Tomorrow is Friday. Friday's the stakeout, where we hopefully find this lycanthrope and finally put an end to this.

We're sitting on Riley's bed, watching *The Outsiders*. I'm lying across the bed, while Riley sits behind me, tinkering away on a small table that I think is meant for reading books in the bath. My vision is blurry, and my eyes feel puffy; I've been crying.

"Here." Riley's voice is sudden and crystal clear. I look back at her as she sets a small pair of pliers down. "See if this stays on."

She hands me a silver chain. At the end is a small stone, mostly white with dark grey chunks that look black in the right light. Riley's constructed a wire wrap around it, which hangs from a small loop on the chain.

I open my mouth and say something, but I can't hear what it is.

I must've said *something*, though, since Riley smiles. "Howlite. Got it from this place inside the mall. I'll have to take you next time."

I don't know what howlite is. I think I say this, but I still can't hear my own voice.

Riley grabs a plastic bag from the floor and fishes a small piece of paper from it. "It says that howlite eases stress and anxiety, promotes a peaceful mind, and *provides support in releasing attachments to old emotional pain*."

She sets the paper down, takes the necklace from me, and undoes the clasp before handing it back to me. Her hand lingers. "I know you've been upset about your dad and the hormone thing. So, until that all gets figured out, I thought maybe this would help settle you. Until you get to be a real boy."

I open my eyes. For a moment, I'm still thirteen years old. I can feel Riley's hand over mine.

It's dark outside. The room is freezing cold. I take a shaky breath in, catch up to the fact that I'm seventeen now, and reach around blindly for the necklace on my nightstand. I grip the chain until the pain of it brings me back to my bed, back to now.

Stop that, I think.

The thought is intended as a plea to whatever part of my brain generates my dreams. I'm not expecting an answer.

sorry

I freeze. My mind races at a speed it's not awake enough to handle.

It's the first time the voice seems to be responding to something. The first time I've considered it capable of responding.

Could you see that? I have no clue how this works, but I do my best to think clearly.

i was looking for it

Oh. Naturally.

Something else occurs to me: the voice is speaking in complete sentences now.

I rub my eyes before I turn to stare at the ceiling. I don't know what to picture. Thinking about a talking wolf feels ridiculous. So I shut my eyes and I don't picture anything at all. Just the dark, endless expanse inside of my eyelids.

What do you care about Riley? I ask.

just curious

The responses are immediate, coming practically the moment I finish my own thoughts.

you hate her you absolutely HATE her but you love her it's this giant angry fucked-up black hole inside your head

I quickly become aware of pressure on my skull, like an exhaustion headache cranking itself up from zero to twenty. I grimace and press my face into my knees.

sorry

Silence. Then, after a minute, the pressure lessens.

There are a thousand questions I could be firing off right now. I might try and ask a few of them if I were more awake, or if I were sure that I'm awake at all. Instead, I press my face into my pillow and wrap my blankets tighter around myself.

do you want to do something about her

I frown. *What does* do something *mean?*

This is the first time the voice doesn't answer straight away.

Outside, I hear Annie Searchwell's voice. "*Miko! Heeeeere, kitty-kitty.*"

I sigh and wrap my pillow around my head as if it'll do anything to dampen the sound of her voice. In the haze of exhaustion, I think a terrible thing: *If you want to do something about anybody, do something about Miko.*

The voice doesn't respond. Of course it doesn't. It's a voice in my head.

I fall back asleep so easily that it's like blinking. One

moment, it's dark. The next, the sun is coming in through the blinds. By then, Annie Searchwell has long since stopped shouting, and it feels like everything has been quiet for a really long time.

16

Dad has already left again by the time Gabe comes by my house after school the next day. When Mars's car rolls up, as the sun sinks low in the darkening sky, Gabe and I are waiting on the sidewalk. I climb into the back seat and Gabe seems right at home up front – and I'm almost better than the jealousy that tries to gain a foothold in my mouth.

No sooner has Gabe pulled the door shut than "Bad Moon Rising" starts playing from the speakers.

A moment passes. When nobody laughs, Mars sighs. "Yeah, figured it might be a little soon for the moon playlist."

Gabe frowns. "I thought—"

"Hey, if *you* can find songs about monkshood, I'd *love* to hear 'em."

The next song – "It's Called: Freefall" – doesn't have anything to do with the moon or wolves, but it doesn't do anything to make me feel better about the state of things either. I glance across the street at Annie Searchwell's house. Her car is parked in the driveway, which means she must've gotten home from work early. She's normally not back until sometime after six.

Gabe speaks up once we've begun driving. "So, what *is* our plan?"

"My thinking was this: she's got water, she's got a decent food supply, and she's got plenty of space to hide if she needs it. Absolutely no reason for her to risk running out and getting flattened by a truck on the highway." Mars glances between me and Gabe. "She's gotta sleep sometime. We check out the same area that Hunter and me found the coyote and fan out from there."

"Wait." I raise my hand. Mars is using an interesting new pronoun. "Why is it a girl all of a sudden?"

"I don't know, feminism?" Mars shrugs. "Anyway, the monkshood is in the bag. From what I've read, boiling it would probably be the easiest way to get her to ingest it, but if we can get close enough to her, there's a dozen ways we can force contact."

She gestures towards her bag on the floor near my feet. I drag it closer and unzip it. The monkshood is wrapped in two Ziploc bags. There's also Mars's elbow-length rubber gloves and a kitchen knife, sheathed in cheap plastic. I reach down and take the knife by the handle, as if getting used to the weight of the thing will endear me to the idea of using it.

It doesn't.

I can still recall the feeling of teeth ripping through my

skin, the ease with which this creature threw me around. It would've easily killed me if Gabe hadn't intervened. There's *no* chance any of us get close enough to kill it (her?).

"Hunter." Mars wiggles her fingers in my face. I jump and drop the knife back into the bag. "I said, we're gonna start on the Sunflower Trail, okay? That keeps us near enough to the water, and we already know she's been around here recently."

I nod, probably too quickly. "Yeah. Sure."

I curl up against the door and stare out the window. A part of me is waiting to hear the voice in my head. But the only voice I hear is my own, repeating my anxieties in an endless loop. Almost unconsciously, I reach up and start scratching at the bits of loose and broken skin on my cheek. It's still tender from where the Band-Aid used to be.

Up front, Gabe asks Mars, "So, have you been doing, like, *any* schoolwork since this started?"

The Henslow and Sunflower trails are effectively the same, one bleeding into the other. We park under a lamp post, and I catch sight of one of Annie's flyers taped to it: DO YOU KNOW WHERE YOUR PETS ARE?

"Do you think anybody's noticed that any of this is happening?" I ask, staring at the paper fluttering softly in the breeze.

Mars hefts her bag into her lap. "No, I don't think anyone else has put together the lycanthrope thing."

"I mean, like—" I pause as we step out of the car. I quickly pull my gloves on. "We're assuming that killing it cures me, right?"

"Uh-huh." Mars hands me a flashlight and a small bag of fruit snacks.

"So, what happens if somebody else gets to her first?" I turn the flashlight on. "What if a park ranger shoots her? Or why *can't* somebody else kill her? Why can't we—"

"Because somebody else is gonna get bit, or die, or they're gonna scare our lycanthrope off and she might *actually* leave the area if she knows she's being hunted." Mars hands Gabe a flashlight and then turns on her own, holding it under her chin. "Anyway, you don't wanna tell your *dad*, but you'd trust a bunch of underpaid, cranky government rangers?"

My eyes narrow at her.

"If you're biologically connected to this lycanthrope," Gabe pipes up, "it'd be cellular. Viral infection is cellular. Maybe whatever... *thing* is driving the infection still has a connection to the queen body. Like bees or ants."

Mars and I both stare at him.

"Oh my God, you read the article I sent you." Mars bats her eyelashes.

Gabe shrugs, and then has the audacity to *blush*.

I shove my free hand into my pocket and sigh. "None of us know anything about biology. I don't know what the hell we're talking about."

"I can send you the article," Mars offers.

"Is it an actual article, or something you ripped from the *Teen Wolf* wiki?"

Mars doesn't answer. Instead, she takes the lead, and Gabe and I follow behind.

I glance back at the lamp post as it shrinks with distance. It doesn't take long before the only sources of light are our three flashlights and the moon, hanging half full above us.

The one nice thing about the Sunflower Trail is that they actually bother to maintain it. Instead of flattened grass, we follow a path of frozen white and brown sand. We're flanked on both sides by dead trees, packed so tightly together that it's hard to see much of anything beyond what's directly ahead of us.

The voice in my head is still quiet. At some point, I should probably tell Mars and Gabe about the fact that I'm *hearing voices* now. But I don't think that time is now, when we're literally walking into the wolf's den.

Worse than that thought is the idea of neither of them believing me. I can't prove a voice. I can't make them hear it. I don't want to say a word until I'm absolutely sure I know where it's coming from.

"Cold?" Gabe's voice suddenly breaks the silence.

I glance at him. My first thought is sarcasm: it's just past six p.m. in the middle of an Illinois winter. *Obviously* I'm cold. It takes another moment for me to remember that until today, I've been constantly overheating.

"Yeah," I answer. It's a strange realization.

I hope it's a sign, some return to normalcy. I don't think I should hold my breath, though.

Gabe nods. He seems equally cold, cheeks and nose the same shade of pink as Mars's hair. He tucks his flashlight under his arm, reaches over, and takes my free hand. Even through two layers of gloves, his and mine, the difference is immediate.

Testosterone really does make you ridiculously hot.

"Thanks," I whisper, grateful that my cheeks were already cold-stained.

Gabe nods like it's no big deal, eyes fixed on the ground.

Up ahead, Mars suddenly stops. Gabe and I stop, too. I listen extra hard, as if our brief exchange caused us to miss something.

"Yo, check this out." Mars glances back at us. If she has anything to say about Gabe holding my hand, it's been deprioritized by whatever she sees ahead.

Gabe and I follow her to the edge of the path, where the ground slopes downwards. Nothing immediately jumps out. Not until Mars lowers the beam of her flashlight to the ground and illuminates the blood streaked on the slush. I *think* it's blood, anyway. It's at least a day old, a shade of brownish black still distinct from the dirt that usually stains the snow.

"How do we know this wasn't one of the coyotes?" Gabe asks.

"Intuition," Mars answers.

She's far too confident. Then I realize that she's pointed her flashlight further down the road, and I crane my neck to see what she sees.

A green quad bike is parked in the middle of the trail. The headlights are dark, the engine isn't running, it doesn't *look* haphazardly abandoned. But in the patchy light of three flashlights, we can all see the decal on the windshield:

POLICE

NAPERVILLE PARK DISTRICT

Nobody moves or says anything. The three of us stand there, probably building the same picture in our heads. The same quad, the same blood, the same disturbances in the snow going further down the hill, like a trail of its own.

Mars reaches over and gives my wrist a squeeze, and for a moment, it feels like the same electric current runs through all of us. Three terrified hearts beating in sync.

"How do we feel about following that?" Mars asks.

"Terrible," Gabe answers flatly.

I nod in agreement. "Let's go."

The best we've got for a trail marker ends up being Mars's yellow beanie, which she hangs from a nearby branch. It's not much, but if we have to run, the neon reflects well enough.

With a departing smile, Mars lets go of my wrist and forges the path ahead. Gabe also lets go of my hand as we navigate the bushes and their gnarled branches, but he keeps our arms interlocked. It's not the best way to walk, but I couldn't care less. I keep my light pointed at the ground in front of us, trying to see any gore before I go stumbling through it.

"Step down extra hard!" Mars whisper-shouts back at us, goose-stepping through the brush. "We can find our way back easier if we have footprints to follow!"

My focus is entirely on making sure Gabe and I keep pace with her. The trail of dry blood quickly peters out into regular dirty snow, but Mars trudges forward with the same determination as if we no longer need it.

"She really wants to end this tonight, huh, Bambi?" Gabe eventually says, just low enough for me to hear.

"Of course she does." I grin, teeth chattering. "She wants to get a good grade in werewolf hunting, something normal to want and possible to achieve."

Gabe's face breaks with a laugh.

"*I can hear you both talking shit*," Mars calls in a sing-song voice.

"*I said*" – I cup my mouth with one hand – "making me freeze to death doesn't count as curing me!"

Mars starts walking backwards, flashlight held under her chin. "We know she's around here somewhere! We're gonna find her."

"And what happens when we do?" I ask.

"Well, obviously, that's why we brought the monkshood."

"Well, *obviously*, I can't just walk up and feed it to her. It. Whatever."

"That is exactly why your two best friends are here to—"

Mars gasps. The flashlight goes out. I freeze.

Gabe, however, doesn't miss a beat and rushes forward to the edge of darkness where she disappeared. He looks down. "Okay?"

There's no verbal answer, but Gabe turns back to me and sighs. "She's fine."

I join him at what turns out to be a fairly steep drop-off. About five feet down, Mars has sat up and begun to dust herself off. Moonlight reflects off the water behind her.

"Found the brook," she sings, sounding like her breath is only just coming back to her.

Gabe shakes his head and climbs down much more gracefully. I sit down to do the same.

hungry

I whip around and stare into the trees behind us.

Hearing it so suddenly makes it feel like it's breathing down my neck, hot and musky and in the shape of the worst word I can imagine hearing right now.

"What is it?"

I look down. Gabe is holding his hand out for me, brow knitted with concern.

"Nothing." I quickly shake my head.

Gabe's eyes linger on me, but he says nothing as he helps me down. Then, he picks up Mars's backpack as she finishes smacking the snow off her pants. He whispers something that sounds like "are you okay?" and Mars looks up at him with this big, toothy grin.

A horrible feeling wraps around my throat.

I think back to the night before. If that *wasn't* a half-conscious dream, then that voice can hear me, too. As I look at Gabe and Mars, I realize it might be the worst possible thing for them to be out here with me, and I make a split-second decision.

"Hey." I clear my throat. "Gimme five, I've gotta take a piss."

Gabe frowns. "Can't you wait until we're back at your house?"

Mars elbows him. "Okay, *Mom*, it's not that deep." She turns to me. "We'll chill here, just make it quick."

I nod and start walking, waiting until the brook bends and takes me out of sight before I pick up the pace.

I should tell them: *Hey, guys, the werewolf is totally in my head right now*. But either this connection goes both ways, or it only goes one, and I doubt that I have knowledge that this thing doesn't. I should tell them, but the words stick in my throat. I'm dangerous, and I'm terrified of them realizing it.

Do you sleep? I think, as pointedly as I can when I finally slow down and catch my breath.

There's a small groove in the bank, which I use to pull myself back up onto solid ground. Out here, there's a whole lot of dead grass and rolling hills, with the next major treeline only a distant promise in the dark.

of course i sleep

I look around uselessly.

We want to help you, I try. *You need help, right? You don't want to be doing this.*

I'm not surprised that she doesn't answer, but it's still frustrating.

My stomach twists with hunger. I grimace and pull the little bag of fruit snacks from my pocket. It should be *something*, but I empty the bag into my mouth and every gummy tastes like ash.

if one of us needs help it's you hunter

A hot chill rushes up my spine. *Why?*

because you're starving

Almost on cue, my stomach growls, wholly unsatisfied with the fruit snack offering.

you need to eat

I exhale. *That's super helpful, thanks.*

well you've already found the water now you need to find the food

For a moment, I have no idea what she's talking about. Then, it clicks: she's close. She's been staying by the water, so it stands to reason that there's a reliable food source nearby. I have to ignore the way my stomach twists with nausea at the thought that *I* was nearly part of that reliable food source. That Norman *was*.

I trudge forward, wondering how in the world I'm

supposed to find the lycanthrope I've only seen *once* since the initial attack, when something rustles in the grass. With a horrible sense of déjà vu, I turn my flashlight towards the noise.

When I illuminate a pair of eyes, my first instinct is to run. But instead, I stay grounded to the spot, and my brain then registers that this isn't our lycanthrope. They are the thin, squinting eyes of a bird no larger than my fist. A black stripe crosses its face like a bandit's mask, and the top half of its beak curves down to a sharp point.

My stomach growls again, as if the bird had turned into a cartoon dinner platter. When was the last time I ate something without feeling sick?

If I could somehow recoil from my body, I would. Instead, I just stand there, engaged in this horrible staring contest with the bird.

I am *not* that far gone. Absolutely not.

Suddenly, the bird flies out of the brush and directly at my face. I instinctively throw my arms over my face and feel something hit me. When I bring my arms down again, there's a tear in my jacket sleeve. A small one, sure, but almost shockingly deep. I can see the blue of the shirt I'm wearing underneath.

Then something slaps against my cheek. A sharp, stinging sensation follows. Distinctly different from the usual sting of the cold. I don't need to check to know that I'm bleeding.

I take off in what I *think* is the direction I came from, although it's all grass and slush and old, twisted tree trunks out here. This is a ridiculous image – me running for my life from a little bird – but I would rather run than find out what happens if I don't.

hunter listen to me

Screw you, I think.

I make three strides before my body seizes up. I'm running, and then the next thing I know I'm on the ground, my forehead pressed into the dirt and everything suddenly aching. *Throbbing* from somewhere deep inside me. I gasp for a breath I can't take.

hunter you should know better than anyone you can't deny what your body needs

Everything is too hot, too tight. I rip my gloves off.

As soon as I've got the second one off, I realize what's happening. It's my nails. They've started to grow again. I stare at my hands as they do. It's not David Kessler's fingers impossibly stretching into paws, but it's enough to shock the breath back into my lungs.

The sensation is like getting my drains pulled out all over again. Except this time, it hurts. *Badly.*

"Stop," I whimper. As if this is something I can ask to stop.

you need to breathe hunter you need to stop fighting it let it happen let yourself become

Suddenly, I'm aware of a presence over my shoulder. The

weight of being watched. Before I can do anything about it, something hits the back of my head. The unmistakable sound of flapping wings fills my ears before the bird reorients itself and flies away again. My scalp stings from where its talons have clawed at the skin.

What the fuck is this bird's problem?

we are beyond their comprehension

I don't love this answer.

The bird is coming around again. I can feel it as surely as I can feel my nails, uneven and jagged in the soft flesh of my palms. I'm not even hungry any more. I'm just *angry*.

Before it can dive at me, I twist myself around and stick my hand out. It shouldn't work. But somehow it does. The feeling of an actual, live bird in my fist is almost startling enough for me to let go. The bird writhes and snaps at me, but my body has suddenly stopped feeling like my body. I don't feel the beak cutting my fingers open. I don't feel anything at all.

I am beyond its comprehension. This creature knows nothing at all except that I'm something to fear, and it is terrified.

I have no recollection of the thought or impulse that leads me to do what I do next. One moment, I'm staring at this bird in my fist in the same way I imagine God looks down upon me, equal parts disdain and pity. Then there's the weight and salt of blood.

My eyes shut. Warmth spreads down my throat and out

through my fingertips. It doesn't even occur to me to be horrified until I've opened my eyes again.

Sitting in the grass directly ahead of me are a pair of large, amber eyes, attached to the biggest wolf I've ever seen. I haven't been this close since she bit me, and, seriously, at the shoulder she's close to being taller than *Gabe*. It's not until those eyes lock with mine that everything suddenly snaps into focus: the ache in my bones, the blood leaking from my mouth, the feather stuck between my teeth.

I panic and I scramble backwards until I find my footing and run. That gets me all of five feet before I fall right back onto my face.

My hand goes into something wet. Something hard *snaps* under my palm and my arm suddenly goes cold.

I don't stop to figure out why or from what. I pull myself back up and run like my life depends on it, until I see the sharp bend of the brook glisten in the moonlight. I don't gracefully climb back down to the bank as much as I drop to my hands and knees and scramble towards it. Like an animal. Like a *thing*.

I go straight over the edge and land on my hands, which sends a jolt of new pain up through my wrists. Somebody screams, then somebody *else* screams, and then there are two flashlights shining in my face.

"Oh my God—" Mars stops. When I look up, she's staring at me with huge eyes.

Nothing comes jumping down after me. There's still a feather in my teeth. My right arm is freezing cold. I finally look down and see the reason why: I'm covered in blood up to my elbows.

I sit back on my haunches. As I do, Mars crouches down. Her expression slowly shifts from one of horror to one of intrigue. Between the brook and my own haggard breathing, it's not quiet, but the silence between the three of us is almost unbearable. Gabe is staring at my face. Mars is looking over the rest of me.

"What happened?" Gabe finally manages.

I nearly open my mouth to say something. About the bird, about the lycanthrope and her voice in my head, about whatever I stuck my hand in that left me drenched in blood. But I can't. I just sit there, staring at my hands, thinking about the last thing the voice said to me: *We are beyond their comprehension.*

17

I don't know how we make it to my house. At some point, Mars helps me to my feet, and we manage to retrace our steps back to the main trail. In some weird way, I'm kind of proud of us for not getting *totally* lost.

I catch a glimpse of myself in the window when we get back to the car and the interior lights turn on. The cuts across my cheek seem quaint in comparison to the blood everywhere on me. I look like Brigitte at the end of *Ginger Snaps*, when she tries to appease her lycanthrope sister by eating handfuls of her best friend's guts: gory and miserable.

It's a short, quiet drive. As soon as Mars parks, I get out and stumble into the house. The last thing we need is for somebody like Annie Searchwell to look out her window and see me covered in blood – and seriously, how much of my wardrobe have I trashed in the last three weeks?

In the bathroom, I rip everything off from the waist up and throw it blindly towards the tub. The blood on my face has already mostly dried. I grab a hand towel and run it under the water. It takes all of my focus just to scrub my face and not try to tear the skin completely off.

One towel becomes two. Two become four.

I still don't know what bloody *thing* I shoved my hand through, but I try not to think too hard about it. I *really* don't want to think about it.

The floor creaks. I glance up. Mars is standing in the doorway, her arms crossed tightly over her chest. I pause, but she doesn't say anything, so I finish washing my arm off. Then my neck and a few spots near my collarbone. I'm thankful the bird was as small as it was; my shirt absorbed the blood before it could stain my chest.

It's only once I've started to wring the towel out, pink water circling the drain, that Mars finally speaks. "I don't think you should leave the house until this is over."

I look at her. Even now, even like *this*, that's inconceivable. "Mars…"

"I mean it. Whatever happened out there can't happen in front of other people."

"I can't put my whole life on pause!" I snap. "I have—"

"You *have* to control yourself," Mars shoots back. "Okay? It'd be one thing if you were a little hormonal, but this is… This is dangerous, Hunter. What happens if you hurt somebody? God forbid you do something worse."

My stomach twists. She's right. I just grabbed a bird out of the sky and ate it because a voice in my head told me it was a good idea.

I realize that the faucet is still running. I turn it off and stare at myself in the mirror. My skin is red everywhere I've scrubbed it. The long, deep talon scratches across my cheek sit right above the spot I've been compulsively picking at. There's still blood under my nails.

"What if I just have to kill myself?" I ask.

Mars's expression doesn't waver, but there's an edge to her voice. "Don't."

My laugh is weak. "I mean, that's where this ends, right? Mars, there's no way we find this thing. We can't *kill it*."

I want to tell her: *I did find it. It was right there, and I ran away.*

I can't.

"We are gonna do whatever it takes," Mars answers, slow and intentional. As if she's trying to make herself believe it, too. Something about this infuriates me.

"Like *what?*" My voice is shrill. "Spend all night outside running around with a kitchen knife? Even if I'm not turning into the fucking wolf-man, I don't want to live like this! I *can't!*"

"You *aren't*. Gabe and I are gonna figure it out."

"There's nothing to figure out! The monster dies!" I take a shaking breath. "In all those movies, you have to kill the monster. You can't cure it, you can't save it, you kill it. You kill it in *Ginger Snaps*, in *Silver Bullet*, even in *Howling II*. If the guy in *American Werewolf* had killed himself like he was supposed to, then all those other people wouldn't have died. And at least if I die, maybe I stop something like that from happening, huh?"

My voice echoes off the tiles. The sound of it makes me want to die. Mars looks like she wants to kill me. Everything suddenly comes back to death, and I wonder when God is gonna finally pull the plug on this whole thing.

Mars's shoulders rise and fall with a deep breath. Then she reaches out and jabs her finger into my sternum. "Why did you do this?"

I glance at my chest, then back up at her, frowning. "You know why—"

"I don't care. Explain it to me like I'm five."

I roll my eyes and push her hand away. "Because I needed it."

Mars shakes her head. "Not good enough. Tell me *why*."

"Not— I don't know, Mars! Because I've spent my entire life hating this stupid body—"

"Yes!" Mars cuts me off, then frowns. "Wait, no. You don't undergo major surgery because you *hate* yourself, you big idiot. *This*" – she grabs my wrist, below the discoloured bite, and holds my arm up between us – "is not you."

With her other hand, she jabs at my chest again. "*This* is you."

"*All of this* is me." I pull out of her grip.

"*This* is you," Mars re-emphasizes, as if that's all that matters. "Good and bad. But you are not a monster. You are not a *quitter*. You are not Benicio del Toro with latex glued to his face, you are a real human being who fought so hard to be here, and I have never once seen you roll over and give up!"

Mars takes another step closer. My feet feel like blocks of lead.

"You are not allowed to give up. Not ever, but especially not now." Her voice warbles. "Promise me."

I want to give her some kind of real answer. I don't *want* to die, and I have to believe that means something, but I don't know that it does. The best I'm able to do is a small nod, and that seems to be enough.

Mars's shoulders finally come down from her ears. She takes a breath and gives me the tightest hug I've gotten since my surgery. I wrap my arms around her and let my face crumble.

"Iron lung, man," Mars whispers against the side of my neck. "You don't get to bail on me like that. And I mean, honestly, I think I could get Gabe to be a backup, but I don't really know him like that yet."

I hate that this makes me laugh. "Shut up."

When Mars finally lets me go, her exhaustion is evident on her face. But she smiles at me, and once again I'm struck by some feeling of failure. I found our lycanthrope and I did nothing. I ran away. I'm the reason this is still dragging on.

Mars leaves me alone from there to find Gabe. I go into my bedroom for a clean shirt. I feel twitchy, like my skin is about to start sliding off the bone. Overstimulation feels like this sometimes, just not usually as visceral. I go through my clothes until I find a shirt that doesn't make the feeling worse, and then I pace the length of my room, kneading the skin on my good arm until it goes red.

I wonder what Mars and Gabe are talking about. Probably the same things I'm pondering: how quickly I might lose control of myself, how much time I have left until then.

A voice suddenly becomes audible from the hall. My stomach flutters with nervous static. I pull my door open enough to stick my head out.

It's Gabe. He's standing at the far end of the hall with his back to me and his phone up against his ear. "I'll be home tomorrow," he says, just above a whisper. "Ma, no, he's sick. No. No, I'm not gonna catch it. Yes, I'm sure."

I pull the door shut and exhale. Generally, as long as we're together, his parents give Gabe room to breathe. But it seems like even they have their limit.

Rather than going back to pacing, I stand there and stare at myself in the mirror hanging on my door. I pull up my shirt to get a view of my chest. I squint and attempt to fuzz out the scars. If I can survive this, I know I can still look normal. It's just the survival part that seems to be the largest hurdle.

What's your name? I think.

The answer doesn't come straight away, but when it does, the voice is clear.

lawrence

A boy. Try as I might, I can't parse gender from the voice. I don't even know how I'm able to differentiate it from my own internal monologue. It just simply *is*.

Okay. Lawrence. I step closer to the mirror, eyes locked with my own reflection. *You ever been to Chicago before?*

if i ever did i don't remember no

I nod. *Where were you from?*

He doesn't answer, and I suppose it is a pointless question. It doesn't matter where he's from and it doesn't matter what his name is.

I cross my arms over my chest. I'm nearly nose-to-nose with my reflection now, half wishing there was a physical sign of *something*. Like all those horror movies where a person's got a hand or an eyeball at the back of their throat. Something I could reach in and rip out.

Maybe amputating the bitten limbs would have worked if we'd done it soon enough.

Why me? I suddenly think, digging my nails into my arm.

Lawrence does not answer. I glare at my reflection.

Answer me, you coward. Why me?

Lawrence remains frustratingly silent. A sudden warmth makes me realize I've dug my nails into my arm too far and made myself bleed.

Then the floor creaks, and before I can connect the dots, the door swings into my face.

"*Ow.*" My hand goes straight to my nose. *That's* not bleeding, at least.

Gabe sticks his head inside and frowns. "Were you just standing there?"

I open one eye. "Do you want something?"

His frown softens. I step back so he can open the door wider, although he doesn't actually come into the room. "Mars is gonna go home for the night," he says.

Her parents are probably also worried about the fact that she's suddenly spending most of her waking moments with me. I nod.

Gabe lingers. The air is thick with *something*; I don't know if it's discomfort or fear or what. Either of those things would be justifiable, but it still feels like getting punched in the stomach.

"I was thinking about going home, too," he finally says. "Unless you wanted me to stay."

I want him to stay more than I want to be alive. I want him to hold my hand again. I want to crawl inside him and know the security of a real male body for *once* in my life. Just once.

"Nah, I'm fine." I shake my head and force a smile. "You guys go and get some sleep."

Gabe's eyes stick to me. My face goes warm with an

embarrassed flush that I hope isn't visible in the low light. "You're sure?"

"Yeah. Totally. I'll see you both in the morning."

It's that easy. Gabe nods and shuts the door, leaving me in my horribly pathetic, solitary company. I glare briefly at my reflection before I stalk over to my bed. No sooner have I buried my face in my pillow than Lawrence's voice returns to my head.

i didn't mean to

It takes me a moment to realize we're continuing our conversation.

I absorb what he's said: He didn't mean to turn me. I was supposed to die.

but i'm glad i didn't kill you

I roll onto my back and exhale. *You ruined my life.*

what life the life where these pieces of shit like ethan grind you under their heel because the only good transsexual is a dead transsexual the life where your dad hates what you are—

I put my hands over my eyes. "Shut up," I whisper out loud.

the life where your friends will always ALWAYS choose each other over you hunter this life would gut you like a fish before it ever let you be

The pressure behind my eyes continues to build until it's nearly unbearable. I curl onto my side. "Shut *up*."

i didn't mean to turn you into what i am hunter but i'm glad i did i recognize you hunter we're the same soul

My eyes snap open. “We’re not.”

yes we are you and me we’re the same hunter you’re just like me

“I am *nothing* like you.”

Lawrence finally goes silent.

I press my face back into my pillow, desperate for this night to end already. My breathing slows. Exhaustion settles over me like a blanket. The house is quiet.

Then, from the far end of the hall, a dog barks.

When I bolt upright, I’m no longer in my bedroom.

18

Missy begins yapping at the back door at just past six. She's a more reliable alarm than any mechanical clock could ever hope to be, and she will only quiet once she hears your feet hit the floorboards. As soon as you step through the kitchen doorway, she begins spinning in circles.

You unlock the door and throw it open, and Missy runs out into the field that stretches out behind the house. A flock of crows scatter in a chorus of dissatisfied cries. Normally, you'd let Missy have some privacy to relieve herself and chase the birds around. But over the last couple of days, something – or somebody – has been killing animals. A turkey farm on the other side of the highway was devastated over the weekend. So, you keep a slightly groggy eye on Missy for your own peace of mind, until she finally comes trotting back inside and you can lock the door behind her.

On your way to the bathroom, you pass by a number of photos on the wall. You framed your brother's wedding invitation since you couldn't show up for the Florida reception.

There's a photo of Cassandra – you've been meaning to take it down for ages – taken nearly five years ago. Her eyes, blue like the summer lakes, squint at the lens. You once again think about calling her, but there's no sense of urgency to it. There never is. The final photo is of you and Missy on the day you got her, seven years ago. A gift from your parents for deciding to go to the college you would eventually drop out of. Way back when you buzzed your hair off and hid the fact that you smoked, because there was still a part of you that worried about what your parents thought.

Then, in the bathroom mirror, there's you.

Your eyes, emerald green, seem too small until you've splashed some water on your face and put your glasses on. Your glasses are large wire squares, not exactly Dahmer frames but close enough. The faint wisp of a beard is only visible when the light hits you right. You run your hands through overgrown blond hair, then return to your room to dress for work.

As you do, you look down at your chest. This is the most unflattering angle because your chest somehow manages to appear protruding and concave at the same time. The incision lines along your pectoral muscles have finally begun to properly scar. For the last month they were simply little red slashes, no thicker than a hairpin. Despite the massaging and the scar strips and the oils, they've still noticeably expanded. Your surgeon told you that keloid scarring isn't indicative of doing anything wrong, but the sight of them raises something ugly into your throat.

Another surgeon could, hypothetically, minimize this scarring later. You've been thinking about getting a tattoo to cover them up instead. Ugly chest tattoos are effectively a rite of passage among transsexual men anyway, and one they happen to share with cisgender men. You plan to scout out tattoo parlours the next time you go into Minneapolis. The long drive is necessary; the closest shop to where you live is co-owned by Cassandra.

It's an uneventful Monday. Like each one before it, you take your smoke breaks with David and listen to him talk about his ex-wife and the jacked-up gas prices. He blames the communists for the aggravating qualities of both. You eat your lunch in the bed of your pickup, staring out at Highway 28. As the only truck dispatcher for Prairie Implement – a farm equipment supplier – to actually live in Minnesota, you have the added responsibility of making sure none of the drivers set the garbage cans on fire with a loose cigarette. It's hardly the most exciting job in the world, but it pays the bills and never keeps you too late.

This place is too small to ever have any sort of traffic. You drive five minutes up the road and you're home again. Everything around here is a five-minute drive. Tonight, you get home as the sun hits the horizon. The colours look like the end of the world, a fireball that should turn your bones to ash.

But the world isn't ending, so you let Missy out and start prepping for dinner. You set your phone on the countertop and play from Rosanne Cash's album *The List*. You tell yourself it's because you truly love this album and that it has nothing at all to do with Cassandra, who loved it first.

You can visualize her across from you, humming along to "Miss the Mississippi and You". She could pitch her voice to mirror Rosanne Cash's gentle twang like it was her own. You're still finding her black-brown hair all over the house.

You should call her.

Missy starts yowling a couple of seconds into "500 Miles".

In an instant, you've dropped your bag of greens and you're running for the double-barrelled shotgun in the closet. Your dad gave it to you when you were sixteen and he thought you were a dyke who'd spend the rest of her life screwing around with girls and running from their brothers and boyfriends. He didn't have the finer details right, but bad math still sometimes gives the right answer. You've never needed to fire the gun, although it came in handy when you lived in Ralston and Monica's brothers decided to try and crowd onto your porch after they caught you two together. The memory lights your adrenaline on fire.

You run outside and holler for Missy. It's already so dark that you can barely see ten feet past your door; your porch light is the brightest thing around here for a mile, beyond the blood moon hanging low and rusty orange in the sky. Missy cries out once more, somewhere north of you, and you take off in a blind sprint.

The other animal comes out of nowhere. When it slams into you, it's like getting hit by a truck. The shotgun goes off when it hits the ground, a sudden burst of sparks lighting up the night. It illuminates the jagged teeth before they clamp down on your shoulder.

There's a scream. It must be yours, but it sounds like no scream you've ever let out before. You manage to grab the end of the gun and swing it, and you feel it make impact against the animal's skull.

The next thing you hear is the snap of your own forearm.

You don't scream this time. Instead, the world slips into slow motion. You look up at the beast as it finally releases you, wild yellow eyes suddenly hovering a few inches above your own. The fur around its left eye is speckled white, although the rest of its face is covered in reddish-brown fur. Blood has turned its mouth pitch black.

Its head suddenly explodes above you with the sound of a whip crack.

The first face you recognize is David from work. The sonofabitch has a cigarette hanging from his lips, which he almost drops into your open wound when he turns and calls for help. A few other guys you vaguely recognize gather. Men who decided to take the animal killings as the perfect excuse to wander around with guns and beer cans and were only coincidentally close enough to hear your shotgun go off. You'd be dead if you'd known even the basic safety rules of running around with a loaded gun.

David drives you to the closest hospital in Glenwood while the rest of the men gawk at the kill. There's nothing left to hang on a mantel, but you recognize the flash of cameras as they snap pictures with the massive body anyway. You've never seen a dog *that* big before.

You're thankful that the hospital nurses keep David outside, because otherwise he would see your keloid scars vibrantly slashed across your chest despite the blood and brains that have painted you the darkest red. Even if David didn't know what the scars signified, he'd still ask you about it, and you'd have to make up some bullshit about a car accident or something else severe enough that he'd never ask about it again. Something cowardly that would remind you of Cassandra's biting, disappointed tone. She hated the ease with which you could deny your transness. You told her it was jealousy. She was always jealous that you could pass easier than she could.

In one delirious moment, as the nurse wipes away the carnage and discovers that the bites don't seem to be as bad as the blood would suggest, you wonder if you can lie and say you got your chest scars from the animal attack. When you hear the nurse tell the doctor that "*she* should be fine to go home tonight", you know you will not be coming back here even if your life depends on it.

You blink and you're in your house. Your silent house, because Missy is dead and you never even got to say goodbye, because the men who sent a bullet through the wild wolf's brains had enough presence of mind to take Missy's body and have her cremated. A bill for two hundred dollars is sitting on your kitchen table, untouched and unpaid, and now Missy sits in a vase in your living room.

This isn't really the way it happened. This house didn't catch fire overnight. The flames spread slowly, day by day, and you didn't *really* notice until it was too late to do anything about it. But here, in memory, it seems to catch all at once.

First, blood runs between your legs in defiance of the uterus you had removed when you were twenty-two years old. It flows like a wound has suddenly opened inside you and you bleed for days and days. Your hair starts coming out in clumps. Your vocal cords shrivel and shrink until you sound exactly like your teenage self. You run hot, then ice cold.

You know what Cassandra would say – her voice echoes inside your head like a living ghost: *Lawrence, go to the fucking hospital* – but you know what you are. You are two things: a transsexual and a coward. You raised yourself on the stories of men like Brandon Teena and Robert Eads who died cruel, painful, preventable deaths because of who and what they were. The names of women like Tyra Hunter and Shaun Smith are branded into your bones. You are one man in a lineage of others who tried to save themselves and there is something in your chest that cannot bear the humiliation of failing.

You won't grovel. You will fix yourself or you will die, but you will not beg for *them* to save you.

You stop going to work, and instead you burn with rage at the shame nestled inside you, nestled somewhere between your kidney and intestines. Your shame tract. You hate the keloid scars and your doctor and the doctors who failed the brothers and sisters who died years before you were ever born and you hate the voice of your college best friend who told you that transsexuality was an invention of the medical establishment, because it's kind of a shitty conspiracy when the doctors just keep letting us die, isn't it, Tayler? The anger hangs in the back of your throat every day for what feels like a lifetime – has it *not* been a lifetime? Has it not been there since before you knew its name? – until one day you wake up and suddenly there really *is* something in your throat that's too big to breathe around, and you stumble out into the hot summer night horrified because it's coming out and it's the kind of birth you've always had nightmares about, where you are alone and terrified and your skin bulges with a creature that will force its way out no matter what you want or what you do, it is *coming*. Your jaw bends with the weight until it suddenly

snaps

19

I wake up when I hit the floor. There's already blood in my mouth and a new welt on my lip from biting it. My head is throbbing as my brain tries to catch up to whatever the hell just happened. I press my fingers into the floor and stare at it.

My floor. It is mine, I realize, with blossoming relief despite how my breath still comes in panicked gasps. I sit up and look around. It was just a nightmare. Everything is where it should be. My beanbag chair is in the corner, my backpack rests against the wall, my shorts are damp with perspiration where they stretch around my thighs, and my chest—

The world comes to a sudden, grinding halt.

My shirt is also damp, although with *what* isn't immediately clear. As soon as I place my hands on myself, a sharp pain makes me jerk away. It fades slowly into a dull, pulsating throb. I freeze, briefly at a loss, before I scramble to get my shirt pulled over my head. There's a tightness along the side of my chest, where the drains went under my skin. I don't bother to stand, let alone try to run to the bathroom. Instead, I crawl to the mirror on my door.

As my eyes adjust to the dark, more of my body comes into focus. Sweat has plastered my hair to my forehead. My whole arm is black and sore and the scab on my cheek has broken open again. Blood or pus or something glistens on my jaw. Something glistens on my chest, too.

This, I'm almost certain, isn't blood. It clings to my skin right where the incision spots from my drains had been healing into tiny white circles. When I reach down and touch it, it clings to my fingers, almost like a mucus. The skin beneath it is hot and sensitive to the touch. Even scraping that little bit off *hurts*.

I raise my hand to my actual chest, the pectorals I spent my whole childhood smooshing down and imagining perfectly flat. I press down on them again.

Something *snaps*.

Pus the colour of spoiled milk breaks through the incision mark. The snap was the scar tissue breaking open. This is what makes me start screaming.

20

Not everybody knows that medical transition doesn't make your life perfect. I think that's where a lot of the more insufferable detransitioners come from. The ones that say trans identity is one big pharmaceutical conspiracy aimed at destroying the idea of womanhood (or something like that). The ones who are angry that they did the surgeries and took the hormones and still found themselves unhappy.

To which I've always thought: *duh*. Transitioning doesn't make you a completely different person from who you were "before". At the end of the day, even if you change your hormonal make-up and go under the knife once or twice, *you* haven't changed. You might have a different body, you might even enter a different social class, but you're still just a kid from Chicago who can't drive. The only difference is that now you're a *boy* who can't drive.

I think we all secretly hope that transitioning will make our life perfect anyway. I believe there's a part of our brain, no matter how small or ignored, that hopes all our issues somehow stem from dysphoria alone, and a couple of snips and pokes will make it so we're never sad ever again. When I woke up in the hospital bed, I remember feeling free, and hoping that that feeling wouldn't go away.

I have no recollection of calling anybody, but my phone tells me that I called Gabe at just past three. I don't hear the car pull up, but I hear the front door slam against the wall. It's Mars's voice that cuts through the grief garroting my brain.

It feels like it takes hours to calm down – with Mars at my back, and Gabe letting me squeeze his hand until his skin turns white – but when they finally help me to my feet, I catch a glimpse of the clock and see that it's barely four. The sun isn't even up yet. They gently guide me to the bathroom to let me clean myself off. I have ten minutes to do so; Mars makes it pretty clear they'll break down the door if I'm in there for even a second longer.

I stand in the shower and let the water wash away the pus and blood for me, numbly watching the changing colours circle the drain. I don't know how to process what I'm looking at. A sob is caught in my throat, and I have no energy to expel it. There's only the horrible dread and the powerlessness of knowing that the worst possible thing that could happen to me just has.

When I come out, Mars is sitting on the floor with a T-shirt in her arms. I recognize it: one of the few shirts I could wear immediately after the surgery, soft and large enough that it never triggered any sensory issues. Having to gingerly slip it on now feels like a cosmic joke.

The words "suicide watch" aren't said at any point, but I don't think there's a better term for what this is. Mars walks with me to the living room, where Gabe is sitting on the far end of the couch, holding my phone.

Maybe not suicide watch. This feels more like hospice care.

I sit down and wrap myself in the blanket closest to me before taking my phone from Gabe. Mars sits down on the floor next to me. The details of my dream are already fading, but I think I have enough to find an anchor in the real world. I *hope*. I pull up the internet browser on my phone and give it a shot.

lawrence + minnesota

That search comes back with exactly as much junk as you would expect. My shoulders slump.

"Hunter." Mars's voice brings me back.

I look up. Gabe has gotten a little closer, hand on my right ankle. Mars is on the floor next to me with her hand fisted up in my shirt. Each of them has a small point of physical contact with me. Like I'm gonna go anywhere.

They both look exhausted. It's almost enough to pull me from the fog of self-pity.

"Are you okay?" Mars asks, in a tone that tells me she's repeating herself.

I nod, even though we all know I'm not.

Mars chews on her thumbnail. "All right. Um, Gabe and I were talking a bit while you were in the shower…"

Gabe finishes for her, "We're gonna try and figure something else out."

I frown. "What do you mean *something else*?"

"I mean what we did last night *really* didn't work," Mars says, "and we're not— I mean, we can't do that again. I don't know what we're gonna do, but Gabe and I are gonna figure something out, so don't worry about it, okay?"

Don't worry about it, I repeat to myself. The idea of not worrying about this is almost funny. But I'm being told, not asked for my opinion, so I nod and pull the blanket tighter around myself as I return to my phone. I try to think of what else I know about our lycanthrope.

lawrence + missing + minnesota

Fewer junk results, but still nothing that brings up the face I'm looking for.

I consider adding *transgender* to the search, but I find myself hesitating over the keys. How else can I identify him? I strain to remember another name. A licence plate or address.

The answer comes to me after a minute.

lawrence + cassandra + minnesota + missing

At last, I see a page that looks right enough to click, and while Mars and Gabe continue to whisper back and forth, I get my first real glimpse of the man responsible for this.

Lawrence Tennison

Missing Since: 06/14/2022

Missing From: Villard, Minnesota

Sex: Female

Age: 27

Height and Weight: 5′8″, 130 pounds

Distinguishing Characteristics: Blond hair, green eyes. Tennison wears square, wire-rimmed glasses and has a small scar underneath his right eyebrow. May go by Larry or Ren.

Details of Disappearance: Lawrence Tennison was last seen in Villard, Minnesota, on June 14th, 2022. He was reported missing on June 15th when coworkers initiated a wellness check. His house was found empty with the back door left unlocked and open. His wallet, cell phone and truck were accounted for at his residence.

Lawrence is transgender. He lives as male but was born biologically female as Nancy Quinn Tennison. His dog had recently been killed in an incident where Tennison was minorly injured as well, and he was reportedly suffering from emotional distress. Authorities do not believe he met with foul play, although the circumstances of his disappearance are unclear.

Source Information:

Glenwood Police Department

NamUs

Facebook page for Lawrence Tennison, run by Cassandra Sweeney

21

What made you choose Lawrence?

I hold his face in my mind as I ask this. I saw it only briefly within the dream, but now that I know Lawrence's name, I can find pictures. He passed well, but he looked trans, too. Maybe that's because I know what I'm looking for, or maybe I just look at him and feel this bone-deep sense of recognition. In looking at a photograph of somebody who I never knew and who never knew me, I still *know him*.

While I wait for Lawrence to answer, I look out my bedroom window. The sun has finally risen, the clouds outside grey and heavy with an impending storm. I'm exhausted, but I haven't slept. I'm terrified to sleep because I have no idea what I'll look like when I wake up. I hold the howlite necklace gingerly, trying to avoid scarring up my hands any more than I already have.

At last, Lawrence's voice softly breaks the silence:

have you ever seen saw

It takes a moment for me to untangle that sentence. I smile. *The first one, yeah.*

i needed a name and just always thought that cary elwes was so fucking hot in that movie plus he's literally a guy who has to cut off a part of himself to save his own life

Are you saying Jigsaw was secretly a trans ally?

ha ha

Laughter is a strange thing to feel echo inside my head. It makes me smile again, even though it's mostly reflexive. My body aches like it's the first day of the flu. Everything hurts. I push my tongue into the back of my mouth and press it against the side of the unnatural tooth.

birth is always painful hunter

I wince. *This isn't birth.*

this is a rebirth hunter you're becoming something better

I grind my teeth against each other.

it's hardest at the end but it's almost over and then you won't have to worry about this body anymore i promise

Before I can ask what any of that means, the bedroom door swings open. I shoot upright.

Mars stops with her hand on the door, a small disposable cup in the other. "Sorry, can I come in?"

I can feel my face turn red. "Yeah. Sure."

I put the necklace down on the nightstand. Mars sits on the edge of the bed. Her hair has been hastily tied back, and she looks like she's gotten about as much rest as I have.

"Did you guys get any sleep?" I ask.

Mars smiles before making the *so-so* motion with her

hand. "A little. I did, at least. Gabe looked like shit, though, so I had him drop me back at my car and give me the house key so he can catch a couple hours of sleep and get his mom off his back. Nice lady, by the way, but, oh my God, how is that boy not *broken* with anxiety disorders?"

That explains how they both got to the house at the same time. They left together, stayed together, hung out together until nearly three in the morning, when I woke up from the nightmare.

do you see what i mean hunter they will always choose each other over you

I twitch and try to ignore him. "What about your mom?"

Mars shrugs with a slight smile. "My parents could give a shit. Far as I'm concerned, I'm living here with you until we get this thing sorted out."

"You're sure?"

She raises an eyebrow and takes a sip from her cup. "Do I look like somebody who's been *over-parented* at any point in my life?"

We both snort at this, though I recognize it's not especially funny. Maybe if my dad were around enough to know what it looks like when his son is becoming a monster, I wouldn't be here now.

"Anyway, I promise I'm not gonna talk your ear off about werewolf stuff. Gabe needs to sleep and I need to think about something else for five minutes." Mars sighs and sets her cup down. “Do you wanna see what I was looking at for prom outfits?”

It’s a paper-thin distraction, but I can humour her. I nod, and she scoots closer to me as she pulls her phone out. Close enough that I catch a whiff of her shampoo, a strikingly familiar citrus. It takes me a moment to realize why: it’s *my* smell.

“Did you shower here last night?” I ask.

Mars looks up quickly, which counteracts her innocent wide eyes. “Uh, yeah?”

“I…that’s fine, I was just wondering.”

Mars nods, still unusually skittish, and opens Pinterest. I rest my cheek on her shoulder and take in the notes of orange in the air between us. My heart starts to take up too much room in my chest.

“Okay, first of all, we would *kill it* in these.” Mars turns her phone to me. She has a photo of what is ostensibly a wedding dress and grey tux, except the tux has a simulated gunshot wound on its shoulder and the entire front of the dress is soaked in fake blood. I laugh, and Mars scrolls on. “But realistically, we’ve either gotta go for matching suits, or something like this for you, at least.”

The next photo she lands on is comically normal compared to the blood tux. It’s a white dress shirt and a gold waistcoat, except the waistcoat looks like somebody threw paint onto it. In a stylish, intentional sort of way. Green paint.

When we were kids, Riley told me she wanted to be a dryad. Her brother taught her about them during a game of Dungeons & Dragons: beautiful maidens who had flowers for hair and whose blood ran green underneath their skin.

I must look as sad as I suddenly feel. Mars locks her phone and sets it aside. "That's a *no*, I'm guessing."

"No, that was nice." I wince and shut my eyes. "Sorry. It's dumb. Green is, like, Riley's favourite colour."

"Oh."

We sit there for a while. There's a bird chittering outside. I turn my cheek against Mars's shoulder and try to stop the spiral before it starts.

"Is she aware that her boyfriend is going, like, full-blown *Carrie* bully on you?" Mars finally asks.

My smile is a reflex more than anything else. "I *tried* to tell her, and it...sorry, this is, like, the least important thing in the world right now."

"It's important to you." Mars reaches down and takes my hand. I flinch, worried about scratching her or hurting her or *something*, but Mars doesn't let go. "You tried...?"

I exhale and stare at our hands. Hers are soft, and the darkness of winter has turned her skin a lighter shade of beige. Mine are pale and bony, and my nails make me feel more monstrous than anything else so far. Hard *not* to feel like a monster when the contrast between myself and Mars is right there in front of me.

"Ever since our fight," I finally say, "I told myself that I hated her. I hate her for what she did, and I hate her for everything she didn't do, and I've talked to her more in the last month than I have in four years and every time I see her, suddenly all I want to do is tell her that I'm sorry."

It's impossible to tell if I really sound like I'm about to cry, or if that's just in my head.

Mars gives my hand a squeeze. "I know this is coming from somebody who didn't even know you then, but there's nothing you need to apologize for."

"I didn't exactly handle it well."

"So? You were fourteen! You know what I did when I was fourteen? I wore cat ears. *All the time*. Yearbook included. And...what's something stupid that Gabe did?"

"Punched Ethan?"

Mars gives me a look, but then relents. "Yeah, sure, my point is *everybody* is stupid when they're fourteen. And Riley—" She stops and takes a very deep breath. "To be completely fair, she was fourteen, too."

I know this. I know that Riley lost me as a friend just as I lost her. I've already spent years going over everything I could've done differently: if I'd shoved Ethan off, if I'd told Riley about it as soon as it happened, if I'd been *believable*.

As if reading my mind, Mars adjusts herself so she's sitting directly in front of me. "You were fourteen. That was sexual harassment, point-blank. There is no world where *overreacting* is worse than what he actually did to you."

I take a deep breath. "Or I could've just not transitioned at all."

Mars looks at me sharply. "Hunter."

I shrug and stare off into the empty space between us. "None of this would've happened if I'd...*dealt* with being a girl."

I'm not even sure if I'm talking about Ethan, Riley or the lycanthrope. All of it, I guess. The root of all of it is that I'm trans, and all of this has happened because of that.

Mars leans further into my space. "So, what, you'd rather be miserable *and* pretending to be cis?"

I glare up at her.

Mars shrugs. "Look, I know I don't know anything about being trans, but I know *you*. I know how bad you wanted this surgery; I remember how excited you were when your voice started cracking all over the place—"

"Yeah, and look where all that got me," I mutter.

It's quiet for a second. Then Mars's hands are suddenly on my face, forcing me to look up at her. "Riley is one shitty friend. She doesn't deserve this kind of control over your life."

In some distant way, I know that. The problem is that I *want* Riley to care about me. Like she used to. I want the Riley who let me borrow her pencils; who helped me cut and dye my hair so I could be Ponyboy for Halloween; who was the first person I told I was trans; who made a howlite necklace for me when my parents told me I couldn't go on puberty blockers.

I still can't reconcile those memories with the girl I'm so angry with now.

Instead of saying any of that, I pull away from Mars's hands. "I think I loved her."

Mars lets her hands fall back into her lap. Her smile is a little sad. "You deserve someone who's gonna love you back."

"Easy for you to say. You're surrounded by people who love you."

Her laugh is loud and startling. "I—This conversation isn't about me, but no. You, Hunter, are surrounded by people who love you. Gabe loves you; I love you—"

"You guys aren't *dating me*. There's a difference."

Mars shakes her head. "Okay? I still love you. I love you because you're my best friend, and you're, like, basically the only person who puts up with my shit. You think what *I* think matters and you don't treat me like an idiot, and every time I think about what happens if I can't figure out how to help you, I feel like I'm going to throw up."

Barely pausing to take a breath, she pushes a few loose hairs out of her eyes. "I'm not even joking about the iron lung thing any more because I don't want to think about what my life looks like without you in it. I know I'm rambling, and I promise I'm gonna shut up here in a second, but just because I have really annoying intimacy issues doesn't mean I don't love you, okay? It just means I suck at talking about it. I love you too much and I don't know how to deal with it."

There's no brilliant thought process to my decision to kiss her.

I think the impulse hits me at the right intersection of *why not?* and *if not now, when?*

It's an awkward, off-centre collision. I'm burning with embarrassment and shame even before I pull back, because Mars wasn't talking about *that* kind of love and I'm feeling especially selfish right now.

The look on her face is hard to read. I dig my nails into the half-healed cuts in my palms. My brain is already starting to throw together a frantic apology when Mars laughs and presses our foreheads together. She sniffles. I feel frozen.

"You're really gonna like prom," she promises me.

When Mars kisses me again, I can taste the lingering burn of coffee on her breath. She's smiling and she's warm and I almost wonder if I fell asleep from exhaustion without realizing it and this is one strange dream.

I don't think it is. The feeling buzzing around my head isn't grogginess or the usual haze of dreams; it's a surreal kind of clarity. The feeling of the world snapping completely into place.

I hope it's not a dream.

Then, something hits the window beside us.

Mars yelps in surprise, and we both turn to the sound. On

the list of things I'm expecting, none of them are an orange tabby cat. It's a little on the small side, standing on its back legs with its front paws braced against the glass.

Once the shock has faded, there's a hot huff of hair against my face. I look at Mars, whose face is scrunched up as she laughs.

"Sorry," she exhales. "What is *up* with the animals around here?"

The cat gets our attention again with a slightly muffled yowl.

I groan and stand. In response, the cat drops down onto its front paws. Its fur fluffs up like it's preparing to hiss, although for the moment it's just staring at me with big eyes.

Thankfully, there's nothing in me that wants to go after this cat. But as I step closer to the window, my eyebrows knit together. There's a purple collar on it. I bend down to try and read it.

The tag reads *Miko*.

The cat finally bares its teeth at me before it jumps down and scampers towards the back of the house. My stomach is in knots.

"What is it?" Mars asks. All the amusement is gone from her voice.

I don't bother to explain. I grab my jacket and my shoes, and Mars, without missing a beat, does the same.

There's a black cat in the front yard, wandering up the

driveway before it sees us and bolts. A couple of paw prints in the snow tell me there's probably more than the two. I stare at the side of Annie's house, at the undisturbed snow sitting on top of her car.

"How long has that been sitting there?" I ask, pointing at Annie's driveway.

Mars shrugs and looks at me. "I don't know. Couple of days? I haven't— Hey!"

I hurry down my driveway and cross the street until I'm pressed against the fence of Annie's backyard. The wood slats don't go any higher than my elbows, just tall enough to be a pain to try and jump over. But a longer look reveals an easier way into the yard: the gate, unlatched and swinging in the breeze. I know Mars sees it, too, because once she catches up with me, there's no wisecrack. She trails behind me as I walk to the gate.

I look at the porch. Another one of Annie's cats is cleaning herself on the steps.

The door is open. Not enough to notice from further away, but enough to reveal a sliver of the dark room on the other side. I suddenly can't remember anything about this door. I can't remember if it's always had a shitty, chipped paint job; I can't remember if Annie's back gate always had problems latching; and I can't remember the last time I saw her driveway empty.

We don't need to go inside. We could call the cops and let them figure out what we both already know.

I force myself to climb the porch steps anyway. I walk up to the door and push it fully open. The hinges whimper as I look into the living room. All the lights inside are off.

If you want to do something about anybody, do something about Miko.

"Hunter?" I look back. Mars is standing at the bottom of the steps, holding her phone to her ear.

She doesn't say *don't go in there*, but her face does. She's not getting any closer to this house that reeks of soiled litter boxes and something much worse, and I shouldn't either.

I step inside, using what little natural light comes in to find the kitchen I was in a short while ago. From there, I shuffle forward and find the hallway. I run my hand along the wall until I find a light switch.

The cheap orange light illuminates the watercolour paintings hung from the wall.

I find Annie at the end of the hall, still clutching the chunks of carpet she tore out of the floor.

22

At roughly the same time the cops are setting up outside Annie's house, a handful of rangers from the preserve find the green quad bike. A few hundred yards away, they find what's left of the officer who rode it. Torn apart, dragged so far the initial blood trail nearly ran out. One rib broken, where I fell on it.

What happened to either one of them was bad and brutal enough, but the news of both at once is probably what sends the city into total panic.

23

Because of the weekend, it takes until late Sunday afternoon for the mayor to put together a press conference.

From that moment, the city is under a seven-day local state of emergency order, due to what they call "an *imminent threat* in the form of a wild canine, which may or may not be rabid". It's a hell of a way to describe a werewolf that's killed two people, though they don't know it. Most of the press conference is a bunch of legalese that goes in one ear and out the other, until the mayor finally gets to the important part: All neighbourhoods within two miles of the preserve are under a general curfew, and outside of "necessary commutes to school or places of employment", nobody is supposed to leave their house at all. After-school clubs cancelled, sports practices postponed.

I watch all this on the TV, alone on my couch.

It takes the city a full day to go from *two bodies* to *lockdown*, but it didn't take everybody else half as long to fly into their own panic. Gabe was lucky enough to still be at home when the news broke. Mars, though, was standing next to me, watching the crowd in front of Annie's house grow, when her phone began ringing incessantly. I stayed at the window while she walked away to take the call, but I could hear how her voice rose with frustration.

What did Annie ever do to you? I thought at Lawrence, though he never gave me an answer.

Then Mars came back, flushed and talking a mile a minute about how her parents have never once cared about where she was except for *right now, when it's actually fucking important*. I realize now that I could've tried a little harder to act like I'm capable of keeping myself alive for a few days, but all I could do was stand there and feel suffocated by dread.

Before she left, Mars had grabbed the monkshood and stuck it inside yet another Ziploc and shoved it into my hands. "Gabe and I will finish this with you," she promised me, "but if something happens, you know what to do."

She gave me a hug. It was tight and panicked and far too short.

The monkshood is, currently, sitting on the floor beneath the TV. I've started carrying it from room to room, like I might need it at any moment.

I feel horribly alone.

There are a few text messages sitting on my phone, technically read but not responded to because I don't have the energy to. The vast majority of them are wellness checks from

Mars that have been coming pretty regularly. Gabe's last text came in a couple of hours ago.

If you need anything text us ok?

I don't know how we'll get to you but we will.

Below him, I'm slowly racking up messages from Dad, too.

About to go up. See you on Tuesday

Don't forget to check the mail please. Thank you

Everything okay?

On the TV, photos of Annie and the dead cop – Krystal Vasquez – appear side by side.

Guilt weighs heavy on my tongue. I might not have killed Annie myself, but that doesn't mean I'm not responsible for what happened to her. She's dead because she *almost* said my deadname. That cop is dead because I lived, and Lawrence stuck around.

Why Annie? I try again.

Silence. Just as I've resigned myself to it, Lawrence's voice suddenly enters my head.

i asked if you wanted to do something and you said do something about miko

I shut my eyes. *Okay, you psychopath, that wasn't* permission *to butcher my neighbour. Why the fuck would I want you to do that?*

because that's the beauty of what we can do hunter

I grimace and turn the TV off.

hunter i'm trying to make this easier for you than it was for me i didn't have anybody to tell me what was coming

"You know what's easy?" I offer out loud, standing up and grabbing the monkshood on my way out of the room. "Not killing people. I've gone my whole life without killing anybody."

just because you tell yourself that you can be like them does not make you one of them

I tuck the monkshood bag up against the side of my window, like it would do anything to stop a lycanthrope if one decided to launch itself through the glass.

if you thought you were like them wouldn't you tell them about me

My hands falter over the bottom of my shirt. I sit down on the edge of my bed and exhale. "I haven't told them because they don't need to think that I'm crazy."

like how annie thought you were crazy

"Annie was a weird lady who didn't deserve to rot into her own carpet, you freak."

Lawrence, wisely, stays quiet. I take my shirt off and look down at myself.

My chest looks like it's covered in road rash, all the wrong colours and aching and hot to the touch. My arm, though, doesn't even look like it's mine any more. The hair is growing thicker. The bruising gives this illusion of muscle that I know I don't have, and it's started spreading down to my fingertips, towards the thick, sharp nails I've resigned myself to.

Lawrence doesn't say anything for a while. When he does, his voice feels closer, like he's standing right behind me and whispering into my ear.

they make us monsters, hunter. they belittle us and treat us like animals. they all deserve it because they make us monsters, but we can make them regret it.

24

That same night, Gabe, Mars and I all sit on a FaceTime call together. Ostensibly, it's an easy way for them to keep tabs on me while neither of them can physically be here. A way for them to have eyes so that if something *does* happen – if Lawrence decides to come after me again, or if my skin starts melting off – they can jump out a window and come running. Or something. No one's really offered any solutions to the problem of the curfew. Or the problem of our parents.

Their parents, anyway. I'm the one without even *a* parent at home. I rest my hand over my shirt and feel the howlite stone against my chest. Right now, I'm desperate to feel anything that isn't bone-deep grief. Even pain.

Mars has spent the last few minutes explaining the irregularity of the patrol schedule near her apartment. She's close enough to be getting an occasional pass, though the cops have mostly stuck to the neighbourhoods directly surrounding the preserve. I stuck myself in front of the window earlier and clocked one car every ten minutes or so.

"The cops aren't even the issue, though," she goes on. "It's my mom and the way she thinks I'll die if I leave to take the trash out. It's so—*God*."

I glance down at my phone. Whatever frustration she's still holding onto, she's taking it all out on brushing her teeth. In his box, I notice Gabe watching her, too. Smiling.

Kissing Mars hasn't dispelled any of my feelings for Gabe. I don't know if that makes me stupid or just a special kind of selfish, but it's not something I feel equipped to sort out on my own. It's not something I want to try and process alone in an empty house. None of this is.

Mars spits into the sink. "Anyway, I figure we can take tomorrow, see exactly what everyone's doing, and we can build a plan from there. My mom is famous for deciding she wants to parent me one day and then going right back to not giving a shit the next."

Gabe hums. "Uh-huh. My mom is famous for whatever the opposite of that is."

"Okay, so either you sneak out of school when we need you to, or we stage a kidnapping so your mom can blame me, not you."

They start going back and forth on the believability of Mars kidnapping *anybody*, let alone a guy who's built like Gabe. As I listen to them, my hand goes to my neck. Under my shirt, the silver chain tickles my skin.

An ugly feeling catches in my chest.

"Hey, guys, I'm gonna go to bed," I interject into the first moment of silence that I can. "Talk in the morning?"

Both Gabe and Mars say something that sounds like goodbyes, but I'm not really listening to them. I hang up and swing my legs over the edge of the bed. "Lawrence?"

yes?

"I don't want them to get hurt by any of this."

He answers: *if they try to intervene, it's only their fault.*

I clench my jaw. "I'm not asking. They don't get hurt, okay?"

what difference does it make? they don't get to stand in the way. i thought you didn't want other people making decisions about what you could become?

I walk over to the mirror on the back of my door and glare at my own reflection. "They're my friends. Whatever they try to do—"

whatever they try, their memories of you will always be shallow and incomplete because they don't have a clue what this is like. they don't have a clue what you're going through.

No, they don't. I shut my eyes and take a deep breath.

Lawrence goes on: *your friends are cis before anything else, hunter. in the end, they're no better than riley or ethan.*

"Bullshit."

they'll always choose each other over you because they are cis, and you are trans. riley and ethan showed you how it works. i know you aren't dumb. i know you know i'm right.

"Shut up," I mutter, but there's no venom to it. The words

settle under my skin, their roots braiding between my veins. "Riley is—"

you don't need to lie to me hunter. i'm literally in your head. i know you. and i'm the only friend you have in the world right now.

I bring my hand up to my throat again. The silver chain tickles, and the more I focus on the feeling, the more it feels like burning. "Okay, sure. You're my friend. So, explain what I'm *becoming*."

something better.

"Do you really believe that?"

Lawrence takes a second to respond to this one. *not at first. but the longer i spend like this, the more comfortable it becomes. the less i miss what i used to be.*

My hand falls to my chest. I can picture the bruises. The blight I can do nothing about but observe as it spreads. "I mean, don't you ever think about—"

no. no, i spent my entire life worrying about getting clocked, about the people who would see me and realize what i am. i hated that feeling of other i hated that i'd spent my entire life correcting myself and for what for some stranger to look at me and decide no none of this matters you'll always be a girl you'll always be transgender never cis never cis

Pressure swells behind my eyes. Pulsating as it intensifies. I grimace and shut my eyes.

when i was lawrence i was never lawrence. i was just trans. never a real man, only a lesser imitation. comparative. nothing i could do to myself could ever change that. but now that i'm this, i am only this. not a trans-anything. just me.

The headache subsides as steadily as it came. I stare at my reflection and think about what Lawrence is saying. He's not wrong, I guess. There'd be no more worrying how I measure up to boys like Ethan. No more *Frankentits*.

Not a trans-anything. Just me.

Lawrence's voice swims around in my head. *when you're like this, your body is yours. nobody can take it from you. a lone wolf is a dead wolf, but you never have to be alone again, hunter. for the first time in your life your body is about to be yours. and you'll have me with you.*

I look down at my hand and flex it, watching the movement of the muscles as they shift under my discoloured skin. If I shut my eyes, it doesn't even feel like it's *my* arm. It feels like I've shoved my hand into a glove, distant and slightly removed from what my brain is telling it to do. I try to imagine this sensation spread out across my entire body.

My chest constricts with claustrophobic panic.

you can't be afraid of it.

I scoff and drop my hand away, shaking it until my skin stops feeling so tight. "Right. Like you weren't afraid *at all*."

you shouldn't *be afraid. i know that now. the body you have now, this life, it isn't worth saving. not when you can have so much better.*

I turn the lights off like it can do anything to obscure the inside of my head, which ping-pongs back and forth between hating what he says and wanting to lean further into it. It doesn't feel like he's just telling me what he thinks I want to hear. He's been through everything I've been through, felt everything I'm feeling.

I sit back on the edge of my bed and stare at my hands again in the almost-pitch darkness. Without all the ugly details that the light reveals – the hard bumps where the skin has risen around the teeth marks, the ugly colours of the bruises – it's a little easier to imagine how something like this might work. I take the slightly disembodied sensation around my hand and apply it to my whole body again, trying to give it a genuine chance. I try to imagine this body as unequivocally mine.

No more *trans*.

Then I remember the dream – the way Lawrence's jaw *snapped* as whatever was inside him clawed its way out – and I get really scared really fast.

Lawrence is silent as I rush into my dad's bathroom. But I know he's there, watching me in whatever way he does. He's a warm, strangely solid presence at the back of my head. For the first time, I wonder if there's a literal *something* growing there. I don't imagine it matters. Even if there was, I couldn't do anything about it.

I find a small toolbox underneath the sink and pull a pair of pliers from it. I take them into my bathroom, wondering if it's presumptuous of me to worry about getting blood in a room that isn't mine. To assume I'm gonna be human long enough to face consequences if I do.

Lawrence doesn't tell me *stop* or *don't*, not even as I press my tongue into the tooth that shouldn't be there. He doesn't try to convince me that my efforts to literally prise the rotten parts of me out are in vain.

Instead, much like God, Lawrence is a passive viewer to my desperation.

There's nothing wrong with the tooth that shouldn't be there, aside from the obvious. It's not rotting out of my skull, but because of the pliers, it comes out much easier than the first tooth did. There's also a whole lot more blood.

I think it's a molar. It's fat and jagged and inhuman. It bounces off the mirror before coming to a skittering stop on the counter, leaving tiny little blood spots in its path.

There are tears in my eyes and a noise coming from my throat with every haggard breath. Somewhere between a sob and a scream.

For a moment, lashing out feels good. It was my choice, and it got the smallest piece of this *thing* out of me. But Lawrence doesn't say anything. He doesn't have to. This is a tantrum that doesn't do anything to hurt him or change what's rapidly coming towards me.

The adrenaline fades, the sting of blood cascades down my throat, and I'm just as hopelessly screwed as I was before.

25

I don't sleep. Some of that is the pain. *A lot of it* is the pain. The only reason my mouth slowly starts to feel better is that the throbbing eventually results in a headache that's thirty times worse.

When I do sleep, it's the kind that feels like blinking. By the time the sun leaks in through the blinds, I feel like I've been awake the whole night. The only reason I know I've slept at all is that I have a number of missed messages.

(YESTERDAY 11:21 PM)
MARS BAR
text me when you wake up or else <3

GABE
just checking in. night okay?

DAD
Give me a call before school today

After a moment, I delete Dad's texts completely.

On some level, I know I'm being cruel, but I'm driven by an exceptionally childish refusal to apologize first. Or at all.

It's just past eight when I pull myself out of bed. My head is spinning from exhaustion and the lingering pain inside my mouth. I don't even remember that I'm still wearing the necklace until I go to scratch my neck, and my fingers catch on unyielding metal.

The pain is the same as when my drains would catch on my shirt; the movement of something that isn't supposed to move.

I stop, breath stuck in my chest. With shaking hands, I pull my shirt away from my chest and look down at myself. The necklace is long enough that I can see the howlite stone resting at the top of my sternum, and where the skin around my collar has started melting away.

The floor nearly falls out from under me. I stumble backwards, fingers twitching around my shirt. My skin hasn't totally closed over the chain yet, but there's a ring around my neck that has the same look as melted candle wax.

The first thought that comes to mind is: *Get it off. Rip it off.*

Instead, I hurry into the bathroom and flip the shower head to its gentlest setting. As soon as I step under its spray, the sting of the water nearly makes me hit the ceiling. I grip the shelf in the wall and clamp my mouth shut to keep from screaming until the burning finally, slowly starts to taper off.

I wait for several minutes longer before I carefully reach back and feel for the clasp.

Unsurprisingly, that's caught in my skin, too. I fumble with it, the water at my feet turning salmon pink whenever my grasp slips and my jagged claw-nails nick the already injured skin. I can feel Lawrence watching, though he never says a word.

Eventually, I shut the water off and sink to the floor. The back of my neck throbs in time with the frantic flutter of my heartbeat. A tingling sensation starts crawling up into the base of my skull, like Lawrence has started moving around. I shudder and scratch at the back of my head until the skin hums with heat.

The whole house feels like it's holding its breath, silent aside from the sound of water dribbling from the shower head and whatever ragged hiccup keeps rising up into my throat.

It never ends. Every time I think I've broached the acceptance stage of grief, something else comes shrieking towards me.

Finally, I dry off and get dressed: long sleeves and snow pants and gloves that are just as much for the cold as they are to hide my claws. My tongue flicks towards the empty space in the back of my mouth. The ticklish feeling across my skin persists, and I finally realize it's not Lawrence (or, at least, not *entirely*). It's the jitters.

Impulsively breaking a government-mandated curfew is a

bad idea. But I'm going to die inside this house if I stay here. Or – I'm going to *turn*, and I'm not sure if that's any better. If I try to wait for somebody else to kill Lawrence, or even if I just wait for Mars and Gabe to find a way to sneak past their parents for a couple hours...

Well, one night alone and I've ripped another molar out of my head. And spending all day arguing with Lawrence won't stop the silver chain from eating even further into my skin.

I have the monkshood. I know where Lawrence is, or I at least have a pretty decent idea of where he *might* be.

getting yourself arrested isn't exactly what i'd call a great plan.

I ignore him and zip my jacket up. Hard enough to know I have to kill someone; harder still to have that someone living inside my head as a now-semi-permanent resident. I grab the monkshood and shove it into my backpack. I manage to take two steps before I stop and think about the logistics of this. How long it'll take me to reach back, unzip the bag, pull the monkshood out, open each Ziploc—

With a sigh, I sling my backpack onto the bed, take the monkshood out, and tuck it under my arm instead. Fewer steps to getting the monkshood if Lawrence is charging at me.

what do you even think you're gonna do? force it down my throat?

"Might start thinking about it," I answer sharply.

I leave the backpack on the bed and my phone on the charger. There's another voicemail from my dad and a few texts from Gabe and Mars that I've left unanswered. My breathing's gotten loud in my own ears as I walk into the kitchen and grab a knife from the wooden block.

seriously, hunter, think ahead for a minute.

"I am," I mutter. "You get catty when you're scared."

and you get stupid. think. what happens when you get caught?

"I won't."

you will, hunter, and then what? you're a minor. nobody's home. you wanna be surrounded by a bunch of pigs when it's time for your rebirth?

I walk into the mudroom and sit down on the edge of the bench, dragging my boots over. I try not to think too hard about the image he paints. "Well, I'm not just gonna sit here and *wait* for my body to explode."

it doesn't explode.

"Whatever."

i'm just asking you to think about what you're doing before you go and do it. or think about what happened on friday and ask yourself what's going to be different this time.

I pull the laces tight and sigh.

what do you need to hear to feel better?

It's such a hard pivot that for a moment, it does stop me. I frown and rest my arms on my knees. "What?"

i mean, i didn't die. i'm trying to tell you about everything that's great about this and you're not listening. so, what can i tell you that's gonna make you not scared?

Not much. Not unless he can tell me that he's cured me from afar and promises to fuck off somewhere where I'll never have to deal with him again. I resist the temptation to make that my genuine answer, though, and hang my head between my shoulders.

"Can you promise you're not gonna hurt my friends?" I try.

It'd be wrong to say that I hear Lawrence sigh, but that's the kind of vibe I get from the stretch of silence between my question and his answer.

wasn't ever the plan to kill them. ain't interested in biting them and leaving them alive, either. not trying to add a bunch of cis people into the mix, and you already know what i think of your friends. if they keep their hands off me, i'll keep my hands off them.

That's probably as close to a *yes* as I'm going to get. I nod and squeeze the monkshood bag. I don't want to ask questions I already know the answers to – like *does it hurt?* – and there's no point in begging for anything he's already refused to give me.

do you remember what i said the other night about what we can do?

I open my eyes and nod.

well, i meant it. i can see all the anger you've got building.

"Okay, you aren't *goading me* into wanting to claw somebody's face off." I shake my head and stand up, wondering why the hell I was listening to him in the first place. "Nobody deserves that."

ethan does.

I falter. "Fuck you."

you've fantasized about hurting this guy too many times, you don't get to act offended because i'm the one bringing it up.

"No, f—" I cut myself off and press my lips together. Then, I bite out, "I'm only leaving this house to kill one person and that's you. So shut up."

I've just pulled the back door open when I hear the sound of two car doors opening and closing.

It shouldn't even draw my attention, except that school's been in session for more than an hour, everybody else is at work, and none of the cops driving by have so far stopped and got out of their car. I frown and step slowly back inside before I walk towards the front of the house.

My first hope is that it's Mars. Of the two, I expect her to sneak out of school far more than I do Gabe. But as I get closer, the voices coming in through the broken window are both distinctly male.

I turn the corner just in time to see somebody's hand push the cardboard off the windowpane. The tape *rips* before the cardboard flutters to the ground.

"Killer aim, dude." Ethan's voice hits like ice-cold water over my skin.

The hand pulls back. "Swore I was gonna miss and hit the door."

That would be Damien. I stand frozen at the other end of

the hallway, listening to them talk to each other. There's the sound of metal against metal.

I take a few stumbling steps backwards, boots squeaking against the floor. The sounds of whatever Damien and Ethan are doing abruptly stop. My mouth goes dry as I stop, too, and wait for one of them to poke his head through the broken window and see me.

"You think somebody's home?" Damien asks instead.

"No," Ethan says. "No, his dad's always gone, and Riley said his mom lives, like, down south. We're fine, just hurry up before somebody sees."

The next sound is that of something heavy and wet slapping against the door.

Pepto-Bismol pink splatters onto the windowpane, even more flecks hitting the floor. I flinch, but even as the sound of Damien and Ethan's laughter fills the air, I don't budge. I stare at the tinier bits of pink paint on the floor until I hear the sudden roar of the truck driving off.

It's objectively the least awful thing to happen to me all week. It still makes me so angry that I nearly throw up.

hunter.

"Shut up." I wipe my eyes on my sleeve and march back to the mudroom. "Just shut up."

Lawrence, for once, does. I'm so angry I think I could walk up to Lawrence and take him down with nothing but my two hands.

I'm still blinking back tears when I rip the back door open and find him standing there.

I scream and fall backwards.

All at once, my brain attempts to jump from anger to survival mode. As soon as I hit the floor, my hands scramble to try and get the Ziplocs open, except my gloves are bulky and I've flown right past *survival mode* and gone to *panic*.

And then my entire body runs cold.

My brain screams at me to run, to get the monkshood and fight like hell. But I can't move. My hand is gripping the bag, but I can't lift it. My other hand is pressed flat into the floor, equally immobile.

The hardwood creaks. I lift my eyes.

Lawrence has nosed the door fully open and stands in the doorway. He's *huge*, and I don't think all of that is just the fact that I'm on the floor. Up close and unable to run away, I can see that his eyes are the colour of dark amber, and his fur is matted in a number of places where blood dried and hardened to crust. Heat and the musk of death roll off him in waves.

He takes a step properly inside, and the spell breaks.

I scramble backwards until my back hits the wall and I take a gasping breath. The bag crinkles against my hand and the floor, and the sob that tears its way out of me hurts as if it were a physical thing.

Once it starts, I can't stop. Everything feels bad, unfair and wrong and no matter what I do or don't do, the worst keeps *happening*. And then I cry long enough that I can't catch my breath, and that exacerbates everything even further.

In between gasps, I realize that Lawrence has slowly padded over. He towers above me silently, not even a voice in my head.

Then, without warning, he brings himself down and presses his snout into my sternum.

Oh.

All at once, my body goes warm. The steady feeling not just of heat, but *comfort*. I take a sharp breath in and at last, I can finally hold it before I exhale.

For the first time in probably a month, I can breathe.

they're not going to stop. you know that.

Half hysterical, I nod. I know.

they're worse than annie was.

My brain doesn't process that one as easily. But as my fist loosens around the Ziploc, Lawrence's voice wraps itself tighter around my head.

you saw what i did to her. imagine what you could do to him.

26

I know that something had to have happened after that. Something in between where that sentence settled and where I wake up with my face pressed into the floor.

There's an awful crick in my neck that aches even worse when I push myself upright. I'm fully dressed, from my gloves all the way to my boots. The back door is open, softly rocking back and forth in a late-night breeze. There's no snow, but my face is stiff with the cold.

It takes about thirty seconds for my brain to move beyond groggy confusion.

Ethan. Paint. Lawrence. Monkshood.

The monkshood.

My heart flies into my throat as I look around. Thankfully, the mudroom is small, and just a few panicked seconds go by before I find the Ziploc bag under the bench. The monkshood is still inside. Only the outermost bag has been opened, like I left it.

Relief.

The next thing I do is scramble to my feet, slam the door shut, and lock it.

I press my head against the door and let out a long exhale. My body feels heavy. I can attribute some of that to the small breakdown I had, because crying and then going to sleep has only ever led to me feeling like death the next morning. But it also feels like...I've shrunk inside my body. Like my skin has suddenly become a size too big for the rest of me, and puppeteering it has subsequently become that much harder.

"Lawrence?" My voice shakes.

No answer, not from inside my head and not from within the house. I leave the mudroom and check each room just in case. Thankfully, I can't find any sign that he got any further inside than the mudroom. Nothing torn apart, no destruction of any kind.

I end at the front of the house, staring at the pink paint splatters on the window tarp fluttering softly in the air. It feels just as much like Ethan is trying to stain me with his idea of girlhood as it does that he is trying to stain me with *himself*. He wants to be the one reminding people of what he thinks I really am.

I sit with my back to the door and exhale, and my attention slowly returns to the monkshood in my hands.

Lawrence doesn't want me dead. That much I already knew; he doesn't want me dead if he can see me turn. But I don't understand why he left me with the monkshood. I don't understand why he came here at all.

The longer I sit here, ears ringing and still half asleep, the more I think I do.

Lawrence isn't gone from my head completely. If I focus, I can feel the distinct weight of him at the back of my mind. That fuzzy uncomfortableness of being watched. That's him. He's not gone completely; he's ignoring me.

He wants me to feel the silence. Wants me to realize what it's going to be like without him. The kind of people and things I'll be returning to.

I turn the monkshood in my hands. I think he's asking me to trust him.

It isn't hard to find where Ethan lives. A couple of hours on Facebook, the right people with public profiles posting the right pictures. A big, stupid blue pickup truck sitting in the driveway.

Not long after, I nod off on the couch, I guess desperate for some rest that isn't on hardwood. I wake up and my phone tells me it's Tuesday, nearly noon. The rest of my notifications are—

Well, I'm trying not to worry about that right now.

Instead, I spend my time scraping at the dried paint on the porch. I make enough of a dent that I can get the door open without major struggle. There's still a giant pink glob on the door, staring me in the face. A hate crime that doesn't even make sense unless you know exactly who I am.

My jaw burns from clenching it for so long.

Back inside, I carefully change and try not to snag the necklace on anything. It doesn't hurt if I don't touch. Once I've put the monkshood back into my bag and left the house, it's not long before the final school bell is due to ring. With my bag slung over my shoulder, I look like another teenager walking home from school. A normal kid who doesn't draw anybody else's eye.

It only takes me twenty minutes to walk to Ethan's house.

Ethan lives in a greyish house on a one-way, sun-bleached road. We're further from the preserve, but it's quiet here, too. I stand across the street, staring at the back end of his truck.

I haven't put a tremendous amount of thought into this next part.

The nervous part of my brain wonders if I *need* to do anything more than this. If Lawrence knows what I know and sees what I see, maybe it'll be good enough to show him where Ethan lives. Maybe he can take care of the rest.

Except I know he won't. Lawrence is silent. I force myself to cross the street.

My fingers curl nervously around my backpack strap as I approach his truck. It's still warm; he hasn't been home long. There are one hundred and one things I could do to this truck alone, but all those ideas end in the same horrible image of hurting anybody other than Ethan. Whatever I do, it has to impact him and him alone.

I get nauseous if I think about it too long.

He deserves it, I try to tell myself.

I slip my bag to my front and partially unzip it. The Ziplocs glisten in the midday sun. I can feel the intense weight of Lawrence's eyes at the back of my skull as I pass the driver's door.

The sound of the TV leaks through the front door of the house. I take a deep breath and reach my gloved hand into the bag.

All I need to do is get a piece of monkshood onto Ethan. That's how easy it would be. Knock on the door, let Ethan open it, hand him a flower that people have used to bring down whales, and never, ever have to be scared of him again.

People die from touching it.

He would deserve it, too. For everything he's said, for everything he's *done*, for the way that he and his friends have treated me. He deserves so much worse than the death this flower would give him.

I just need to knock on the door.

Slowly, though, I realize I've been standing here for a long, *long* time without moving. I haven't even taken my hand out of the bag. The silver chain has started to tingle around my neck again, and I'm trying really hard not to think about it getting even further embedded in my skin.

He deserves it, I tell myself again.

The first move I make is a half step back.

One step becomes two, and before I know it, I'm wheeling backwards off the porch. Past the truck and onto the sidewalk. The only thing that stops me from going into the street is that the backs of my legs slam into something metal.

I catch myself and look at the car I've run into. It's a dark green Mini Cooper. A pink and purple dreamcatcher hangs from the rear-view mirror, but it doesn't obstruct the bewildered expression Riley's got on her face.

She blinks. "Hunter?"

Her window is down, voice crystal clear. It makes my stomach twist with dread.

"What are you doing?" she asks.

I open my mouth, but it takes a moment for something to come out. "Walking home."

I watch Riley's eyes flit between Ethan's house and me. Then, she reaches back and presses a button on the door. I hear the sound of locks disengaging.

"Get in," she says.

I shake my head. "I can—"

"You're not walking. Get in."

She doesn't need to say it three times. I bite my tongue and get into the car, setting my bag on the floor and kicking it under my seat.

The twenty-minute walk from Ethan's house to mine is easily a three-minute drive. Barely the length of one "deathwish". My whole body is thrumming with horror and panic and a dazed internal monologue composed entirely of *what the fuck*, but I'm prepared to handle three minutes in awkward silence.

Except we aren't moving.

"What are you doing here, Hunter?" Riley asks, hands gripping the wheel at ten and two.

I briefly debate the merits of scrambling out and sprinting for home. "I wasn't doing anything."

She shuts her eyes. "Hunter—"

"I wasn't!"

"Okay, so I don't see you at school for two days, and then I find you hanging out in front of Ethan's house in the middle of a *lockdown?*"

"You're not gonna believe me no matter what I say, so why even bother asking, Riley?"

I put a gloved hand on the door. Before I can do more than that, Riley hits the lock button, and all the doors *click*. It doesn't *actually* prevent me from simply unlocking the door and getting out; it just makes me stop and think about it for an extra second. The longer it takes me to get home, the higher likelihood that someone notices me.

Then, Riley says, "Ethan admitted to the poster."

It might not be the last thing I'm expecting to hear, but it's certainly near the bottom of the list. I turn to her, frowning. "What?"

Riley winces, like she regrets saying anything in the first place. "When I asked the first time, he told me it wasn't him. But then I asked him again a couple of days ago, and he said it was… I don't know what the hell his excuse was, but he swore to me the poster was the only thing he did. He told me he was sorry about it."

At first, I don't know what to think. But as I settle back into my seat, the silver chain around my neck pulls against my skin. And the ugliness of it all rises quickly back into my throat.

"So, you still believe him over me," I summarize.

Riley stares at me. "*That's* what you got from that?"

"I told you everything he's been doing to me, and the only thing you believe is what *he* told you!"

"He apologized!"

"To *you!*"

Riley's eyes flicker to something behind me, and that's all the warning I get before someone's knuckle taps against the passenger window. I jump, and then hate myself for jumping.

Ethan is right there, leaning up against the side of the car. Staring at me.

I look away and fix my eyes to my shoes. Beside me, Riley sighs and rolls my window down. I flinch at the sound and shrink into my seat. My fingers dig into my legs. Even through the gloves, I can feel the sharp edges of my nails testing the fabric.

“I’m gonna drop Hunter off at his house, baby,” Riley says. “He’s not feeling well. He’s just down the road, I’ll be right back.”

“Oh? That’s too bad.” Ethan’s face comes down to my level, and I force my eyes shut so I don’t have to get a good look at him. “I didn’t realize you lived so close, Hunter. What the fuck did that to your face?”

Rage surges into my throat like a beast of its own. I dig my fingers deeper into my legs to keep from taking a swipe at him.

Then, Riley chimes in, “I told you he still lives near the preserve. After we saw him at the movies. Near where—”

“Oh, right, yeah.” Ethan quickly cuts her off, voice clipped.

All at once, Ethan’s sudden haunting of my house makes sense. Not stalking or even random luck. Riley just *told him*.

“Well,” Ethan sighs and slaps a hand on my shoulder, which sends a cold wave of nausea into my core. “Get home safe, right, buddy?”

I don’t move. My teeth grind into each other. I don’t want him to hear my voice. Not sounding like *this*.

By some miracle, Ethan lets go of me and steps back, and then Riley rolls the window up and finally pulls away from the kerb. If she tries to say anything to me, I don’t hear a word of it. My ears ring. My shoulder burns like Ethan’s hand somehow passed through all my clothes and grabbed me by the bones.

hunter.

I inhale sharply, and Riley turns to stare at me. We're on Eighty-Seventh Street. I can see the edge of my house coming up ahead. I stare at it and try to block out everything else, but all I can think about is Ethan touching me again. All I can hear is his voice.

Nothing wrong with a girl's body.

It'd be fucked if you ruined yours.

Riley slows down. "What happened to your door?"

I grab the door handle and open it. The car jerks as Riley slams on the brakes, the automatic alarm *beep*ing for the open door before I put my feet down on the asphalt.

hunter.

"Shut up," I breathe, running a hand over my face.

"Hunter!" Riley's voice comes on Lawrence's heels.

I ignore them both.

I rush inside, and the moment I have my back to the door, I scream. It's short and shrill and it echoes off the walls. It doesn't even give me the small dignity of making me feel better.

you get stupid when you're scared.

"Shut *up*," I mutter, slapping my hands over my ears as if it'll do anything.

I squeeze my eyes shut and try to remember how to breathe. How stupid am I? To go running after Ethan to try and hurt him. To try and *kill him* when I can't even look at him.

No matter what I do or don't do, it keeps coming back to Ethan. No matter what I do, I'm still defined by *him*.

I drop my hands and rip my gloves off. Before I can think twice about it, I pull the collar of my shirt aside, wrap my hand around the howlite stone, and give it a violent tug.

It does not snap the chain. But pulling it so taut so fast finally rips the chain out from under my skin. My teeth clack with how hard I clamp down on the scream that rumbles through my throat. Blood quickly starts to trickle down my chest.

Trembling, I slide the chain to the side, enough to get the clasp in my hands. A couple seconds later, the chain *finally* falls into my palm. Each breath comes out ragged and uneven as my body pulsates with fresh pain.

It's only then that I remember my backpack – and the monkshood – is still sitting under the passenger seat of Riley's car.

27

While I'm trying to get in touch with Riley, Dad tries to call me twice.

Both times I send him straight to voicemail. I don't have time to deal with him and whatever lecture he wants to give me about what a terrible kid I am from whatever corner of the country he's in. I text and call Riley relentlessly, but there's no acknowledgement. No answer. Nothing but me and my own horrible decisions.

The number of missed calls on my own phone is well into double digits by this point. Even still, I'm startled when I finally break and call Gabe, and he picks up after just two rings.

"Hunter?" His voice is tight. "Are you okay?"

All I manage to get out is: "I think I fucked up."

I don't call Mars. Instead, I wait at the door for what feels like ages, watching the late afternoon sun slowly creep lower in the sky, until I finally hear the sound of car doors slamming shut. I glance out and observe Mars scramble out of his passenger door.

they're just like ethan and riley. they don't need you any more.

I wince and shake my head in a feeble attempt to dislodge Lawrence's voice before I open the door. Gabe is already halfway up the driveway, Mars right behind him. I hear her start to ask, "What the hell is the paint—" before she sees me.

She breaks into a sprint, and I barely have the time to brace myself before she barrels into me. I wrap my arms tightly around her. Then Gabe pushes us all inside and shuts the door behind him.

"Are you okay?" Mars puts me at arm's length and looks me over before quickly zeroing in on the flesh wound around my neck. "Oh, holy shit—"

"What happened?" Gabe asks.

"I'm getting a towel, that's still fresh." Mars lets go of me and runs for the kitchen.

My head feels like it's spinning. There's not even the joy of seeing my friends again. Just the same stress and nausea twisting around in my guts.

Gabe looks as panicked as Mars is acting, but he's holding himself extremely still. One hand is white-knuckled around his equipment bag, which apparently hasn't left his side despite the curfew. His gaze flickers down to my neck in short, brief ticks.

"Riley has the monkshood," I blurt out.

Tactful.

Gabe frowns. "What?"

I wince. My mouth feels dry. "I left my backpack in her car by accident—"

"What were you doing in her *car?*"

I open my mouth to give some kind of answer, but then Mars's boots come squeaking down the hall. She's moving a mile a minute, though her hands are gentle as they pull the neckline of my shirt aside. The wet towel she presses into my skin is freezing. I flinch away.

"Sorry," Mars whispers. She doesn't stop, though, just keeps wiping at the dried blood she can reach without taking my shirt off.

Gabe makes a noise. Almost a laugh. I look up at him.

His jaw is a hard, clenched line. "We were calling you. Two days of trying to make sure you were okay, you can't even send a thumbs up, and you left the house to be with *Riley?*"

Something ugly twists in my chest. "I wasn't *hanging out* with her."

Mars looks between us, like she's only just become aware of the tension in the air. "What about Riley?"

Gabe ignores her. "Then what were you doing?"

I don't know how to begin to explain that. I shake my head. "Nothing."

"Nothing," he repeats. "Just talking to Riley. Not us."

Mars opens her mouth.

I beat her to the punch. "I was alone, okay? And I wasn't thinking, and I got scared, and I thought that—"

Gabe's eyebrows go up. "You thought what? What's Riley done that Mars and I haven't been doing this entire time?"

Mars turns to him. "Dude, chill."

"You don't get it, Gabe," I grit out.

"What don't I get? You're my best friend—"

"And you're not trans!" I snap. "You will never know what any of this is like, so stop pretending that you do!"

Something dark passes through Gabe's expression.

Before I can keep going, Mars finally puts her body fully between us. "Okay, *both of you*, chill the fuck out."

I'm still holding the argument on my tongue, but Gabe turns on a dime and literally stomps away. There's no slamming of any doors this time, but just like that, he's gone.

A second ticks by in the tense, lingering silence. The anger coagulates into something cold and claustrophobic in my stomach. I feel nauseous again.

Mars glares down the hall after Gabe, though her eyes soon return to me. "Are *you* good?"

Not at all. But now that everything has slowed down for a second, I feel like I can breathe. "I'm good," I manage.

Her expression slowly softens. She nods, exhales, and gives me another hug, this time taking care to gently wrap her arms around my chest and not my neck. It's not a lot of comfort, not when it feels like the whole world is starting to melt around me, but it's not nothing.

"How did you guys get here?" I ask into her shoulder.

Mars huffs and pulls back, fumbling with her coat before taking a folded piece of paper out. "*Necessary commute*," she says, unfolding the paper to reveal the schedule from work. "Gabe was gonna pretend to be Bryan if we got pulled over."

"But your—"

"All parents are at work, and we're lying through our teeth every time they ask." She smiles bashfully. "We probably have two hours before they get home and call the cops."

Before I can say anything more, I feel my phone start buzzing in my pocket. I jump, my thoughts going straight to Riley as I take it out.

It's Mom.

That stops me. Mom *never* calls. Especially if I haven't called her first. My brain floods with sudden, paralysing fear that something might've actually happened. What could've happened that she'd be calling me?

Mars puts her hands on my cheeks and lifts my face to hers. "Take it. I'll handle Gabe. We're good."

Things could not be falling apart more completely nor at any faster rate, but I can only handle one unending disaster at a time. I nod. Mars smiles and presses a kiss to my forehead before hurrying down the hall. I wait until she's out of sight before I carefully reach back, open the door, and step onto the porch.

I leave the door open a crack, and stand facing the preserve. Just in case.

Then I finally pick up the phone. "Hello?"

"Hey. There you are." It's my dad's voice that comes through on the other end.

I wince. "Dad. Hi."

I quickly pull the phone away from my ear to check the contact name, like I might be hallucinating. It does say *Mom*, which I guess tells me that Dad's ended up in Texas.

"Sorry if I scared you," Dad says. "You weren't picking up for me, so your mother thought we might give her phone a try."

"Right. Sorry, it's, uh… I've been meaning to call you."

I'm a terrible liar.

Dad hums in acknowledgement. "Well, I'm not allowed back inside until I talk to you, so I'm glad I got you on the first try."

That startles a laugh out of me as I suddenly picture him sitting on one of the porch chairs, my mom watching him from the window, her arms crossed sternly over her chest. It almost makes up for the faint but emerging sense of disappointment that it's not *her* on the other end of the line. And the confirmation that he's only doing this because he *has* to.

For what it's worth, I've never been able to figure out the dynamic between my parents. They never had massive fights when they were married – fighting would necessitate my dad being home – but the divorce made them strangely more amicable towards each other. Whenever he ends up in Dallas, he usually crashes in the guest room at Mom and Gary's house.

"Right. Uh, what's up?" I ask, carefully sitting down and trying not to make a noise when a sharp pain zaps through my chest.

"There's...well, I guess the first question is, are you okay? Your mom and I saw something about a lockdown. What's happening?"

"Oh, uh, just some coyote with a wild hair up its ass. They're trying to keep people inside while they hunt it down," I lie, hoping that downplaying it will make this conversation go faster.

Dad grunts. "You seen anything?"

My eyes flick towards the preserve. A patrol car rolls by at a glacial pace, the cop behind the wheel giving me a sideways glance before he continues past. "Nope."

"Good. Stay inside until that's handled."

"I will," I promise absently.

Then Dad says, "Well, anyway, I wanted to talk to you for a minute. Mostly about what was said in the car last week."

I wince again. No matter how poorly it'd go over, there's a part of me that wants to try and explain my way out of this. *Listen, Dad, I could turn into a complete and total monster any second now, all because I let Norman out to pee, so could you please cut me a little slack and parent me some other time?*

"I don't think we made a mistake with you," he continues.

"I mean, to be honest, your mom and I figured you were gay pretty early on. The whole trans thing never occurred to me. *Now*, obviously, we know this was the right thing for you, but back then, my concern was that you were trying to rush into something serious that maybe you didn't fully understand yet."

My molars grind against familiar grooves of frustration. "I knew I was trans a long time before I ever told you or Mom. I didn't *come up with it* on the spot."

"I know, and I'm not…" Dad sighs. "Not trying to make your life any harder than I know it is, kiddo."

I don't say anything to that. I pull my knees into my chest, uneasy about the fact that we haven't started snapping at each other. In fact, this is the most we've talked about *emotions* in…I don't even know, ever?

He goes on, "I still think you're too young to be making these kinds of decisions for yourself, but—"

"But you trust me when it comes to everything else," I interrupt. "You let me stay home by myself all the time. You've been trusting me to keep myself alive since I was twelve."

"That's different, Hunter."

"No, it isn't. You trust me to eat and shower and get to school and not burn the house down. But then you act like me being trans is this impulsive, stupid decision when it's, like, just another responsibility, you know? This is how I'm trying to be responsible for myself. And I— I wish you trusted me with this like you do with everything else, because it's *not* different."

Dad doesn't respond right away.

I take a breath and look out at the preserve and the sky that's slowly started to turn orange with the impending sunset. Mars and Gabe need to get home before their parents. They're both in danger here.

"I still don't understand," Dad says.

I shut my eyes and sigh. I don't have the time or patience for this conversation on a normal day.

"But are you happy?"

I frown. "What?"

"Are you happy? With your transition, the surgery, all that?"

For a moment, I don't know how to answer. My body's been falling apart on me for the last month, and even before that, I hated the thought of looking trans. I hated the idea of being my mom's trans son.

Then I hold Dad's question under my tongue for a little longer and realize how stupid that all sounds. I'm still Hunter.

"Yeah," I answer. "I'm happy."

"Okay. That's all I need. You can help me understand it all some other time."

It's not funny, but it makes me smile a little anyway.

"You all right?" Dad asks.

I nod and swallow the knot that's come into my throat. "Yeah. I'm good. And Dad?"

"What?"

"I don't want to live with Mom."

He chuckles. "We'll keep that between us, okay?"

I nod, but before I can think about anything else to say, my phone buzzes against my ear. I frown and look down at the screen.

The sight of Riley's name makes my heart leap into my throat. I force myself to swallow it and hurriedly put my phone back against my ear. "Hey, Dad, I gotta go. I'll talk to you later, okay?"

"Sure. You'll probably be asleep by the time I get home, so I'll try and catch you before school tomorrow."

My mouth opens, but my response falls apart at the back of my tongue. "You what?"

"I told you; I'm flying in tonight. Leaving once I'm done talking to you, I should be back in Chicago anywhere between nine and ten. I'll talk to you in the morning?"

It feels like my heart's gotten stuck where it sits in my throat. "Okay," I manage. "Talk to you then."

It's only after I've hung up that I realize how much tension has found its way into my shoulders. I wonder if I should've said something different. Told him I loved him. Something that a good, considerate son would do.

Except if he's coming home tonight, he's gonna come home to maybe the least safe house on the block. To the least safe *son* on the block.

I quickly find Riley's missed call. I press my thumb against her name and stare at the screen for one, two, three rings before I see the call connect.

"Riley?" I take a breath before the words come falling out. "Listen, I'm sorry about earlier. I know I was being a jackass, but I really need—"

"Holy shit, is *that* what you sound like on the phone?" Ethan's voice stops everything. "You sound like my sister."

My heart starts racing. "Where's Riley?"

"Bathroom," he answers dismissively. "Doesn't matter. She's not interested in talking to you because of whatever you two were arguing about earlier. What *did* you do this time?"

"None of your business."

"Really? None of my business why Riley caught you crawling around in front of my house like the little freak you are?"

My eyes flit to the pink-stained door to my right. "Doesn't feel great when somebody stalks your house, does it?"

"If I ever catch you—"

"I don't fucking care about your house, dude, I just want my bag back."

There's the distinct sound of rustling. "Your bag, yeah, I got that from the hundred texts you sent. What do you got in your bag that's so—"

He goes quiet. The sound of my own breathing suddenly becomes too loud in my ears.

"The fuck is this?"

I don't give an answer, stuck on imagining Ethan's nails digging into the monkshood stems.

Ethan sighs. "You know what? Fine. You're losing your mind over flowers. Stop bugging us about it and get it tomorrow."

"You bring it tonight, I'll apologize," I blurt out.

I don't have a clue where that comes from. Although I've never responded very well to someone else having their hands around my reins. It's a knee-jerk, desperate appeal to the one thing I know he cares about: his ego.

Ethan's tone is reserved. "Apologize for…?"

"You know what," I snap, already losing my nerve. "You come over here tonight, and I'll do it, otherwise you're gonna spend the whole rest of your life wishing you never touched me."

I hang up before Ethan can give me an answer.

It's a stupid gamble. But if I know Ethan at all, he's not going to give me the last word. Won't even let me think I had it. And, just as my stomach starts to twist with the dread of knowing what I've set in motion, my phone buzzes again.

5pm

28

Gabe and Mars are gathered on the couch in the living room when I come back inside, and Gabe is looking just about everywhere but at me. It's tense. As soon as I step into the room, my hands are suddenly sweaty, but I force myself to (very basically) recap the phone call.

Even though he's staring at the seat cushions, Gabe's reaction is immediate: "That's the stupidest thing you could've done."

"I know." I nod and slip my phone into my pocket. It's not an apology.

Mars makes a face, then shrugs. "Well, he's also got the monkshood, so…what can ya do?"

That hangs in the air for a moment. Our apprehension is mutual and palpable. Ethan has no reason in the world to do me a solid, even when there's *not* an active state of emergency. But at least like this, I've put the ball in Ethan's court. I can worry about what I promised him later.

Gabe sucks his lip between his teeth. "Hunter shouldn't be the one who goes."

My head snaps to him. "Bullshit."

"I don't love the idea of you two being out there alone," Mars agrees.

I sigh and shrug. "Then I don't go alone."

"I'll do it," Gabe says.

Mars and I both respond *no* at the same time.

Gabe startles and looks between us.

"I say this with so much love and respect for what I know you *want to do*," Mars goes on, "but this is not the time, place, or situation for an ass-kicking, Haymaker."

I watch Gabe's face twitch.

Mars scoots closer, so she and Gabe are practically knee-to-knee. "Hey, you and Hunter both have, like, five years of hating this prick under your belts. I've only got a month. I'll go with Hunter, I'll keep everything short and sweet, and we'll have the monkshood so we can get back out there and kill a werewolf. Sound good?"

Gabe, in response, looks at me. I stare back at him, confused. What does he want me to do, vouch for his ability to punch his way out of (or into) a problem?

Before I can decide on saying anything, Mars grabs my hand and Gabe's, and suddenly we're all way closer than I was ready to be.

"We work together, we get this done together, and we start having some normal weekends together." She puts my hand over Gabe's. "Hunter and I will get the monkshood. As for using it—"

"If we boil it down, we'll have an easier time using it as a weapon," I interrupt. "Worked for ancient whale hunters, right?"

Mars beams at me. "Then Gabe can get us ready to boil while we're dealing with Ethan. And if we need a tough guy, Gabe, you'll be right here. After that, we can worry about how we get onto the preserve, but *all of it* is done together. Okay?"

We stare at the hand pile: Gabe at the bottom, me in the middle, and Mars on top. It's childish. It's also the first time in days I feel like there's the smallest pinch of hope for me.

"Together," I echo.

"Together," Gabe echoes, but with half the feeling.

He pulls his hand from the pile, gives Mars and I both a tight smile, and stands.

"I'm gonna go…prep, then," he says, gesturing vaguely at nothing before walking towards the kitchen.

As soon as he's gotten slightly out of earshot, Mars turns fully towards me. "Do you *want* to come with me?" she whispers.

I am fleetingly entertained by the idea of Mars going out there and single-handedly wiping the floor with Ethan. Then I return to reality. "I don't have a choice," I answer.

Mars frowns. "Yeah, you do. I don't want to immediately contradict the motivational speech I just gave, but *your* job is surviving. I can handle Ethan."

I shake my head. "No, I don't have a choice."

It takes a second, but my meaning finally reaches her.

For a myriad of reasons, I *have* to do this. Because I'm the reason we're here in the first place, because I need to stand up to Ethan properly for once, because I am so, *so* sick of cowering every time I'm faced with the possibility of just being around him. It can't be Mars, and it can't be Gabe who does this. It has to be *me*.

A slow smile creeps across her face. She nods and sticks her fist out. "Iron lung?"

I complete the fist bump. "Iron lung."

The moment is half good. Because Mars and I are here, but Gabe isn't. And I should probably deal with that now while I have the time.

"I'm gonna go see what's up with him." I nod in the direction of the kitchen.

Mars grins. "Have fun with that."

She winks, which makes my face go hot before I hurry out of the room.

I walk too quickly for my own good. Before I've even prepared myself for what I'm going to say, I'm at the threshold of the kitchen. I come to a loud, awkward stop.

Gabe doesn't even glance in my direction. He's standing near the sink, next to the wooden knife block, making sure each knife is sharp before sliding it back into place. His hair hangs over his face, which is set in an expression of intense neutrality.

The stupid, teenage-boy part of my brain takes a picture for later.

"You know where the pots are?" I ask.

Gabe stops, finally looks up at me, and makes a face. "Of course I do."

It's a small miracle that I don't snark back. Gabe sticks the last knife back into the block and turns to the cabinets to the left of the sink, indeed where we keep our pots and pans. I take the chance to step into the kitchen properly and come up to Gabe's side. When he places the pot in the sink, I turn the faucet on.

For a moment, as the pot fills, we're both quiet.

Finally, I take a breath. "I know you want to help. I'm not trying to shrug that off, it's...well, you're always getting pissed about me *not* standing up to Ethan, right?"

Gabe doesn't say anything. He stares at the stream of water.

Right as I resign myself to being ignored, he shuts the faucet off and braces his arms on the counter. Easily distracted animal that I am, my eyes fall to where his fingers grip the edges of the sink.

Okay, Hunter, seriously.

"I don't want you to get hurt," Gabe finally whispers.

That helps me focus. In fact, the world quickly narrows to Gabe and only Gabe.

I swallow and half joke, "Hey, I'm tough."

It works. Gabe cracks a small smile. "I know."

"I can take care of myself. Or, I could *start* to, at least."

"You can. You *do*, you..." Gabe trails off and looks at the ceiling.

Something in my chest gets skittish in the silence. Eventually, Gabe crosses his arms on the counter. His hair falls over his face again.

"I'm supposed to protect you," he finally breathes. "I'm supposed to get you to school, I'm supposed to help you with your shots, I'm supposed to *be here* when you need me, and I've been fucking that up ever since that thing attacked you, and if something happens again and I'm not there—"

"Hey." I put my hand on his arm to stop him. My chest suddenly feels hollow. "This isn't *your fault*."

Gabe's silence is its own answer.

I take a shaky breath. "I'll be okay. You'll be right here, and I'll have Mars with me."

"Mars isn't *me*," Gabe says.

I blink. Then, as honest as I've ever been, I agree. "Nobody's you."

Gabe goes quiet again. I watch his face, heart beating painfully hard against my ribs.

Would I be an idiot if I said that I didn't realize Gabe felt this...*strongly?*

Well, yes. Because I did know that. This is Gabe we're talking about. The same guy who threatened to kill Damien Hulme in front of our entire gym class. Who beat sparks off Ethan the moment he could engineer the flimsiest excuse to do so. Who, according to Mars, went out of his way to practise injections on oranges so he wouldn't hurt me. Who has been here every single day since this began. Since the bite, since Riley turned her back on me, since Mr Silberg stuck us on a bench together.

But I guess I've known it exactly as it's been laid out here. In chunks. In individual, unrelated incidents. It's not until now that I realize I can fit the pieces together and create a much larger picture. It makes me feel light-headed.

To seem like my brain hasn't started slowly melting, I shrug. "You've also already saved my life this month, so maybe be nicer to yourself."

Gabe finally looks at me, and although he smiles, it doesn't reach his eyes. "Doesn't really matter if I let you run into the same burning building again."

I force myself to hold eye contact with him. "Except I'll come out, 'cause I know you and Mars are counting on me to come out."

The longer we stare at each other, the hotter I feel my face become. Gabe's expression is unreadable. Or, rather, I don't trust my reading of his expression. I don't feel like I've said anything at all, and yet something in my gut tells me I've said too much.

"You look like you want to say something," I finally manage.

His nod is a ghost. "Trying to decide how stupid I want to be."

I crack a smile. "You've been stupid since the day I met you."

Everything that happens next happens fast, but in well-defined actions. Like snapshots. Gabe straightens, reminding me of the several inches he's got on me. I look up at him. There's a long, heavy moment where we're both staring at each other with the same frustrated loneliness of two people on opposite sides of the world from each other, and not people who are close enough to feel the other's body heat.

He's the one who kisses me, but I meet him halfway.

It's not a rough kiss, though it's not gentle, either. It's very *intentional*. A kiss that nearly makes my legs fold under me like a cheap lawn chair. My hands fly to Gabe's arms to keep myself upright.

For the second time in my life, as I'm desperately kissing him back, the world snaps perfectly into place.

I miss the exact moment that Gabe's warm palms come to rest on my cheeks, but they're there when his mouth leaves mine. My eyes open. Gabe is staring at me, his expression once again a jumble of unreadable things. I feel like I can't breathe.

In another world, I must get the chance to do more than gawk at him.

But in this world, we both hear Mars's boots coming up the hall towards us.

Gabe lets me go and takes a step back right as Mars enters

the room. I don't *think* we seem like two people who have just kissed, but I watch Mars pause to look between us anyway.

My face burns. Kissing Gabe hasn't dispelled any of my feelings for Mars.

This is the moment that the exceedingly obvious finally occurs to me: I love them both.

I can't make sense of how that works, let alone how to handle that or what that means for Gabe and Mars, but the thought pops into my head like it's inherent. The sky is blue, it's cold in winter, I'm in love with both of my best friends.

Mars's eyes land on me. "Hey. Big blue pickup truck outside the house."

She tosses my coat to me, which I catch despite my slightly shaking hands.

I look at Gabe. His face betrays nothing. He just nods, and I nod back, and then I'm following Mars to the front of the house.

I put on my coat and zip it up to my neck, wincing when the cold zipper rests against the broken skin. Mars and I both gaze through the broken window and out at the blue bed of Ethan's truck, parked across the street. In front of Annie's house, yellow crime scene tape flutters in the breeze.

Mars and I look at each other, sharing the same expression of distrust.

"Clock's ticking," she breathes, before opening the door and stepping out.

I shut the door behind us and shove my hands into my pockets. My gloves are somewhere inside the house; I have to hope the onset of dusk will make it less obvious that I'll be grabbing my backpack with clawed fingers. As we walk over, the tension in my shoulders incrementally worsens. Especially once I'm close enough to identify Ethan standing near the back of the truck. In the truck bed itself is Damien, his legs dangling off the edge.

He's a surprise. A very bad feeling squeezes my chest. And that's before I realize that Riley is standing there, too.

She's standing on the sidewalk closest to Annie's house. When the breeze kicks up, the deep red of late sunset shines through her hair as it billows behind her. The street lights flicker on right as Riley finally looks up and makes eye contact with me.

If I were feeling generous, I'd almost say that she looks nervous. Ungenerously, she looks impatient. Jittery.

"I'm impressed." Ethan's voice brings me back. "You kept your dog inside."

I turn to him with a glare, and then my eyes lock on the backpack hanging from his shoulder. My lifeline.

The *snap* of a tab directs my attention to Damien, who grins as he sips from a can of Monster.

Mars's laugh is flat. She looks at me and jabs her thumb at Ethan. "He has jokes."

A grin spreads across Ethan's face. "What's your name again?"

"Mars. Pleasure to see you. Now, it's cold and none of us want to get arrested for breaking curfew, so we're just going to say *thank you* for the bag and—"

She takes a step in, and Damien suddenly plants his feet on the ground between her and Ethan. Mars doesn't flinch, but she does stop. I carefully come up to her side.

"*Easy*," Ethan urges as his grin falls. "I've been trying to catch up with this guy. If you don't want to talk, go back inside."

Mars doesn't budge. After a moment, Ethan's eyes return to me.

I swallow and try to find confidence in my voice. "You got it?"

Ethan unzips the backpack, enough to partially pull out the monkshood. Triple-wrapped in Ziplocs.

"Gotta admit, I'm still a *little* curious about this." Ethan tilts his head.

Just as I open my mouth to tell him to fuck off, Mars beats me to the punch. "It's monkshood," she says. "We're trying to kill a werewolf."

I kick her ankle. "*Mars*."

She gives me a look like *I'm* the crazy one, but then Ethan snorts and draws our attention back to him. "Come on, seriously."

Mars echoes him, laughing without a hint of humour. "Seriously. Take it out of the bag if you don't believe me. That shit's crazy poisonous."

I don't think Ethan believes her, but there's an interesting skittishness that flashes behind his eyes when he glances down at the backpack again. Mars is a wild card; he doesn't know her tells for when she's lying.

I look over his shoulder at Riley. She's standing about as far away from all of this as she can be, with that vaguely troubled expression on her face.

"Sure. Monkshood." Ethan shrugs and zips the bag up. "Whatever."

He stops there, and several long seconds of silence tick by before I realize what he's waiting for. Ethan's fulfilled his end of the bargain; now it's my turn.

I take a breath, trying to recover whatever confidence had made me offer this false apology in the first place. But my mouth feels like it's suddenly been shoved full of cotton balls.

Before long, Ethan sighs. "Okay, Hunter, we can make this easy. Riley said she's already told you, but I'll say it again – I'm sorry for what I put in your locker. It was immature and inappropriate."

He couldn't sound more like he was reading off a script, not even if he had the paper physically in his hands. "Thanks," I respond flatly.

Ethan rolls his eyes. "I have apologized, and – hell, Damien, you throw an apology in there, too."

Damien pulls the tab off his can and smiles. "Sorry for what I said about your dick."

Mars scoffs.

My eyes rove over to Riley. Her eyebrows have knitted together as she watches this all unfold, but she still hasn't bothered to interject in any way. I glare at her until Ethan speaks again.

"See? We're all cool here." Ethan drums his fingers against the front of the bag. "Now you apologize, and it's yours."

Mars looks between us and seems to understand what he's asking of me in the blink of an eye. "You want him to say *sorry?*"

"What I want him to say's got nothing to do with *you*," Ethan snaps, "so if you've got a problem with it then you can go right the fuck back inside."

At the same time that I say "*Mars*," Riley finally, warningly says, "*Ethan.*"

"No, don't baby him." Ethan throws a warning hand back to Riley. "He asked for this. He doesn't get to pussy out now."

Mars grabs my hand but doesn't otherwise move. Like she's not sure yet if she should let this play out or drag me back inside herself.

Ethan continues, "It's simple. We were all friends, everything was fine, and then *you* lost your mind over nothing. Instead of being a man about it, you ran to Riley and you lied. And you've been trying to cover your ass ever since." The smile slowly drops from Ethan's face. "I want you to admit that you lied to Riley about me."

On paper, this is as simple as Ethan says it is. I don't have to mean it. I never *intended* to mean it. All I have to do is say two words, burn my pride, and live to hate myself for it later.

I've spent my entire life swallowing back horrible things and kicking down emotions for the sake of keeping the peace. I'm a good trans kid who doesn't complain and doesn't make waves. I keep my mouth shut and head down.

And look where that's gotten me.

"He's a pussy," Damien chirps. "He won't."

"Knock it off," Riley cuts in.

All of a sudden, I understand why Gabe hates her so much.

Ethan pushes off the car and takes a few meandering steps closer. "It's two words. Hell, you can make it one."

He dangles the backpack just out of reach.

I know what it means if we don't get the monkshood back. I also know that what it takes to get the monkshood is contorting myself into the shape of Ethan's lie. And I don't know if that shape is something I'll be able to get out of again.

I squeeze Mars's hand. She looks at me. "You okay?"

"I can't," I whisper.

Mars's expression is tight, a thousand thoughts swirling behind her eyes. "You're sure?"

"You can lie for four years, but you can't fake it for *two words?*" Ethan's voice shifts, however slightly, into something truly angry.

Mars looks up at him with a resolve of steel. "No, we don't

negotiate with fucking terrorists."

"Hunter, please." Riley's voice comes through the air like a small, sharp needle into my chest.

For maybe the first time in my life, it doesn't freeze me to the spot.

"Okay, Hunter, go!" Ethan throws his arms out and the bag swings wildly. Mars starts pulling me back towards the house. "You go, and I'll be sure to tell everybody what they already know. That Hannah Wakesfield is a lying—"

Something inside me snaps. I whirl around and punch him right in the nose.

The tension that had been coiling around all of us explodes. Damien scrambles to his feet like a dog let off the leash. He grabs me by the collar and shoves me to the ground.

My head bounces off the sidewalk and my ears ring. I catch a glimpse of Mars, face twisted in panic as she surges after me. Then Damien cuts her off and pushes her back.

Ethan hauls me to my feet like I weigh nothing. He shoves me into the side of the truck, one hand balled up in my shirt. The other grabs my jaw and forces me to look up. I go still at the sight of blood on his face, a nasty, jagged cut going across his nose.

Claws, I suddenly remember. My thumb must've nicked him.

"That feel good?" Ethan growls. His fingers dig painfully into my cheeks. "You hit like a girl, Hannah. You hit like a *girl*."

A guttural scream tears its way out of me. I start thrashing, trying to get enough distance to land a real punch again.

"Stop it! Both of you!" Riley's voice is a panicked shriek.

Even through the frantic buzz of adrenaline, I still manage to think: *Both of us? Are you kidding me?*

Ethan picks me up and throws me to the ground again. I land on the dying patch of grass outside Annie's backyard, and a new wave of nausea keeps me down. I try to swallow the knot in the back of my throat, try to stand and run, but Ethan easily rolls me onto my back and holds me there. He looks down at me like he's disappointed that he expected any better of me.

The knot rises into the back of my mouth, and I can suddenly taste something *hot*. It tastes like salt and has the consistency of mud, clumpy and strangely dry. For a moment, I worry about choking on my own vomit.

Then, I remember my nightmare. Or, rather, Lawrence's nightmare. The way that the lycanthrope finally forced itself free of his body.

No. I start panicking. *No, no no no no.*

Ethan grins, a manic slice of teeth and giddiness from a man who's finally doing what he's probably always wanted to do. I want to scream, but I can't. There's the weight and heat of liquid in my mouth. Rather than pouring down my throat like blood, it's clawing its way up my tongue. It presses against my teeth. My jaw aches with the effort it takes to keep shut.

Ethan bends down as he drags me up by the collar. He opens his mouth.

Then, in a sudden blur of motion, he's gone. Something sharp clips me on the side of the head, and the world goes fuzzy.

29

For what feels like way too long, all I can hear is a high-pitched ringing. I don't think I lose consciousness, but the world suddenly gets cold and dark and I can't move, let alone think. I sit there, pressing my face into the ground and sucking air in through my nose until I can finally hear the sound of my own breathing.

The weight in my mouth slowly creeps back down my throat.

There's still a very fragile sense of nausea, but while I fight back the urge to vomit, I manage to bring my head up.

A large chunk of Annie's fence has been demolished, bits and pieces of broken wood littering the ground in front of me. From where I am, I can't see the exact path of destruction, but if the streak of glistening blood is any indication, it's gone into the house. As the ringing in my ears continues to fade, I realize how *quiet* it is.

A quick look to the street reveals Riley standing at the front of the truck, mouth slightly agape. Damien and Mars are both near the bed, frozen and staring in the same middle distance behind me. Nobody moves.

Lawrence? I dare to think.

There's no answer. My head feels heavy. So does my entire body.

Nevertheless, I force myself to my feet. Somebody says my name and it passes through my brain like white noise.

I follow the blood streaked along the porch steps and discover that the back door to Annie's house has been completely smashed open. Inside is dark, but I can still see the patches of gore that glimmer in the moonlight. Further in, at the mouth of the hallway where I found Annie's body, is where I see the edge of a blue backpack strap.

Before anybody can stop me, I run for it.

The house is unsettlingly silent, save for the groaning of the floor where my boots hit. At the mouth of the hall, I drop to my knees and grab the backpack. I give it a quick shake, and I can hear the Ziplocs crinkle.

Then, in the darkness ahead of me, I catch a whiff of rot.

My breath hitches in my chest, and I start to stand—

And my body goes cold again.

Lawrence stands in the half-light a couple of feet away. As my eyes adjust to the darkness, I can see there's something hanging from his teeth. I can't tell what exactly it is, but it's not big enough to be a whole body. Just a piece.

The only sound in the world is the blood that drips from

his maw onto the already saturated, crusted-over carpet.

I try to move, to get up off my knees and run back outside, but the most I can do is stare back as my breath comes faster and faster. Lawrence steps closer, the hot stench of blood close behind him. I expect to hear his voice in my head again, but it's silent between us.

When Lawrence presses his nose to my chest, the ringing in my ears vanishes. The aches go away. I'm warm again, and I hate how the first proper move I'm able to make is to bury my hands in Lawrence's fur and cling to him.

The moment ends with a thick *thud*. Something heavy smashes against Lawrence's head, and suddenly *I'm* freezing—

Damien backs up until he bumps into the living room couch, holding a splintered board from Annie's broken fence in his hands. From what little I can see of his face, he looks *terrified*.

Lawrence flies at Damien with bared teeth. He gets him by the meat of his throat and takes him to the ground. There's no scream. Only a gasp, and then a *crunch*.

I grab onto the backpack with both hands and run for it.

Belatedly, I realize that Damien just tried to save me.

I burst back into the yard, where I nearly plough into Mars at the bottom of the porch steps. She catches me and keeps us both upright, and I watch her eyes take me in in pieces: the backpack, the blood smeared on my jacket, whatever horrified expression is on my face.

Mars says nothing, just grabs me by the wrist and pushes me ahead of her.

As we clear the broken hole in the fence where Lawrence took Ethan through, I see Riley, still standing beside the truck and staring at Annie's house. She hasn't moved an inch.

I stop so quickly that Mars runs right into me.

As I hear her start to say, "What the—" I pivot and impulsively run for Riley. Because she can't just *stand there*. I grab her arm, with the intent to drag her into my house and figure out the rest later.

Riley screams and immediately attempts to rip herself out of my grasp. Startled, I let her go and take a step back. She looks down at her arm, and then at my hand, still outstretched in her direction. I watch her eyes linger on the jagged edges of my nails.

"What the fuck is wrong with you?" she asks, barely above a whisper.

My heart takes a funny beat in my chest.

Just as Riley takes a few shaky steps away from us, Mars grabs my arm and yanks me backwards. Lawrence tears through the empty space and slams into the side of the truck.

The truck screeches sideways a couple of feet, but miraculously stays on all four wheels. I don't think Lawrence *meant* to hit the truck as hard as he did, but it doesn't take more than a few seconds for him to shake it off. I watch his eyes focus on me and Mars behind me, who's still trying to drag me back to my house. Then, he turns and locks onto Riley, whose face has gone totally white.

A low growl fills the air.

I don't think. I just swing my backpack as hard as I possibly can.

It's practically empty, although I think this ends up working to my advantage. It means that all the little zippers and the handful of enamel pins pick up a decent amount of speed before slamming into Lawrence's side.

It can't possibly hurt him, but it gets his attention. Lawrence whips around and *snarls*.

"*Don't*," I snap. Like I'm talking to just another dog.

I can see Riley over his shoulder. The moment Lawrence turns his attention to me, she takes off. Doesn't throw so much as a backwards glance, or anything that'd indicate I just saved her life.

she came here with ethan she's stood by him all this time she would've let you die if the roles were reversed

Lawrence's voice echoes inside my head, louder than it's ever been before. So loud I almost forget that Mars can't hear it. I take a few steps back, and she thankfully stays behind me as I do.

"I don't care," I breathe. "She doesn't matter any more."

Lawrence's lip pulls back, canines stained red.

In the distance, I hear a door slam. I look up and see Gabe running down the driveway.

Lawrence's jaws snap at the backpack, and I don't know how I manage to yank it back in time to avoid losing it all over again. I swing the backpack at his face and hope that I manage to get something in his eye, where it hurts. Then I let Mars grab me by the arm and we finally run.

Gabe stops at the edge of the sidewalk as soon as we come out from behind the truck. I can tell the exact moment that Lawrence comes after us, because that's the moment that Gabe's expression shifts. Mars sprints past him, like a bullet going straight for the door. I can hear the clatter of claws on the asphalt behind me.

Lawrence doesn't want to kill me. I'm not worried about that. I'm worried about what he'll try and do to either Gabe or Mars, or what he might try to do to neutralize me until it's too late.

Gabe grabs me by the arm and tugs me forward right as I hear Lawrence's teeth *snap* over my shoulder. Missed me by inches.

We practically fall through the threshold into the house. I blindly throw my bag further inside before spinning back and slamming the door shut – onto Lawrence's snout. He yelps. I open the door enough to slam it again and again until he finally takes the hint and jumps back. Even once I've closed the door, I can still hear him whining as he slinks away.

I curl up on the floor and put my head in my hands. My brain is a haunted house, a myriad of ghosts dancing across my eyelids. Ethan's grin. The *crunch* of Damien's neck. The way Riley looked at me when she asked, *What the fuck is wrong with you?*

I take a shaking breath in, then out.

A hand comes down on my shoulder. I look up. Gabe kneels next to me. He touches my forehead and gingerly traces his finger along what must be a new bruise. The skin is tender where he touches.

"Uh, Ethan's dead," Mars announces, voice shaking. She's lying down, rubbing her eyes with her palms and breathing heavily. "Just…by the way. He's like, super, *really* dead."

Gabe looks between us.

"Damien, too," I breathe, just loud enough for him to hear.

Gabe's expression becomes sombre. Behind us, Mars sits up and sniffles. We all signed up for this, to some extent, but watching a person die is *a lot*. Watching someone die like *that* is another thing entirely.

Something *slams* into the front door. Everybody jumps. Gabe drags us both to our feet as Mars grabs the backpack. A moment later, Lawrence's snout comes through the broken window, teeth-first. He's too big to fit through, but the entire wall shudders with the force of the impact before he withdraws and slinks away again.

Mars grabs Gabe and me by our jackets and starts dragging us further back. "Okay, *she's* pissed, let's—"

"He." I cut her off.

She stops. "What?"

"It's *he*. *He's* pissed."

Under normal circumstances, I can imagine the kinds of jokes that Mars would make – *Even the werewolves are men? Can't women have anything around here?* – but she just stares at me with the same expression as when I called her Marcy. Even Gabe is looking at me sideways.

"How long have you known he's a *he*?" Mars asks.

Anything I could say is only varying degrees of wrong, because I didn't tell her the moment I started hearing Lawrence in my head. My silence quickly becomes its own answer.

Lawrence slams into the door again, something *cracks*, and Mars grabs Gabe and me again. "Okay, *he's pissed*."

We run back into the kitchen, where Gabe has set us up to boil the monkshood down. A box of rubber gloves sits on the counter beside a cutting board, and the burner is on underneath the pot of water. Mars pulls a pair of gloves on before taking the monkshood out and dropping it on the cutting board. She quickly begins severing the roots while I slip out of my jacket and make a mental note to myself: *Power wash the shit out of that cutting board when this is over. And probably everything else in this kitchen.*

"I thought I was dreaming," I try to explain. "It was random at first, just words. The longer it went on, the more I could understand him."

Gabe frowns as he grabs a pair of gloves. "So, you can hear him?"

I flip back through our conversations. "Sometimes. He was just a voice at first, but then I realized he was poking around in my head, looking at memories, and I think trying to… connect with me?"

Gabe's frown deepens, but Mars beats him to the punch. "And what exactly is our lycanthrope telling you right now, Hunter? What part of your *connection* is that?"

I know she's just stressed. I still bristle at her tone. "Look, I thought I was losing my mind, I wasn't trying to *harbour him*. I thought if I told you guys, you wouldn't believe me—"

"Why the *hell* would we not believe you?" Mars asks.

She stares at me like such a thing has never even crossed her mind. And, I realize, it's a fair question. It's what sets Mars and Gabe apart from Riley: they believe me.

They've *always* believed me.

"Hey," Gabe softly puts his hand on my shoulder. "You said it goes both ways?"

I blink back tears and shrug. "I think so. I don't know, it's a *voice*, I don't know how any of this works."

It's as quiet inside my head as it is outside. My stomach flips when I realize I don't know how long it's been since I heard Lawrence.

Mars nearly goes to wipe her eyes before she remembers the monkshood residue on her gloves. She huffs and puts her hands on the cutting board.

"I'm sorry," I offer weakly.

Mars nods and finally wipes her eyes against her shoulders. "It's okay. Ugh. It's okay, I'm just trying to think. There's a lot happening in my brain right now."

Gabe comes up to Mars's side and gently takes the knife from her. She smiles at him, wordlessly thankful. On the stove, I can hear the water starting to bubble. We're at a boil.

I suddenly remember one of the things Lawrence told me a few days ago: that all of this isn't worth saving.

The hell it isn't.

"Hey, guys?" My voice comes out wobbly. I wince.

Mars and Gabe glance at me, an afterthought to the task at hand. "Yeah?" Mars asks.

I swallow, trying to keep my nerves from slipping away. "I wanted to say something. Now, while I have a chance."

Gabe is halfway to the stove, cupping the roots in his hands, when he stops. Mars kicks him in the ankle, and he quickly continues on. "Go 'head, Bambi," he says anyway. "Mars, what's the plan for when this is ready?"

Mars scoops the monkshood flowers into her own hands. "Maybe Hunter plays some Marco Polo with the werewolf and finds him right away."

I frown. "It's not a GPS."

"Yeah, well, a girl can dream."

I clear my throat.

"Right. Sorry. Go."

My hands are shaking. I stare at the table, which feels like the only thing in the room without a judgemental pair of eyes on it, before taking a deep breath.

"Um, I just wanted to say thanks. For still being here." My voice traitorously wobbles. "You're both my best friends, probably the only reason I'm not dead right now, and I love you both more than anything. I mean that in the way that anybody loves their friends, but I…I mean that I really love you both. I love you both so much it scares me, and I don't know what that means, but I wanted to tell you because I kissed you *both* and I really thought that would clear it up, but all it did was make it weirder because it's still…it's both of you."

When I look up, Mars and Gabe are both staring at me.

Then they look at each other, like it's the first time they're seeing each other. I don't know if this is a good thing or if somebody's about to throw a knife.

"Okay." Mars softly breaks the silence and turns to me, suddenly calmer than she's been all night. "We can definitely talk more later. Yeah?"

Well, it's not flat-out rejection. I manage a jerky nod.

"Um, shit. I didn't have anything prepared." Mars peels her gloves off and sets them aside. She thinks about it for a minute. "This has been a really fucked-up month," she finally says, "but I can't imagine anybody else who I'd want to do all this with. So, yeah. What Hunter said. You both mean the absolute world to me now. I love you guys."

My heart swells. Then my eyes drift to Gabe, head down as he squeezes his hands together, and my nerves crackle back to life. His lip is between his teeth. Just as I open my mouth, he speaks.

"I don't think I'm cis," he says, flat and quiet. "I don't know if that makes me trans, or— I don't know *what* it makes me. That's all."

The room was silent before, but this sucks the air out of it.

Mars's eyebrows have shot practically up to her hairline. "Okay," she manages, audibly uneven. "We can talk about that later, too."

Gabe nods. Then he looks at me.

A good friend would say something. A good friend would crack a joke about how I've known this for months and I was waiting for Gabe to finally tell me, and then we'd all laugh and feel perfectly fine about the whole thing.

But I had no idea.

Gabe's trans, I repeat back to myself. *Gabe is trans. Gabe. Is trans. Gabe.*

My head is spinning.

At the base of my skull, I suddenly feel the weight of being watched.

Before I can say anything, the lights go out. I must jump half a foot into the air.

"Oh, sweet baby Jesus." Mars gets her phone flashlight on first. The weak light jerks all over the place. "Matches. Do we have matches? Do we *need* matches?"

"Drawer. Right of the oven." Gabe's voice is steady as it moves around me. There's the rustling sound of his gloves coming off, and then shoes thudding down the hall. When he comes back, his phone flashlight is on, too, and he's got his hockey stick in hand.

My hands are shaking as I pull my phone out. Something about the silence makes my ears ring. It takes a moment longer to place: the heating is off. The power is totally out.

Mars's phone light swivels to the pot. I hear her exhale with relief. "Flame's still going."

"He's here," I finally manage to breathe.

Both flashlights turn to me. "Where's the breaker box?" Mars asks.

From the mudroom comes the horribly familiar sound of wood cracking. Once, twice, then nothing.

Nobody moves. Not one of our lights turns towards the sound. Beside me, the floor creaks.

"Mars," Gabe begins, "in the same drawer as the matches, there should be a big flashlight."

The drawer slides open. Mars shuffles through it. I nervously step backwards. Left foot, right foot, left foot, until my back hits the fridge with a quiet *clank*. Mars swears under her breath. Down the hall, something breaks with a crisp *snap*.

A beam of light finally floods the room and connected hallway, and a mouthful of teeth comes snarling out of the dark.

Gabe swings. The stick *cracks* against the side of Lawrence's head. It doesn't do a lot to slow his momentum, but it probably lets Gabe keep his face. Lawrence skids into the table and knocks it askew, the corner slamming into the stove between Mars and me. Everything goes clattering to the floor.

I jump back, but then Gabe moves into the light and I freeze. The blade of his stick has already broken and limply swings in the air as Gabe readies for another go. Lawrence recovers and launches himself, jaws clamping down onto the stick before they both end up on the floor.

Mars, blessedly, whips into action. I hear the slide of metal, and I look in time to see the light reflect off the knife's blade as she takes it from the wooden block.

For a moment, I think *thank God*.

Then, like a nightmare, I suddenly remember the lycanthrope that bit Lawrence. The one whose head exploded in a shower of gore. Rightly or wrongly, two dots connect.

The lycanthrope that turned Lawrence has been dead since the start. Bloodline severed. Except Lawrence had nothing to do with it.

I scream "*Don't!*" but it's too late. Everything happens at once: Mars brings the knife down into Lawrence's back. Lawrence wails. *Somebody* shouts. Mars rips the knife out so quickly she falls backwards. Then Lawrence takes off down the hall, perhaps injured but very much not dead.

My legs only remember how to move once Lawrence

disappears into the darkness. I run to Mars first, who's sitting with her legs splayed out in front of her and the knife clutched in both hands. I grab her shoulder and she turns to me with wide eyes.

"Think that got him?" she breathlessly asks, smiling with adrenaline.

I shake my head. "You can't kill him. It has to be me."

She frowns. "We know this for sure?"

"*I* know."

That's all Mars needs. She nods and firmly puts the knife in my hands. Even in the poor light, I can see the blood dripping from the blade. Mars only stuck it halfway in. There's a whole expanse of glistening, untarnished steel left.

In front of us, Gabe tosses the broken hockey stick aside. Mars and I scramble to him.

"Are you okay?" Mars asks.

Gabe's mouth is a hard line. "Not really."

Panic seizes me. My eyes frantically comb his body, looking for the injury that I finally find on his calf. It's hard to tell at first, because his snow pants are already dark navy, but then he shifts, and the slashes in the fabric reveal themselves. He's bleeding.

Mars, patron saint of level-headedness in a crisis, pulls her sweater over her head and tells Gabe, "Face me."

He adjusts himself, and Mars ties her sweater around the wound. It's not much, but it's something. I give Mars a once-over and, for whatever reason, focus on the fact that if we end up outside again, she's going to only be wearing trousers and a grey tank top. I grab my jacket from the floor. Once my hand touches the fabric, I realize that I'm shaking.

"Good job stabbing it," Gabe breathes.

Mars shrugs. "I think I just pissed him off."

I hand Mars my jacket. She takes it with a smile.

Here's a fun thought experiment: the lycanthrope that bit Lawrence is dead. But because Lawrence wasn't the one to kill it, he transformed into the lycanthrope that bit *me*. In order to keep from fully turning myself, I have to be the one to kill Lawrence.

Now remember that Lawrence took a swipe at my best friend. Broke the skin. Infected him. How does that affect my next step?

If I were to be able to answer that question for myself, it wouldn't be now, with adrenaline clogging my veins and a slurry of emotions making my mouth taste something like rot. How does this affect my next step? I have no clue.

The panic shifts suddenly into anger. Still clutching the knife, I push myself to my feet and surge towards the hallway. "I told you not to hurt them, you—"

My feet stick to the floor right as I reach the threshold of the hall. I tremble, although I'm at least partially expecting the immobility this time, as well as the snout that comes into the light.

You want me? I glower. *I'm here.*

Lawrence comes more fully into view. His head tilts.

you're still fighting it.

Against my will, my feet wheel my body backwards. Lawrence moves with me, a step closer for each one I take back. From the corner of my eye, I see Mars help Gabe to his feet. They watch the knife clutched in my fist stay there, motionless at my side.

You want ME, I reiterate, though it feels suddenly less like a fact. I say it because I need it to still be true. *Mars and Gabe have got nothing to do with this. It's you and me. We're a pack.*

a pack of monsters, Lawrence agrees, pushing me further back. *me. you. gabe. think about it, hunter. think about what we're capable of and multiply it by the thousands.*

The blood drains from my face. He heard Gabe's confession, too, and it gave him an idea.

Instinctively, I try to raise the knife. It's like trying to lift a hundred-pound weight. I can manage a couple of shaky inches, but the blade never goes any higher than my waist.

can't you see it? town by town, one transsexual at a time, until WE are the ones with OUR teeth against THEIR throats. none of us will ever be alone again.

An agonized whimper drags itself out through my clenched teeth.

put it down, hunter.

An invisible hand prises each of my fingers open, one by

one, until the knife hits the floor between my feet with a sharp clatter.

don't worry. it will be easier for gabe. he'll have both of us.

Just as I start to feel weight on my knees, encouraging me to submit in subservience to this higher power, a heavy *whack!* startles us both. Lawrence whips around, mouth pulled back in a snarl.

Mars has the broken hockey stick raised like a baseball bat. Her eyes widen. Knowing her, she didn't think much further than *distraction*.

Behind her, Gabe catches himself against the wall. Then he disappears into the dark with a horribly off-balance limp.

Mars taps the side of the table with the end of the stick. A growl fills the air.

"Yeah." Her grin is manic. She's edging backwards. Baiting Lawrence towards the darkened hallway, I realize. "You still gotta deal with me, bitch. You want me?"

Lawrence snaps his jaws at her. A warning. Mars jumps, but it doesn't scare her off.

"Come get me," she taunts. "You want me? *Come on.*"

She's already taken off when Lawrence turns to give proper chase. He doesn't move at a sprint, but a trot. This is a race he knows he's already won.

As soon as Lawrence's focus leaves me, my legs turn to Jell-O. I grab onto the counter as I sink to the floor, gasping for breath. It's not that it's *unfamiliar* to have Lawrence in my head. But this has been markedly different. He's stronger. Or I'm weaker. Either way, he's not just a voice in my brain, he's a *force*.

I wonder, absently, what would happen if I stayed here. Lawrence has clearly decided that I'm not a threat any more, if I ever was one to begin with. This night can end very quickly, and very simply. All he has to do is leave me here to fully turn, kill Mars, and begin crafting Gabe as his next great find. The next monster.

It could all be over in a matter of minutes. Which is why I pick the knife up and use the counter to pull myself back to my feet.

As I do, my stomach pitches. I grimace and shut my eyes, until I realize that it's not just nausea. Something inside me is moving again. Something is pressing against the inside of my ribs, pushing out into the tips of my jagged fingers. Something wants *out*.

Down the hall, I can hear the sound of breaking wood. There's a shout.

I take a deep breath. At some point, the flame on the burner went out, but a testing tap against the pot reveals that it's still searing hot.

I hesitate for a moment before lifting my hand. It shakes around the knife, and then I worry about what happens if I drop it into the boiling vat of poison. I worry about what happens if we fucked up and only succeeded in making spicy plant water. I worry about this not working in any way whatsoever.

I slowly lower the knife into the water, inch by inch, until the entire blade is submerged. The air above my hand is smouldering. I only manage about ten seconds before the heat is too much. When I pull back, though, I can see the gentle shimmer of substance on the blade. It seems almost like a very thin, watery jam.

I very nearly reach out to poke at it, to see how it feels.

Thankfully, I have enough of a brain left to *not*, and instead stare down the dark hallway before me. The sound of commotion has not completely stopped, but it's suddenly quieter. I force myself forward, step by heavy step, and my lungs pinch with every breath.

I walk blindly through the dark, my free hand out in front of me, until my palm comes into contact with the end wall. From there—

Well, I can see the moonlight pouring into my bedroom, which is not a great sign. I hurry through the entryway, past the door hanging from only one of its three hinges, and look around my room. No Mars, no Gabe, no Lawrence. But there is my window, which has been pushed open. There's blood smeared on the wall beside it.

I reach back and stick the knife carefully between my belt and the belt loop. It's not especially sturdy, but it gives me two free hands as I hoist myself through the window and into the side yard. It's not hard to follow the action; there are all sorts of boot prints and bloodstains in the snow around me. They veer right.

The path that Lawrence took to get here is immediately clear. And the fence around the yard is, decidedly, the most useless thing ever. It's been pulled apart again, pretty much where the new chain link ends and the old, rusty stuff begins. Despite the snow, I hurry as fast as I can. Mars isn't down yet; I can hear her voice at a steadily increasing volume.

It seems that she and Gabe got into the yard through that new hole in the fence. I catch myself on the edge of the broken chain link. Mars has got the hockey stick in her hands, protectively standing over Gabe, who is halfway on the ground and turning ghostly white.

"*Hey!*" I shout. My voice breaks.

Everybody's attention snaps to me. I don't have the capacity to figure out the look on Mars's face. Gabe, however, tries to stand so quickly that he falls straight to the snow.

I step into the yard. Just as Lawrence's body twists, a defensive snarl on his lip, I do the first thing that comes to mind: I put my hands out and drop to my knees. The ground is cold and hard and burns even through my trousers.

In the back of my mind, something lets up. Like a boot slightly lifting, but not all the way gone yet. Lawrence was expecting to stop me. He wasn't expecting submission.

Please, I think. *I don't want to be alone.*

There's a moment where nobody moves. Then, slowly, Lawrence stalks over to me. I hang my head and shut my eyes, praying to any god that isn't Lawrence that I don't die here.

His snout softly presses into the side of my neck, and that warm sense of comfort swaddles me like a blanket. I take a gasping breath. I reach out and place my hand on Lawrence's face again, scrambling for a hold amid such an intense feeling of *clarity*. Despite the patches of both dried and fresh blood, his fur is still soft.

you're not alone, hunter.

I understand the appeal of what he's offering me. The sense of *calm*, the brotherhood. The promise of being able to make a family of my own. At any other point in my life, I'd be running for it with open arms.

With my other hand, I reach back and slowly wiggle the knife loose.

Lawrence's nose drags up my neck, nuzzles against my jaw, and then repeats the motion. The third time he does it, I feel the knot rise back into my throat. His snout guides it, drags it up towards my mouth.

We stare at each other. No words or thoughts. Just heavy amber eyes in which I can observe my own reflection.

breathe, Lawrence finally says. *don't forget to breathe.*

I wait until the substance dribbles onto my tongue before I allow myself to exhale. My grip on Lawrence tightens with equal parts panic and resolve.

"I'm sorry," I whisper.

I'm still staring this lost brother in the eye when I stab him in the chest.

The howl that comes is sharp and short. I haven't even fully processed what I've done when something smacks me in the face.

I go down and the world spins. Snow flurries everywhere. I curl up on myself instinctively, but no further assault comes. There's a ringing in my ears, and both of my cheeks are burning. It takes a moment to realize that it's partially because I'm pressing my face into a pile of snow slush.

I get halfway upright before a violent cough tears its way out of me.

Blood splatters onto the snow, as well as something *black*. Slimy, like mucus. There are little fur tufts in the thickest of it. I cough until I'm light-headed, and my throat finally goes dry.

It's over quickly. I stare at the viscus, sizzling as it sinks into the snow and stains it. Once I've processed that I'm not dead, my brain moves to the next point of concern: Lawrence, who's stumbled towards the porch, leaving a warbled trail of blood behind him. He makes it to the base of the stairs before unsteadily lying down.

"Hunter?" Mars's voice comes from somewhere far away.

My legs shake as I stand, but they hold my weight long enough for me to clumsily drop myself onto the bottom step. Each breath comes slow and heavy. A mirror of Lawrence.

For a moment, we sit together. I look down at him, and he looks out into the dark, somewhere far away from the cruddy fence and hard, lumpy snow. He doesn't say anything to me. I don't know if I would want him to.

Even still, I reach out and place my hand on his head. I want him to know I'm here.

I don't know if it's a comfort, but it's all I can give.

When he finally stops breathing, it almost takes me by surprise. A chill washes over me that makes my entire body shudder. It's horribly, horribly quiet. I swallow and the noise of it makes me wince.

I slowly bring my hand back into my lap. Once he's been still for long enough, I lie back against the stairs. As the adrenaline crashes, the aches of a dozen injuries suddenly push their way to the front of my mind. I press my hand to my cheek and come away with bloody fingers.

"Hunter…?"

Mars stands on the other side of Lawrence's body, clutching the hockey stick with both hands. I look behind her and find Gabe using the fence to hold himself up at the other end of the yard. I can't tell if he's waiting for Mars or if he's given up on trying to move, but I can tell that he's bled through the sweater wrapped around his leg.

He's still bleeding. When Lawrence bit me, I stopped bleeding within a matter of minutes. It's strange that the sight of blood sends relief rushing through my chest.

Mars takes a few steps closer, eyes darting uncertainly between me and the body. "Okay?" she asks.

It's an unanswerable, horribly unspecific question. I'm not okay. I will probably never again, in my life, be okay. I'm also *okay*. I'm alive, and the longer I sit there with that feeling of *emptiness*, the more it starts to settle that *I am okay*.

To make things easier for Mars, I nod, and the noise that bursts out of me is somewhere between a laugh and a sob.

Mars stands there for an extra second, eyes wide, but I think it finally reaches her that I'm all right in all the ways that matter. She sits in the snow with a hard exhale, which turns into a giggle, which becomes a full shoulder-shaking laugh of relief as the wail of sirens begins to steadily rise, somewhere down the road.

30

It used to be that when trans people died, they might only be outed on the autopsy table. They could manage to live their whole lives as one gender, only to die and suddenly be deemed liars. Monsters. The subject of debates for decades after their death, all because they didn't have the resources or desire to transition in the way people do today.

James Barry, Billy Tipton, Joe Monahan, Charley Parkhurst. And, hell, those are just the ones I know about.

In a similar way, nobody can agree on what happens to a dead werewolf. Some stories, like *An American Werewolf in London*, give their monster the very small dignity of humanity in death. But in most, like *Ginger Snaps*, the monster stays a monster. Either way, a dead lycanthrope can't rise from the grave to explain the intricacies of its identity to you, whether it identified more as a monster or a man. It's just dead.

Lawrence's body does not become human again. The only indication he was ever human in the first place are his eyes, which slowly shift from amber to a deep emerald green the longer he lies there.

The cops are the first to arrive, but they quickly swarm to the trail of destruction at Annie's house. The EMTs arrive second; they're the ones who finally pull me away from Lawrence. They clean my face enough to get some butterfly stitches over the cuts on my cheek. They start to try and check me for any further injuries, but I quickly insist that those cuts were the only injury I took.

While they shift their focus to Gabe and his leg, and while the cops are still dealing with the gore in Annie's house, I return to the back porch and stare down at Lawrence from the steps. For now, the street is still somewhat quiet. But it won't be long before everybody hears about the dead wolf in my yard. There'll be a crowd, news vans. Animal Control will eventually take Lawrence away.

I don't have a clue what they'll do to him, but for a dizzying moment, I'm thankful his body didn't become human again. For as much as he was in my head, I got a good look inside his, too. I could feel his rage and shame. The *loneliness*.

I reach for the warmth at the back of my head, only to find a whole lot of nothing.

The sound of footsteps on the hardwood startles me back to earth. I look back to find Gabe, putting most of his weight on his right leg before carefully making his way over to sit beside me. I can see gauze wrapped around his leg through the rips in his pant leg.

Neither of us says a word. I try not to get lost inside my head, but now that I'm the only one in there, it's not as easy as you'd think.

I think I miss him. God knows he was horrible company under horrible circumstances, but he was *like me*. We had the same anxieties, the same anger, but he…

Lawrence was angry because he didn't want to be hurt. Angry because he didn't want to feel regret. Angry because he thought his transness was something shameful. After so long, that anger curdled into something worse. Something uglier. Something so big that it stopped having focus and just became an excuse to make the world hurt the same way that *he* was hurting.

He couldn't conceive of a trans life for himself that was worth living.

It doesn't feel fair that he's just *gone*. That he didn't get the same chance I did to realize we were both wrong. That our lives were always worth living.

My eyes prick with tears. It's not fair.

"He *is* dead, right?" Gabe suddenly asks.

I come back to the moment and take a deep breath. "Yeah. He's dead."

Gabe nods, probably repeating this fact to himself.

We're already sitting pretty close together, but I scoot a little closer so I can rest my head on his shoulder. A moment later, I feel his fingers on the back of my neck, slowly rubbing circles into the top of my spine. I let my eyes shut and melt into the touch.

It's quiet for a minute.

"How do we *know* he's dead?" Gabe presses.

I open my eyes and sigh. "Your leg still bleeding?"

"Yeah. Why?"

"Remember how fast I healed the night he attacked me?"

As soon as Gabe connects the dots, I feel his shoulders relax. I healed so quickly because of the lycanthropic infection. It kept me alive so it could continue to spread.

Lawrence is dead now. Bloodline severed. The blood soaking Gabe's bandage is one hundred per cent human.

"I could feel it, too," I add, gesturing to the back of my head. "When he was *there*, there was this warm feeling. Like a heated blanket, I guess, but really, really concentrated. It's not there now."

Gabe sits with that. I feel him breathe in before his arm pulls me impossibly closer.

"Do you want me to call you a different name?" I ask.

I watch Gabe process what I'm talking about. He turns pink and stares at his lap. "Gabe's okay," he finally says. "I don't know, I haven't thought about it."

I carefully lift my head from his shoulder. "Why didn't you say something before?"

"I didn't want you to tell me that I was wrong."

"Why would I tell you that?"

"Because if anybody's gonna know if I'm trans or not, it'd be you. And if you told me I'm not, then..." Gabe takes a shaking breath and curls up on himself. "I thought if I ignored it, it'd go away, and when I realized it was still there, I thought it was too late for me to ever do anything about it, so..."

I find his hand and squeeze it as tightly as I can. "Pronouns?"

Gabe is quiet for the longest time before finally smiling. "*They* is okay, I think. For now."

I try it out in my head.

Gabe is my best friend. I love them more than anything.

"Jesus Christ, it's *freezing* out here." Mars's voice comes from behind. "Why are we just sitting here?"

Gabe straightens and covertly wipes at their eyes. Their voice is deceptively steady. "Not any warmer inside, is it?"

The busted fuse box is hanging on the wall just a couple of feet away. Mars rolls her eyes and plops down on Gabe's other side before looking down at Lawrence. "Still dead?"

"Still dead," Gabe answers.

She nods, then rests her head on Gabe's shoulder. I smother a giggle. The three of us make a strange sight, but I kind of like the feeling that settles over us. Security. Certainty.

"So, do you...feel any different?" Mars asks, suddenly looking over at me.

I glance down at myself. I don't feel as bad as I *did*, but I wouldn't call it completely fine. "Kinda? Everything hurts."

Mars nods. "Figured. What about you, Mighty Duck?"

Gabe carefully pulls their pant leg up and shows the bandage off. They'll definitely need to go to a hospital for stitches, but it might be a little hypocritical of *me* to suggest that. "Could be worse," they answer. "Gonna have the gnarliest scars once this heals."

I smile and feel the butterfly stitches strain against my cheek.

Mars sighs. "You guys are dorks. Anyway, uh, a few of the cops are out front now. They want statements. It's quick, though, I just told them Ethan and Damien were returning a backpack for school. Wolf attack happened, Hunter got lucky with the killing blow."

She hoists herself to her feet and extends her arm to Gabe. It takes a little manoeuvring, but she's able to get them to their feet with minimal winces and curses. I start to stand, but Mars sticks her shoe out and stops me.

"*You* are also injured. Sit here, I got 'im," she promises with a smile.

I huff, but Mars is steady as she takes Gabe's weight and helps them through the house. In the ninety seconds that I'm alone, I try to unravel *that*. The Mars and Gabe Thing.

It doesn't suddenly start making sense with an empty head.

Mars is back before my anxiety can rise to anything more than a simmer. She sits down, exhales, then turns to me and smiles. "Hi."

"Hey." I grin.

Mars takes my hand between both of hers. She's just as cold as I am, but it's a kind gesture. I flex my fingers. I think the first thing I'll do once I'm done talking to the cops is finally cut my nails.

"You're thinking super loud right now," Mars comments, very matter of fact. "What's up?"

I blink, then clear my throat. "Um, about what I said earlier…"

I stall again, trying to figure out what exactly I want to say. Mars rewinds the night until she realizes what I'm talking about, and then she squeezes my hand.

"That's a really big conversation that we can have on a night when you haven't killed somebody," she promises me.

It's not said like she's letting me down easy (nor is she acting like it), but there's still a skittishness that won't settle under my skin. "I didn't freak you guys out or anything?"

She glances at the door, then scoots a little closer. "Can't speak for our Mighty Duck, but I think he's got a lot on his mind right now."

"They," I softly correct her.

Mars's mouth quirks up. "They've got a *lot* on their mind. But, no, didn't freak me out."

Her smile turns a little more devious, teasing, and I can feel my whole face cycle from pale to pink to deep scarlet. "I mean," I press, "I don't…I don't know how this works. Dating. One person or two. How does that – how do we figure that out?"

I watch Mars's expression shift again. Something close to a frown. "Well, to start, you know I'm not monogamous."

I frown. "You aren't?"

"I have a whole bumper sticker about it, what do you mean?"

It takes me a moment to realize what she's talking about. "*I practise ethical non-monogamy with your mom*? Oh, yeah, sorry for not taking that one at face value."

Mars throws her hands up. "I mean, *listen*, have I been pulling bitches left and right? Absolutely not. I will happily fight to the death for your affection if it comes to it. Gabe's injured, I have the advantage."

I elbow her.

She elbows me back. "*Or* I can throw together a PowerPoint and we can take a democratic vote the old-fashioned way and figure it out together. All up to you, my guy." She stops. "Well, up to all three of us, technically."

I try to wrap my head around this idea. I have no frame of reference for it, no concept of what something like this would look like outside of the few scattered fantasies I've cobbled together, fantasies that are too bogged down with embarrassment and shame to spark much hope. But…

Well, I've thought a lot of things that I've now learned to be emphatically not true.

Mars brushes my hair out of my face. Her fingers linger on my cheek. "Let's give the cops what they want, and then we'll get you somewhere warm, okay, Bambi?"

Wordlessly, my eyes fall to Lawrence. I can't just *leave him here*.

Mars looks down at him, too, before giving my cheek a pat. "He ain't going nowhere. You go out front, and if anybody comes for him, I'll shout for you."

I let her help me to my feet.

Inside, guided by the patches of moonlight and muscle memory, I take stock of the house. Two broken doors. Broken front window. Obliterated fuse box. Fence torn apart. The bucket's worth of paint still caked to the front door. All the blood and scuff marks on the floor that'll need to be buffed out. The thought of it all gives me a headache, so I nearly disregard the sound of voices until they suddenly rise.

A male voice, stiff with authority, tells somebody to *step back*. I slow, wondering if we've finally begun to draw a crowd, before walking faster towards the front of the house. Another, angrier male voice starts speaking over the authoritative one, insisting that this guy needs to move, he lives here, he needs to see his *fucking son—*

I break into a sprint. If the front door hadn't already been open, I probably would've run right through it.

Despite the swell of emotion that makes everything suddenly blurry, I catch the moment that Dad sees me. I watch the anger fall from his face. He sidesteps the cop and has his arms open when I barrel into him for the tightest hug we've ever given each other.

31

Graft rejection is what happens when the reconstructed nipple doesn't get the right amount of blood flow. It suffocates, basically, and the tissue dies. For all I've read, I haven't found what actions or behaviours definitively result in graft rejection. Nor is there anything proven to prevent it. Like many things, it's all about luck.

My rejection happened at the end of February.

Until then, my body had been making a slow return to something resembling normal. My voice lowered to where it was before, the colour came back to my skin, and my nails no longer grew in as claws. The worst of the lingering damage was the scar tissue. Small rough spots on my arm and leg where the bites were and in uneven patches around my neck. Two small defined lines from Lawrence's claws have scarred my cheek, too, running from the outside edge of my cheekbone down to my upper lip. Nothing severe, but enough to be noticed.

My left nipple eventually regained its colour and recovered.

My right, though, was the reason I got my dad to drive me back to the surgeon's office. There, the surgeon told me that the rejection was only partial, which meant I had two options. I could wait to see how it progressed and *maybe* keep my chest symmetrical, or I could get a pre-emptive, total removal of the graft.

There's been no research done on the effects lycanthropy can have on nipple grafts. Nevertheless, when my surgeon lays it all out for me, I can't help but feel like it's Lawrence's final effort at punishing me. I rejected the body *he* wanted to give me, and so he's made sure that the body I'm returning to won't ever be the one I used to lie awake at night and dream of.

Both pectorals share a reddish scar along the curve of the muscle, where the surgeon opened me up the first time. They're noticeably raised, having had to heal *twice* instead of just once. My right pec has an additional small scar that puckers where my nipple used to be.

I would say that this secondary scar is a reminder of Lawrence, but Lawrence left plenty of other marks behind. Lawrence is the scar on my leg and on the inside of my forearm. He's the claw scars on my cheek.

Riley is the scar that wraps around the base of my neck.

When I look in the mirror and see the scar on my chest, it reminds me of the funerals I attended in the weeks afterwards. Annie. Damien. Ethan. It reminds me of seeing Riley at the last one and watching her pretend that I didn't exist. It reminds me of all the news coverage Lawrence's death got as the experts tried and horribly failed to explain his abnormalities.

It also reminds me of the nights and weekends that Mars and Gabe and I spend together as spring melts the snow. The time that Dad and I carve out for each other when he's home, and especially when he isn't.

The scar on my chest is not from something *taken* from me. It's a mark of everything I chose to let go of in order to keep myself alive. So when I look in the mirror, I get to be proud that I'm here to have scars in the first place.

EPILOGUE

It costs thirty bucks to bribe the kid working the Bolingbrook Golf Club to turn on the sprinklers during prom. It's absurdly easy, and so, so worth it.

We make a break for the parking lot before we can get properly kicked out of the venue. Mars drives us further east into Romeoville and straight into a drive-thru. We blow far too much money on the largest cups of pop they'll sell us and then we keep on driving even further, until Mars pulls off onto a service road with a Dead End sign posted in the grass.

This far on the edge of town, the only sound for miles is the music coming from the car speakers, out through the open windows and into the humid night. We've got a three-way Spotify jam going, which is mostly Mars playing "Red Wine Supernova" over and over while Gabe and I try to break it up with any other song.

"We gave those nerds the most memorable night of their lives, that is *well* worth thirty bucks," Mars declares, putting the car into park and unstrapping her shoes from around her ankles. "Should've picked better running shoes, though."

She swings her feet over the centre console and into Gabe's lap, whose side-eye is undercut by the smile on their mouth. Gabe – who isn't any closer to choosing a new name but has started experimenting with *she* as well as *they* – turns the volume down on the stereo as Mars sticks her head out of her window, face turned towards the sky.

I watch both of them from my spot in the back seat, rolling my sleeves up to my elbows.

"I was just saying, *one of you* could've told me before you did it," Gabe says, pulling her hair back in a tie.

"You would have tried to *stop us*," Mars, very correctly, counters.

At this end of the service road, there's only one dimmed street light. It makes the dye in Mars's hair seem a much brighter lime green than it actually is.

Mars and Gabe playfully bicker back and forth about the sprinkler prank, while one of the Cavetown songs I put into the queue softly fades in. I get comfortable in the back seat, face warm with lingering adrenaline and the mid-May air. I maintain that there's nothing like a Chicago winter, but for the first time in a long time, I really am enjoying spring as it melts into summer.

The howl that cuts through the night stops all of us.

It's brief, and nowhere near where we've parked in the dirt. Still, there ain't nothing around here but a bunch of dead land. No people, no safe place to run to. We all go quiet until the cry finally tapers out a couple of seconds after it began.

Mars is the one who breaks the silence: "How many lycanthropes do you think are out there, anyway?"

It's a question both she and Gabe have raised before, as if I might have some secret insight on the answer.

I don't. I only know that Lawrence is dead, as is the lycanthrope who turned Lawrence. But that's only two generations of the family tree. The roots have to run deeper than that.

"Probably a few," I finally offer. I take a long sip of Diet Coke until the straw rattles against the ice. "Big country. Big world."

Up front, Gabe makes a contemplative noise.

"You think they still got some in Minnesota?" Mars asks, staring up at the crescent moon.

Have you given any more thought to summer? is the question she's not asking.

There's been no research done on the effects of lycanthropy on nipple grafts, and there's nothing online that walks you through the process of telling a stranger that you killed her ex-boyfriend because he'd been turned into a lycanthrope and went homicidal. But Cassandra Sweeney still posts to the Lawrence Tennison Facebook page. She's still looking for him. I don't know what I can offer her, if anything at all, but—

Well, Gabe has been letting me drive the Jeep in the

parking lot after hockey practice. And we've got a long, three-month stretch of summer ahead of us before college starts in August.

"Please, they're gonna be all over Canada if they're gonna be anywhere," Gabe answers.

Mars snorts and puts a hand over her mouth. "Sorry. Thought about hockey. Werewolves on ice."

While that launches a whole conversation about which professional teams are or aren't led by lycanthropes, my attention wanders to the dark night. The wolf out there that I can't see.

A pulp novel cover paints itself in my mind. The first in a series of many. The three of us with comically oversized silver crosses in our hands, monkshood flowers curling around the spine. An old, ugly church would loom behind us, like the artist who drew it wasn't sure if it was supposed to be a refuge or a prison tower. Mars gets to wear the Indiana Jones fedora, at least on this first instalment.

I can't help the smile that overtakes my face.

The wolf howls again, and this time, I swear it echoes against the metal body of the car.

It takes a moment longer to realize that the sound isn't echoing. It's being answered. A small symphony of responses bounce off one another as more wolves answer the call.

Wherever that wolf is, it's found its pack.

If you have been affected by the issues raised in this book, please go to qr.usborne.com/2ctma or scan the QR code below for links to organizations who may be able to help.

ACKNOWLEDGEMENTS

The first time I wrote this story, *The Transition* was a 104 page story about the horrors of Being Trans Under Capitalism. My first *thanks* must go to the people who have been with these characters from the very beginning: Micah Stack and Laurene Debord-Foulk, Mike Corey, and especially Daithi and Coley.

Thank you to Krista Marino, Emma Leynse, Becky Walker and Lydia Gregovic for being such warriors in whipping this book into shape. Seriously, if I could call dibs on you guys for the rest of our professional lives, I would. Thank you for being phenomenal editors and for going above and beyond in every possible way. Of course, thank you to Chloe for your almost supernatural ability to be doing the best work 24/7. I'm not convinced you ever sleep. I am so thankful that you're the one I get to continue forward on this journey with.

For their unbelievable work on their respective covers, thank you so much to Mx Morgan and Zoë Van Dijk.

And thank you to the other folks at Usborne: Katharine Millichope, Sarah Cronin, Gareth Collinson, Debbie Sims, Rebecca Hill, Jacob Dow and Jessica Feichtlbauer.

Thank you, James, for being my hockey liaison and only occasionally laughing in my face over my stupid questions. If there are any Blackhawks fans in the audience, blame this guy. Thank you again to Mom and Dad. For buying me smoothies and helping me with my drains and making sure I didn't smash my head to pieces when we took the bandages off and I decided to almost pass out. Everything I do is for you guys, always and forever.

In no particular order, thank you to Dia, Ash, Maddie, Sari, June, Jay, Vanna, and Paige (Nixon *and* McClure). Thank you to Dwynwen, Tori, Michelle, Brooke, Carter, Ivanna, Benji and Blue. Thank you to the Hayes, Peterson, and Fleisher families. Further thanks to Lily Besinger, Maegan Stebbins and her blog, maverickwerewolf.com, and to Meaghan Good and the Charley Project website.

I dedicated *Old Wounds* to "everyone gone [and] everyone still going". I would like to emphasize and extend that dedication here. This book is for the trans kids. For the trans kids who didn't know they were trans kids until after they'd already grown up and for the kids who figured it out early. For the kids we've lost – Nex Benedict, Brianna Ghey, Leelah Alcorn, Blake Brockington, Onyx John, Nova Dunn and the countless others – and for the kids who survive, who are brave enough to stand tall and ensure our dead are not forgotten.

Finally, Alex. You let me talk at you for *hours* on our second date about this book and you never once tried to tuck and roll out of my car. You told me this book was perfect even when it definitely wasn't. I love you and all that you bring to my world.

Discover the pulse-pounding horror-thriller from Logan-Ashley Kisner...

Erin and Max are two trans kids, trying to get to California. Max is desperate to finally transition, and Erin wants to understand why she's on this trip to begin with, after Max broke up with her two years earlier. But when they find themselves stranded in the creepy woods of rural Kentucky, they suddenly have much bigger problems.

First, there's the creature that, according to legend, feeds on girls. And then there are the locals, who are searching for a female sacrifice. If either of them hope to survive, Erin and Max will have to stop running: from their attackers, from each other, and, ultimately, from themselves.

"Subversive and scary, with compelling characterisation… a pulse-pounding debut." *The Guardian*

"Had me on the edge of my seat." Bill Wood, bestselling author of *Let's Split Up*

"Terrifying, tender, and unflinchingly honest." Rory Power, *New York Times* **bestselling author of** *Wilder Girls*

Logan-Ashley Kisner is a trans and queer author born, raised and still residing within Las Vegas, Nevada. He has a BA in Creative Writing and minored in Film Studies at UNLV. On top of being an author, he is also a transgender horror historian, cat dad and horror addict (his favourites include *Ginger Snaps*, the *Evil Dead* series and *Sleepaway Camp*).